*Portrait of a Married Woman*

SALLY MANDEL was born in New York in 1944. She is a descendant of the Oneida Community, a nineteenth century attempt to create a Utopian society. Her third year of college was spent at the University of Hull in Yorkshire.

She currently lives in New York City with her husband and two children.

# SALLY MANDEL

# *Portrait of a Married Woman*

FONTANA/Collins

First published in Great Britain by
William Collins Sons & Co. Ltd 1985
A Continental edition issued by Fontana Paperbacks 1986
This edition first issued by Fontana Paperbacks 1986

Copyright ©S.E.M. Production Inc. 1985

Made and printed in Great Britain by
William Collins Sons & Co. Ltd, Glasgow

FOR MY MOTHER

# One

~~~~~~~

That day Margaret Hollander saw two people dressed as chickens on Ninety-first Street. They were a young man and a young woman with great yellow-feathered bodies and heavy chicken feet sitting on a bench by the Cooper-Hewitt Museum smoking cigarettes. Later, even years later, the strange creatures always came to mind as the harbingers of the unexpected in what was once an orderly life.

Morning started out as always. Matthew, Fred, and Susan sat around the table, each absorbing the shock of a new dawn in his own fashion. The children ate in silence, Fred consuming prodigious amounts of cinnamon toast in an effort to fill his ever-yawning twelve-year-old stomach, and Susan extricating the raisins from her cereal and leaving the bran flakes to grow soggy. Matthew pored over the first pages of his *New York Times* with ferocious concentration as if he feared that confronting today without yesterday's *data vitae* would be to venture forth unarmed.

Maggie stood propped in her usual spot at the counter waiting for the caffeine rush from her first cup of coffee. She was a tall, slim woman, five feet ten in her bare feet. Even now, while still groggy from the warmth of her bed, she stood very straight. For Maggie, mornings were always wrenching. Nearly two hours would have to elapse before her senses fully awoke. Until then, sounds and images seemed fuzzy to her as if filtered through a gauze screen.

Suddenly the sunny room erupted in a jumble of requisitions. Matthew's deep baritone won out. 'My blazer hasn't come back from the cleaners, has it Mag? I need it for tomorrow night.'

'You didn't tell me.'

'Yup. And I need longer laces for my black wing tips. Think you could get ahold of a pair today?'

5

'Haul that barge, tote that bail,' chimed Susan. Her grin flashed a mouthful of braces. Matthew reached out with his folded newspaper and tapped her on the head.

'I suppose you don't have a single item to add to my list, Suzie Q,' Maggie said.

'As a matter of fact . . .' Susan began.

Maggie interrupted her. 'I'm to pick up your costume and drop it at rehearsal at three, and Fred, you forgot to buy Michael a present and his party's this afternoon.'

Fred's tongue was rendered helpless by half a banana. 'Mrthma bmp?' he asked.

'You want me to get him something.'

Fred nodded and took a gigantic swig of juice. 'The new *Corpse* tape would be sensational.'

'Oh God, all right. It'll be with Sue's stuff this afternoon. I'm here 'til seven. Otherwise feed yourselves. There's lamb in the fridge.'

Matthew sent crumbs flying as he opened the Metropolitan section. 'I ought to be home by nine. Want to wait and have dinner with me?' he asked with nose buried.

Maggie envied him his powers of concentration. She once dreamed that she had set fire to a corner of the *Times* as he read at the breakfast table. Matthew had simply continued reading faster and faster, racing the flames to the bottom of the page. He held the charred paper between his fingers gingerly until the words fell into ashes. Without comment, and without glancing up, he merely swept the soot away and began the next section.

'Mom's not going to be here to take care of you, Daddy,' Susan said. 'Hey, maybe you guys'd like my famous hamburgers *au roquefort*.'

Fred clasped his stomach and gagged convincingly.

'Not here?' Matthew asked.

'Jeez, you're out of it sometimes,' Susan complained. 'It's Tuesday night. Bridge night.'

'So it is,' Matthew declared. 'Whose house?'

'Phyllis's.'

Matthew grimaced. He had never liked Phyllis, but Maggie always asked him not to exhibit his antipathy in front of the children.

6

'She thinks she's seventeen, the way she dresses,' Susan said.

Maggie shot Matthew a look that said *See what you encourage?* But he was reading again.

'She's got great legs,' Fred remarked. 'I don't see why women have all those rules about what they should wear and what they shouldn't wear. If you've got it, flaunt it, I always say.' As he warmed to his subject, Maggie poured herself another cup of coffee and smiled at him. She enjoyed Fred's speeches. Even when he was tiny, he used to deliver solemn lectures to her about why it was advisable to sleep with twenty-two stuffed animals or why the pink gelatinous canned spaghetti was so much better than home-cooked pasta.

'You're all slaves to the fashion industry,' he went on. 'If some old bag wants to wear something young and sexy, why shouldn't she? You won't catch us men . . .'

Susan cut him short. 'Mother, that's your third cup! You drink too much of that stuff!'

'Why don't you lay off, Motormouth?' Fred said, stung at the interruption. 'God, you're going to be such a nag when and if you ever grow up. I was right in the middle of a sentence.'

'You don't even care if Mom gets breast cancer and maybe even dies.'

'You think you're the big medical expert just because you got an A in your Personal Health report.' Fred's round face was beginning to redden. 'Besides, I care about Mom's breasts as much as anybody.'

'Hoo *hoo*!' Susan howled.

Fred half rose from the table to lunge at his sister. She leapt up and flattened herself against the refrigerator, out of reach.

'That'll do,' Matthew said. 'Your mother's breasts are in no immediate danger as far as we know.'

'Well, maybe not from cancer anyway,' Susan said with a smirk as she sat down again.

'You're disgusting,' Fred said. 'She doesn't have one iota of class. You know what she did in lunch line yesterday?'

'Don't you dare,' Susan whispered.

'She farted. Everybody heard her, a real ripper. Loverboy Bobby Posner looked right at her and said. "Can't hold what you don't have in your hand, right, Sue?" It was classic.'

7

'Mom,' Susan asked sweetly, 'when do little boys stop worrying about castration?'

'Never, babe,' Matthew muttered. He stretched, stood up and embraced Maggie. 'Take care of 'em, will you?' he asked. Maggie wondered if he meant the children or her breasts.

Susan and Fred traipsed out of the kitchen after him with Susan making a running commentary on Matthew's attire.

'Daddy, look how preppy you are with the button-down collar. *Très* Reaganesque, you know, like you've been embalmed in the fifties or something. Next thing you'll be wearing plaid pants . . .' Her voice disappeared down the hall. Good, take on your father for a change, Maggie thought. She slumped into Matthew's vacant chair with a sigh. A few moments later, Fred called, 'Don't forget Mike's present, Mom!' The front door slammed and they were gone.

Maggie sat with her chin in her hands. She had what her mother always told her were 'good bones', which Maggie supposed meant that she was homely. 'You'll grow into your face,' Mother said, and at age thirty-eight, Maggie was still waiting.

Normally she sat for half an hour after breakfast and skimmed the *Times*. But this morning the silence seemed hollow as if she was entombed in a cavern so vast that the ceiling could barely be seen for the shadows. She got up and began transporting dishes to the sink. Her body moved automatically, with a kind of swaying grace. She remembered Fred's remark about Phyllis's legs and poked one of her own through her robe. Not bad, she determined. If perhaps the face was lacking a certain Hollywood panache, she was still all right from the neck down. She knew the power of an attractive body. At cocktail parties, she was accustomed to men speaking to her chest rather than to her eyes. Sometimes she would amuse herself by recapturing the attention of a distracted male by crossing her legs or moving her shoulder in a certain way. Men were so preoccupied with her breasts or her knees that if she were to unscrew her head and place it next to the salted nuts, she wondered if anyone would notice.

A saucer slammed against the rim of the sink and chipped. In the nine years since she bought the set, this was the first time she had broken anything. The jagged edge of the plate cut her thumb. She found a bandaid but as she tried to apply it, she noticed that her hands were shaking. Maybe Susan was right: too much coffee.

Moving around would help, the faster the better. It was a good day to attack her closet, get out her summer things, clean the shelves, and make a list of the clothing she needed to buy this season. That would take care of the morning. Then there were plenty of errands: a note to her ailing father; Mother's Day gifts to choose; groceries to order; medical insurance forms to fill out for Fred's persistent ear infections.

She marched towards the bedroom, keeping her eyes averted from the other rooms with today's curiously eerie quiet. They had bought the place just before the upswing in cooperative market prices would have barred them from the market forever. It was a pleasant two-bedroom apartment in a brick pre-war building on Seventy-ninth between Lexington and Third Avenues. It had Maggie's two prerequisites: the ceilings were high and there was a fireplace in the living room. The children had flipped a coin for the extra bedroom. Susan won, relegating Fred to a small maid's room near the kitchen, but it had worked out fine. Fred liked his privacy, and also his proximity to the refrigerator.

Maggie had taken pride in decorating the place on her own in a comfortable not-very-contemporary style. The living room faced south, and was a rain forest of palm fronds and ferns. Maggie often played the stereo for her plants, maintaining they were partial to Debussy. The colour green was evident throughout the apartment. Matthew theorized that Maggie was unconsciously trying to reproduce the lush atmosphere of her Stafford, Connecticut, childhood.

Maggie opened her closet door, grabbed an armful of dresses and hauled them to the bed. She flopped down with them, and found that the dress on top of the pile was her old madras shirtwaist with the lilac and green plaid. It was hopelessly out of fashion and so faded now that the colours were barely distinguishable. Every year she told herself to quit being foolish and get rid of it, and every year she retrieved it from the giveaway pile and hung it back in the closet.

9

With the soft fabric between her fingers, she felt her anxiety succumb to a pleasant dream-like sensation that she had experienced several times in the past week. It was as if she were periodically checking out of the present in order to take a long walk in the past. It had happened in the supermarket waiting in line at the deli counter. That time she was transported back to her wooden desk in the first grade where she could swing her legs without her feet touching the floor. It happened again yesterday in Bloomingdale's giftware department. Suddenly she was in Rockport, walking along the beach with her father as he tried to explain to her about menstruation. A store clerk had startled her by asking if she was ill.

The dress sent her back to that first afternoon with Matthew. It was the beginning of Senior year at Radcliffe and the air was so crisp that it almost hurt her eyes. The trees had begun to turn; Harvard Square was littered with awed Freshmen and brilliant leaves. Maggie was dashing to the subway for a trip to Filene's and, as she rounded the corner of Boylston Street, she suddenly found herself hooked to the elbow of Matthew Hollander.

'May I have this dance?' he asked. He seemed to have simply materialized out of the shimmering autumn light. 'My name's Matthew Hollander. You're Maggie Herrick.'

'I know who you are.' Everyone knew Matthew Hollander, with his earnest handsome face and lean body that performed athletic feats with simple ease. Like every other woman at Radcliffe, Maggie had enjoyed watching the sheen of sweat on his back and shoulders as he leapt into the air to hurl the basketball through the hoop with a decisive swoosh. But she wondered how he knew her. Surely he didn't recognize her from the only class they had shared, Renaissance Art, which was a glorified slide show occurring mostly in total darkness.

'Come and have a cup of coffee with me,' Matthew urged. He still held onto her elbow. Maggie looked down at her watch to hide a burning face. 'And a hot fudge sundae. I know you like those.' She glanced up at him. 'I saw you in the window at *Brigham*'s one afternoon with Phyllis Jacobson,' he went on. 'You shoved the whipped cream off but ate the cherry.'

Maggie laughed and fell into rhythm with his long stride.

She only hoped she would pass someone she knew. All the way to *Brigham*'s, she kept saying to herself: Here I am with Matthew Hollander. She wanted to remember exactly how it felt.

Pain brought her back to the bedroom. She had clutched the old dress so tightly that her shoulders ached. With a sigh, she stood and hung it back in her closet. She would keep it a while longer even though the wonder and excitement it evoked had faded along with its once-bright colours.

She walked across the carpeted floor towards the window. It was Maggie's habit to poke her head out over Seventy-ninth Street and appraise the air first-hand before dressing for the day, but this morning she felt an odd reluctance. She regarded the window thoughtfully for a moment, then threw it open and looked down.

The air was cool and thick with moisture from an early morning shower. It washed around her like a gentle whirlpool. The traffic noises rose in bubbles that popped to release their sounds just under her face. The vehicles and pedestrians below were like bizarre sea creatures with shapes distorted by the glassy surface of the water. Maggie swayed, seaweed drifting. How pleasant to dive into the soft transparent waves. She closed her eyes against a sudden lurch of nausea and stumbled away from the window. Cold sweat clung to the fringes of her hair and plastered it to her forehead as if she had indeed been immersed. Perhaps she was drowning. Perhaps as the water closed over her head, she would continue to relive the years, newsreel style, just as they tell you, except that it would take weeks for her to submerge completely.

# Two

Maggie was on her way out of the door for her bridge game when Fred and Susan arrived home.

Susan looked at her closely. 'You getting your period?' she wanted to know.

Startled, Maggie shook her head.

'Well, you look weird.' She moved past her and Maggie heard the pile of books crash down on the bed.

'Thanks,' Maggie murmured.

'I don't think you look weird, exactly,' Fred said, leaning against the wall. 'But something's wrong.'

Maggie felt a lump growing in her throat. 'Not a thing,' she said. 'Gotta go. Don't forget your leafy greens.'

Fred gave her a quick kiss. 'Knock 'em dead, Mom.'

Phyllis's apartment was within easy walking distance, but Maggie dawdled. Either she was having a nervous breakdown, she decided, or menopause was setting in early. She remembered last night's television advertisement that touted a disaster film about an airplane that plunged into the ocean and sank to the bottom. In the film clip, flames raged, waves crashed, wounded and dying passengers screamed with terror. A stout-voiced fellow, presumably the hero, shouted from the midst of the seething maelstrom, 'Don't panic!' Maggie likened the voice in her brain to that stalwart person; she had been hearing the same command all day. Except that there was no disaster in her life. Everything was perfect, really perfect.

She shook her head and half a dozen tiny seedlets fell to her shoulders. The spring trees were shedding in a strong breeze from the south. A pair of joggers passed, a man and a woman wearing matched shorts. They were laughing. Were we ever like that, Matthew and I? Maggie wondered, and she was off again, back in Cambridge, Massachusetts.

He had called her that same night and asked her out for dinner on Saturday night. Maggie refused, due to her long-standing Saturday commitment to Frank Pearson. She felt as if she had just turned down the Nobel Prize, but ten minutes later Matthew called again, this time to ask if she could see him on Sunday. She agreed.

Frank Pearson and Maggie used one another for sex. At first, Maggie had tried to convince herself that she was in love with him, but her room-mate, Phyllis, had set her straight.

'He's a good fuck, that's all. Don't make it into the romance of the century.'

'But he was my first and only,' Maggie protested.

'Nu? My first was my thirteen-year-old cousin. Think I should marry him?'

Matthew took her to Nick's place, known at Harvard as The Greasy Greek's. Neither of them spoke much at first. Matthew watched her, while under the table Maggie rolled and unrolled her napkin.

'Why are you staring at me?' she asked finally.

'You have an interesting face.'

Maggie smiled. 'Good bones, my mother says.'

'Your mother's right. Do you mind not being pretty?'

'I did when I was fifteen. Not now.'

He nodded as if she were confirming something he already knew.

'Do you mind being pretty?' she asked him.

'Yes,' he answered instantly. Then they both laughed, and Maggie began to relax.

They had talked about art that night, Maggie remembered, and she was impressed with his sensitivity and profound admiration of creative performance. On the way back to her dormitory, he had tried to kiss her.

She pulled away. 'Why are you doing this?' she asked him.

'Doing what? Kissing you? I like your gap.'

'I beg your pardon.'

'The gap between your front teeth. It's sexy.'

'I mean all of it. Taking me out, giving me the rush.'

'You're cute.' He tried to draw her close but she resisted.

'I may be many things, but I am not cute. I'm a novelty, that must be it.'

'I'd say special.'

'You don't even know me.'

'I want to. I'll tell you something else. I've been thinking about you all summer.'

'Why?'

'I saw your pictures at the student exhibition. I liked them a lot.'

'Listen, I'm just an ordinary person with an ordinary talent. I'm no Mary Cassatt.'

He held her by the shoulders and shook her slightly. 'Why are you giving me such a hard time?'

'Because you could make hash out of me.'

He was silent a moment. 'I won't do that,' he said at last.

'How do you know? It can't be easy to break the beauty-queen habit.'

'I think I'm going to kill you,' he said, then kissed her and held her very close to him the rest of the way back.

He called her every night but Maggie, though cordial, told him she was busy. Phyllis paced their little room. She was beside herself.

'What does he *say* when you turn him down?'

'"God damn".'

'You've got the Adonis of Harvard hot after your ass.'

'He doesn't want me really,' Maggie explained. 'He just thinks he does.'

'So what, so what? If you pass up a chance to sleep with that man, I'm transferring you to Mass Mental.'

'Phyl,' Maggie said, 'I like him. He's not just another pretty face.'

Phyllis held out her hands in a gesture that said *So, then*?

'I'm going to get mangled and shredded by this one.'

'Then have a night or two of bliss to remember the remainder of your mangled and shredded life. Am I right or am I right?'

Maggie regarded her silently. Phyllis had penetrating green eyes. 'Stop zapping me with those things, I can't think.' She and Maggie had been paired as room-mates in their Freshman year. Maggie remembered being appalled by her language. It

14

was one thing to read the word 'cunt' sprinkled among abstruse paragraphs of Chaucer, but quite another to be confronted with the actual spoken word. As the weeks went by, it became clear that Phyllis's formidable mouth was matched by an equally formidable intellect, with which she was just as generous. If Maggie was baffled by a Statistics problem, Phyllis was always there to explain. She shared her Biology lab notes and read all of Maggie's English term papers, offering patient, tactful criticism. They had continued to room together except for Junior Year when Phyllis spent the year abroad and Maggie had missed her terribly. When Phyllis asked Maggie to analyse her reactions to Matthew Hollander, it did not take Maggie long to get up off her bed and telephone him.

'It's me,' she said. 'Can I take you to dinner?'

'Yes,' Matthew said, and it began in earnest.

The sight of Phyllis's apartment house roused her from her reminiscences. The newsreel was happening again, Maggie thought, visualizing dark water closing over her head. Eventually she would work her way up through the years and then what? Something cataclysmic, surely.

The linoleum flooring in the lobby was coming up around the edges. Even the plastic plant by the elevator seemed dustier and more forlorn than usual. But Phyllis was fastidious about her apartment. It was decorated in beige and white, sparsely so that the cramped space seemed larger. There were touches of rattan here and there, and lots of mirrors. Maggie marvelled at the contrast between the orderly home and the chaotic marriage that inhabited it.

The others were already sitting at the card table. Three pairs of eyes stared at Maggie as she let herself in. She found refuge in Robin's, which were deep brown and, as always, filled with warmth. Robin was five months pregnant, but even in profile, her figure barely showed it.

'Did somebody die?' Phyllis asked. The long dark braid of Radcliffe days had been replaced with an attractive cropped haircut.

Maggie shook her head and sat down. There was a glass of white wine beside the pile of cards Hilary had dealt her. 'Thanks,' Maggie said, and took a swallow.

'Gee, in all these years, I think you're the only one who's never been late,' Robin said. The soft eyes were plainly worried.

'Sorry. I was attacked by Marcel Proust on the way over,' Maggie hurriedly arranged her cards.

'You going to explain that?' Phyllis asked.

Maggie shook her head. 'Not to worry.' She had a good hand. The second time around the table she bid two no-trump.

'Oh, Christ, I always forget what I'm supposed to say to that,' Hilary moaned. Even with her face screwed up in dismay, Hilary Vonderhyde was beautiful. Maggie had known her for years, and still never tired of looking at her. She had thick wavy hair, honey-coloured but streaked pale around her face. Her eyes were light brown, almost gold, and her skin always seemed tanned. Her eyebrows and lashes were dark, making the blonde hair suspect, but the fact was, Hilary was one hundred per cent natural. She drew her long fingers through the tangled mane.

'You must be asking for another suit,' she murmured.

'No hints,' Phyllis warned.

'Oh, three no-trump,' Hilary finally decided. The others passed.

'Damn, I hate playing no-trump,' Maggie muttered.

Robin led the six of diamonds and Hilary laid down her hand. Maggie looked it over in silence. There was a conspicuous gap in the diamond suit and, as always, Robin had ferreted it out. Somehow she always seemed to know her opponent's weakness. She was the kindest, gentlest person Maggie knew, but she was deadly at the bridge table.

'I'm sorry, Mag,' Robin said mournfully as she ran through the last of her six-card diamond suit. It was a joke with them about Robin's talent with cards. She was good, she was lucky, but she could not bear the fact that someone had to lose. Sometimes she seemed almost exultant when she drew a three-point hand and was unable to bid.

Maggie watched helplessly as the pile of cards accumulated in front of Robin, and was amazed to feel her eyes sting. She was losing it all. She glanced up and saw Phyllis studying her. Damn it, Maggie thought, she never misses a trick. The pun was awful, but it served to dry up the threatening tears.

Maggie took the next trick with her queen of hearts but then proceeded to relinquish transportation from her hand to Hilary's strong club suit. She finished the game down four. 'Sorry, partner,' she sighed.

'I left you in the lurch. Those were sucky diamonds.'

'What's the matter, Margaret?' Phyllis asked.

'Nothing,' Maggie replied.

'Oh, yes, dear,' Phyllis said.

'Getting my period. Whose deal?'

'Mine,' Phyllis said, 'but I think I'll wait until you tell us what's with you.' She tapped the pack of cards on the table and stared morosely at Maggie. Maggie doodled on the score pad. She was continually making cartoons at the bridge table. This was a drawing of a chicken with human features.

'Do you feel as if you've changed?' Maggie asked them. 'Over the years, since college, I mean? Oh, I don't know what I mean.'

'I've gotten a hell of a lot older,' Hilary said.

'That's not . . .' Maggie began, but Phyllis interrupted her.

'I remember the energetic, confident young thing who was going to conquer the art world, first Boston, then New York.'

'I used to go after the things I wanted, didn't I?'

'You got a case of the regrets?' Phyllis asked.

'I don't know *what* I've got.'

'Talent. Which you don't use,' Hilary said.

Maggie drew heavy pencil marks through her doodle.

'I don't think she needs criticism tonight,' Robin said. 'Go ahead and deal, Phyl.'

Phyllis began to distribute the cards. 'What she *needs* is a lover.'

Hilary laughed incredulously.

'All you ever think about is sex,' Robin protested.

'All anybody ever thinks about is sex, honey.'

'See what happens when you spend eight years getting your head shrunk?' Hilary said.

'Don't get so defensive, Hilary,' Phyllis blew out a huge cloud of cigarette smoke. 'The ideal Hollander marriage is not about to crack up just because Maggie needs to get laid. One club.'

'I promise I'll go right home after this and attack Matthew,' Maggie said. 'You bid a club? I pass.'

Phyllis's eyes narrowed. 'That won't do it, but you go ahead and give it a try.'

'She's got late-thirties ennui. It's practically an epidemic,' Hilary said. 'It'll pass, Mag, really.'

Maggie was beginning to feel dizzy and feverish as if she had had too much wine.

'Are you okay?' Robin reached her hand out to touch Maggie's arm.

Maggie nodded. 'Fine, but I think I'd like to play some bridge.'

'Two hearts,' Robin said.

'Jump shift, that bastard,' Hilary murmured. 'I pass in the face of rampant balls.'

After that, the hands got interesting and Phyllis concentrated on her cards instead of Maggie. It was past eleven by the time the last rubber was finished and they had chosen Robin's house for the first Tuesday in June.


Matthew was sitting in front of the television set when Maggie got home. There was always restraint between them on bridge night, particularly if Matthew preceded her home, as if somehow Maggie was supposed to be there first, waiting for him. Neither of them spoke of it, but Maggie was always conscious of an impulse to rush if the game lasted past ten-thirty.

'So how's Robin?' Matthew enquired as she dropped her bag and sat down next to him.

'So far so good. This week's the five-months mark.'

They were silent for a moment. Maggie thought of her remark at the bridge table about attacking him. It seemed like a pledge. He had changed into his faded brown corduroys, v-neck sweatshirt and battered topsiders. The hair on his chest was soft and pale, several shades lighter than the hair on his head. 'How tired are you?' she asked, giving him a half smile.

Matthew grinned. 'What did you ladies talk about over there?'

'Oh, this and that.' She leaned against him and turned her face up for a kiss. He reached behind her neck, and at his touch she felt herself grow lethargic. She felt sleepy, sensuous, deliciously helpless.

'Come on,' he said, taking her hand and pulling her up off the couch. 'Let's go to bed.'

Maggie stumbled to her feet as if he had roused her from a pleasant dream. 'Why?' she asked.

He was halfway down the hall as she trailed along behind him. 'More comfortable. And besides, the kids.'

They stood on opposite sides of the bed. Matthew threw the covers back crisply and climbed in.

'Turn off the light, okay?' Maggie asked. She crept in next to him and he began to stroke her body. Maggie trailed her fingernails lightly up and down his back. She knew that within a minute, he would be kissing her breasts.

Later he asked her what happened.

'Overtired, I guess,' Maggie said. Between her legs, she ached from straining to achieve the impossible.

'You seemed interested enough out in the living room.' His voice was thick with impending sleep. Matthew could never keep his eyes open after sex. Maggie, on the other hand, found it rejuvenating and would often slip out of bed to balance her chequebook or tackle some long-neglected chore.

'I guess I lost it on the way down the hall,' Maggie said.

But he was already breathing deeply. Maggie felt tears leak out from under her closed lashes. She let them come. They trickled into her hair and grew cold. Then she put her hand between her legs as if to soothe a wound and finally fell asleep.

# Three

Maggie heard the children's key in the lock with the usual relief. It was past six-thirty already.

She held out her hands for their backpacks. 'Your father and I are going to the ballet with the Brodys tonight. I can't imagine why I forgot to tell you.'

Susan shrugged off her light jacket. 'That's two nights in a row, Mother,' she protested. 'Why can't we ever sit down and have dinner together like a normal family?'

'You always have rehearsals,' Fred said. He headed for the kitchen. 'What's to eat?'

'You're getting chubbier every minute!' Susan called after him. 'Better have a grapefruit!'

'Tell me about it, Jaws!' he shot back.

Susan looked at her mother furiously. 'I'm the only person in the whole universe who's got braces at fifteen years old. Why didn't you do it when I was nine and sex appeal didn't count? Fred's don't show at all and I can't even *smile* without blinding somebody. Is there any chocolate cake left?'

'You'd better hurry or there won't be.'

Fred had sliced a square of cake for his sister and set it on the kitchen table. Susan smiled at him. Maggie always marvelled at the way their animosity converted to good will. A display of affection between them, however limited, filled Maggie with a special kind of pleasure, perhaps because she and Joanne were strangers, or worse.

'Is it just because I'm your mother,' Maggie asked, 'or are you two extremely engaging?'

'We're extremely engaging,' Fred replied.

'It's because you're our mother,' Susan said.

'Don't eat any more of that because there's something else I forgot to tell you,' Maggie said. 'You're invited to eat with

20

Veronica at the Brodys.' She dipped her finger in Fred's icing and licked it.

'She's always snorting coke in the john,' Susan said.

'I can't believe that. She's just a baby.'

'You'd better believe it,' Fred said. 'I'll go anyway. Mrs Brody's a great cook.'

'How come you're forgetting all this stuff, Mom? It's not you.' Susan looked at her mother with concern.

'Momentary lapse, I guess. Do Robin and Jackson know about Veronica?'

'Mother, don't you dare tell them we said anything!' Susan cried.

'Mrs Brody's not dumb, Sue,' Fred said. 'I bet she already knows her stepdaughter's a looney-tune. Anyway, stepmothers are required to hate their stepchildren. It's in all the fairy tales. Except stepmothers are supposed to be ugly, and Mrs Brody's a piece of ass.'

'Fred,' Maggie complained. She realized with a shock that her discomfort rose not so much from Fred's language as from the realization that he was becoming a sexual person. It was happening too fast.

'You're a horny little thing,' Susan said, setting her dish in the sink. 'First it's Mrs Wheeler's legs and now Mrs Brody, and she's even pregnant.'

'That other friend of Mom's not bad either. Vonderhyde.'

'I can't stand it,' Maggie said.

Later on, she sent them off to the Brodys in a cab. The housekeeper would be there as chaperon, but still Maggie worried.

'We'll be fine, Mom,' Fred assured her. 'If Veronica wants to rot holes in her nostrils, that's her problem.'

'Anyway,' Susan added, 'as Marie Antoinette said, "Let them snort coke."'

Maggie shut the door and heard them chattering on their way to the elevator. They seemed so confident that nothing terrible could ever happen to them. When Maggie was growing up, she was always convinced that catastrophe was imminent. She read statistics about leukaemia, automobile accidents and spinal meningitis, and assumed they applied to her, if not today, then first thing next week. Somehow, her children had eluded the paranoia of her own adolescence. Perhaps it was because they had no older sister like Joanne to create emotional pandemonium.

An hour later, Maggie arrived at the *Café des Artistes*. She liked the place, with its lovely murals and dim light that was mysterious rather than oppressive. The European ambiance here was a respite from the raw pounding energy of the street outside. When Maggie felt like plugging into New York's potent current, she chose one of the bustling Third Avenue restaurants. There, plate glass windows revealed the mob inside to the mob outside, not like the *Café* where even the entrance was covert.

Robin and Jackson were already seated. Jackson, always gallant, rose to greet Maggie and settle her in her chair. Maggie would not have been surprised to have her hand kissed. It would be a natural gesture for Jackson Brody, though she had never met another man who could have got away with it.

Jackson was sixteen years older than Robin. He looked like General Robert E. Lee in a Brooks Brothers suit. Tall, elegant, silver-haired, he should have been Savannah bred, but in fact he was born in Jackson Heights – hence his name – just across the East River. Jackson had spent most of his life scrambling to support his parents, both now dead, and an alcoholic sister. He had met Robin – and Maggie, too – while working as an advertising executive at the mammoth *Woman's Companion* magazine. Then recently separated from his wife, he had lost his secretary besides. When Robin showed up for an interview, tripped over the extension cord, landed on Jackson's lap and said 'Hello' with perfect equanimity, Jackson hired her on the spot. They were married as soon as the divorce went through.

'The kids have an extra baby-sitter tonight,' Robin said.

'Aunt Titmouse from Dayton,' Jackson explained. Each of Robin's multitudinous relations was named after a bird.

Robin ignored him. 'My Auntie Wren is here overnight on her way to Boston. I'm glad she's around to keep an eye on the nest.'

'Do they need it?' Jackson asked.

'Veronica does,' Robin replied.

She knows, Maggie decided. And Jackson doesn't, or doesn't want to. The waiter, who had perfect white teeth, asked Maggie if she wanted a drink. She ordered a glass of wine. As another customer squeezed past their table, the waiter pressed against her bare shoulder. After he had gone, the small area on her skin throbbed pleasantly.

'Hello, troops,' Matthew said. He kissed the women and shook Jackson's hand. There was always an initial formality between the men, but after an evening together, Matthew invariably declared that Jackson was a terrific guy and he was going to set up a lunch date. Somehow, however, he never seemed to get around to it.

'Where'd you get that nice-looking corsage?' he asked Robin as he sat down next to Maggie. Robin wore a small bouquet of exotic blossoms over her left breast.

'Oh, Jackson's always bringing me flowers.' In her mid-Western drawl, the word came out 'flaahrs'.

'I think I last brought a bunch to Maggie when she was in the hospital having Fred. She's not the flowers type.'

Maggie stared at him.

'I made Jackson some beaded ones for his office,' Robin said. She looked extra pretty tonight, Maggie thought. Part of the glow was due to her pregnancy. After two miscarriages, making it past five months had added extra sparkle to her eyes. Her hair puffed around her face in a bubble that was the envy of every female two decades ago and the despair of Robin right now. But Jackson liked it, so that was how it stayed.

The waiter arrived with Maggie's wine. She wished he would press against her again, but dinner was served expertly without so much as a feather touch. The conversations soon split into duets: Jackson and Matthew on real estate; Robin and Maggie on the merits of bearing children.

'Jackson thinks I'm crazy to keep trying and I know he worries,' Robin said, 'but look, Maggie, you've got your art . . .'

Maggie laughed. She studied the scrap of paper she had been doodling on. She had sketched a cartoon of the waiter with the perfect teeth. 'This isn't exactly my idea of art.' Maggie crumpled the paper and tossed it in the ashtray.

Robin retrieved it, smoothed it out and examined it thoughtfully. 'I don't have much of a brain,' she said.

'You're a killer at the bridge table.'

'That wouldn't get me far in the world of high finance. I want babies. Maybe it's because I come from a big family, who knows? I just want at least one.'

'You don't have to defend yourself, Rob. I think it's a fine idea.'

Robin shook her head. 'Do you realize I've been pregnant almost non-stop for two years? And I get nuttier all the time. I lost Jackson's coffee yesterday. I picked up his cup to fill it, went into the bedroom to fetch something, I don't remember what, and when I came back to the kitchen, the cup was gone. We looked everywhere. I was ready to check into Bellvue.' She folded Maggie's cartoon and slipped it into her handbag. 'I finally found it when I went to change the sheets. It was in the linen closet.'

Maggie laughed. 'I remember. I always got this thing about open doors. I couldn't bear any door that was even slightly ajar. And I was always drifting off somewhere. I'd wake up and wonder where I'd been. At work, on the bus, it didn't matter.' She thought for a moment. 'As a matter of fact, it's been happening again lately, a little like that. Only, well, I know I'm not pregnant.'

'I was hoping it'd go away once I had the baby.'

'A lot of it did for me. Except that once you've got a child, you're not in control any more, and I don't know if it ever comes back completely. Maybe when they're all over twenty-one. I'm still waiting. Why did you save that cartoon?'

'I always keep your stuff. For when you're famous.'

Maggie laughed. The men's voices had risen to an impassioned pitch, so Maggie and Robin turned to listen.

'He bought in 'Sixty-eight – three bedrooms on Park for twenty-five grand!' Matthew exclaimed.

'Jesus!'

'How come you guys get so worked up over a pile of concrete?' Robin wanted to know.

'There's a great deal of magic in the rise and fall of co-op prices,' Matthew explained.

'Uh huh,' Maggie said.

They were nearly through with their coffee when a couple drifted past the table. The woman stopped and swooped on Matthew with a little cry.

'Matthew!' Her voice, like her face, was unmistakably that of Helene Sargeant, the actress. Matthew half-rose, but she placed her fingers with the long painted nails on his shoulder. And left them there, Maggie noticed.

'Please don't get up,' said Helene. She turned to her companion. 'Darling, this is the marvellous attorney who saved me from those dreadful piranha at Lunar Pictures.' 'Darling' was obviously doomed to remain nameless, so Matthew made his introductions.

'. . . and my wife, Margaret.' Maggie watched Helene's face and waited for the inevitable shock. It came, reading: *What's brilliant, gorgeous Matthew Hollander doing with a dowdy number like you?* Maggie wondered how difficult it would be to peel those white fingers off Matthew's suit.

Helene soon swept off in a cloud of chiffon and subtle perfume.

'Whew.' Jackson was awed. 'Do they always talk like that?'

'Yes,' Matthew said.

'I feel like a lump of pie dough,' Robin said, looking down at her pregnant bulge. 'She weighs ninety-two pounds with her jewels on.'

Maggie watched Matthew curiously. As always, he was unimpressed, by both Helene's celebrity stature and by her seductive interest in him. Maggie had attended cocktail parties where glamorous women draped their cleavages all over Matthew. He was polite, sometimes even flirtatious in the friendly manner he applied to his interchanges with the fat Hungarian lady who cleaned his office at night. Maggie would watch with amusement as Matthew's admirers became increasingly frantic in their efforts to engage his libido. Finally, if the attentions grew too heated, his face closed shop and he would move away. He didn't like obvious women, he said, which was his major complaint about Phyllis Wheeler.

'Helene reminds me of Phyllis Wheeler,' Matthew said.

'Lucky Phyllis,' sighed Robin.

'It's no compliment,' Maggie said.

'Helene's much more attractive,' Jackson said. 'More feminine.'

'Phyllis is about as feminine as Attila the Hun,' Matthew pronounced.

'Fred thinks she has nice legs,' Maggie said. 'Anyway, it's getting late. We ought to get the check.'

'Better watch out,' Matthew went on. 'Phyllis'll have our Fred in the sack before he knows what hit him.'

'That's a little too young, even for Phyllis,' Maggie said carefully. She drained her wine glass and looked around for the waiter. Something moved in her stomach, and she visualized her half-digested pasta coiling and twisting down there in the dark, as ugly as disloyalty. Matthew knew how his contempt for Phyllis pained Maggie. If Maggie was only more like her sister, Jo, she would stand up and deliver a diatribe right here in the subdued murkiness of the restaurant.

'Phyllis came to see me every day when I was in the hospital,' Robin said. 'She always brought something, a little gift. She acts tough, but she's a softie, really.'

'She'd seduce Jackson or me without a qualm,' Matthew said.

'That's different,' Robin said.

The men laughed.

'You guys don't understand. That's just sex,' Robin insisted.

'Just sex,' Matthew echoed. 'So Mags, how would you feel if I nailed Hilary Vonderhyde?'

'You don't have Phyllis's problems,' Maggie said. Her face was blazing.

'Well, she's an aggressive bitch, not to mention nymphomaniac. I don't know why you hang out with her.' Matthew now sounded as angry as Maggie felt.

The people at the next table had turned to look at them. Maggie dropped her voice and articulated with clipped deliberation. 'She can't help it. It's a sickness with her. She was raped by her cousin when she was eight years old and she's never gotten it all straightened out. Who could?'

'She probably raped *him*,' Matthew said.

Maggie forgot about the curiosity of the neighbouring table

26

and blurted furiously, 'You can't stand her because she's not a goddamn clinging vine like the rest of us.' As she glared at Matthew, Maggie felt that the only way to stop the trembling of her fingers would be to encircle his neck with them and squeeze hard. The fantasy terrified her. She dropped her eyes and murmured, 'I don't know where that came from.'

'I suggest you find out,' Matthew said in his attorney voice.

Robin was staring at them with the pain of a child watching its parents quarrel. Her lips moved as if she were trying to find the words to make it all better.

Maggie reached over to take a sip from Jackson's wine glass. 'It's all right, Robin. I'm all done being a bore.'

'My flowers smell like cigarettes,' Robin said sadly.

During the ballet, Maggie tried to concentrate on the dancers but was distracted by Matthew's body beside her. He was a shadowy hulk she could barely see out of the corner of her eye and yet every time he shifted in his seat, she startled. She felt frantic to do something about that substantial shape but could not think what it was she ought to do. Halfway through the performance, she began to feel trapped. She was four seats from the aisle. What if there was a fire? She'd never make it to the exit. She was perspiring and sick at her stomach. It seemed forever until the ecstatic audience allowed the ballerina to make her final bow.

Robin and Jackson got out of the cab first. In the elevator, Matthew said, 'Nice music. Did you enjoy it?'

Maggie nodded.

'Jackson's a good man,' he said serenely. 'Think I'll call him up and have lunch.'

'You do that,' Maggie said.

# Four

Maggie stood on the corner of Fifth Avenue and Fifty-third Street and closed her eyes. When she and Joanne were children, they had often played the blind game, tying scarves around their faces and stumbling about the house to see what it felt like. Maggie had watched her own children do the same thing. But this spot in front of St Thomas's church at noon on a sunny spring day seemed likely to short-circuit the sensitive auditory system of any blind person. Ornate, exotic languages eddied around her: Chinese, French, Spanish, something Slavic. Beyond the traffic sounds of Fifth Avenue, a vendor hawked t-shirts, announcing designer names like station stops on a commuter train. To her right, a trio – violin, flute and clarinet, she guessed – performed Vivaldi at the bottom of the church steps and, down the avenue, she could hear the plink-plank-plunk of Caribbean kettle drums. She wondered if a blind person could identify his locale simply by listening to the sounds of a given corner. The subdued din of Madison and Eighty-first must differ from a street in Soho or some busy intersection in the financial district.

As the light changed again, she was jostled out into the street. It was pleasant to move along with the crowd, and besides, she wanted to be prompt for her semi-annual lunch date with Hilary Vonderhyde. Ordinarily, Hilary needed three weeks' advance notice to squeeze a social lunch into her schedule, but this time she had called only yesterday. Maggie was so curious that she cancelled the appointment with her gynaecologist and agreed to come.

Maggie had not visited CinemInc since Hilary's last promotion. Her new office was vast. It had corner windows and a plush, colourful decor. On the walls were framed graphics of CinemInc's latest films. There were two medium-sized trees on either side of the couch. Hilary stood behind a sleek blond desk. She waved at Maggie and continued her telephone conversation.

'No, get me Phil Kessler. I don't *want* Mason, he's no damn good. I gotta go. Just do it, okay, hon? I know you can. 'Bye.' She hung up and came to give Maggie a kiss. Her electric blue silk blouse and grey slacks showed off her figure. She was as tall and slender as Maggie, though her breasts were fuller. She rarely wore a bra.

'I always like standing next to you,' Maggie said. 'With Robin, I remember those awful days when I was tallest in the class.'

'I know. I wanted to cut off my feet. Or head. Anything. I ordered us some salads. They ought to be here in a minute. Yikes, it's been a zoo around here today. We've got two productions going in Manhattan and there's an awful hassle with the sanitation department. Come and sit.' She led Maggie to the couch and they each took a corner. Maggie leaned back into the cushions and sighed.

'It's a beautiful office. Congratulations.'

'Not bad. They were scared shitless I was going to leave, but of course I wouldn't have.'

'You're still loving it.'

Hilary tapped her knee with her fist. 'It's my hedge against chaos, this place. It's only outside I get into trouble.'

A young man appeared at the door with two paper bags. He had a beard, a pony tail and a necktie with bright-red tongues on it. His eyes were innocent, ethereally beautiful, but his jeans were very tight. There was a bulge on the left side of his crotch which Maggie tried hard to ignore.

'Be a love, Tom, and don't let them get to me for half an hour.'

Tom nodded and left.

'Do you have to be gorgeous to work here?' Maggie asked.

'I think that's one of the reasons I'm comfortable in this place. Everybody's so attractive it's boring already. I don't get looked at here, not like on the street.' She prised open a tin-foil container and handed it to Maggie. 'The best fruit salad and frozen yogurt in town.'

'Is it really so terrible being beautiful?'

Hilary smiled at her. 'I'm thinking of getting a nose job.

29

I'm going to find some quack who'll bust it all to hell for me, and while he's at it, he can break a few teeth or rearrange them all snaggled and give me little squinty eyes. Maybe I'll order banana boobs and spindly legs.'

'I don't think you'd enjoy it.'

'I suppose not, but I'd like to try it for a day or two. You look pretty smashing yourself.'

Maggie was wearing the loose black dress that showed off her long legs. Sunglasses with immense round lenses were perched on her head.

'You seemed kind of down at Phyllis's,' Hilary went on. 'Is everything okay, really?'

'Not to worry.'

'She was on your case about your sex life.'

'I went right home and raped the elevator man.'

Hilary watched her in silence.

'Really, Hil. I'm fine. Lord.'

'Okay, but I don't like thinking you're off-centre. You're the most stable person I know.'

'Aren't I entitled to a nervous breakdown like everybody else?'

'How'd you like a job?' Hilary asked abruptly.

Maggie set down her plastic fork.

'Yeah, a job. Full time. I need somebody to do publicity posters. The guy we're using's a schmuck. Everybody comes out looking like Richard Burton or Elizabeth Montgomery.'

'Why me?'

'You can do likenesses. You've had plenty of experience at *Companion*'s.'

'Are you doing this because you're worried about me?'

'You just told me not to worry.'

'I haven't had a job in ten years. More. I'd have to talk to Matt. The kids.'

'What do they have to do with it?'

'Lots. It would mess everything up, me working. I don't even have the room at home, the materials.'

'You'll work here, lovey. What do you say?'

'I say . . . God. I don't know what to say.'

'The pay's good. Four hundred a week to start.'

'I think I made one-fifteen at *Companion*.'

'So you'll do it?'

Maggie laughed. 'Wait.' She sat still while her yoghurt melted into sugary soup. 'What if you had to fire me?'

'I'd be ruthless.'

'What about our friendship?'

'I can handle it if you can handle it. If I dump you, I guess we might have a couple of tense bridge games.'

'I'm flattered.'

'Don't be flattered, just do it. I need you. Now let's forget it and finish our lunch. Yuck. It's all mush.'

'I feel exactly the way I did the night Matthew called and asked me out.' She waved her hands in front of her face as if she were erasing a blackboard. 'Okay, okay, I'll forget it. You still seeing Bill?'

'I'm doing my best not to. Why am I so magnetized by bastards? It's a classic case of self-contempt. I'm always inflicting these sadists on myself. If they're nice, I just want them to go away.'

'What about the detective, isn't he nice?'

'Oh, Lou's all right. I let him touch me above the waist now, but I don't think he'll ever graduate to down below.' She stirred her yogurt absently. 'Sex has become an awful bore. Here I am in my prime and orgasms are like great big yawns. Maybe I should get into group gropes or necrophilia. Oh, Christ, Mag, I look at you and Matthew and wonder if it'll ever happen to me.'

'What makes us so great?'

Hilary leaned forward earnestly. 'You're friends. You respect one another. It shows in the way you relate.'

Maggie was beginning to feel the familiar panic again. It suddenly reminded her of being stuck between stations in the subway. It was always dark and hot and there was a dangerous smell. Perspiration slid down her sides.

'You're absolutely the best married people I know,' Hilary declared.

'What about Robin and Jackson?'

'That's strictly father-daughter. Who needs it? Besides, I'm too tall to be anybody's little girl. Come on.' Hilary unfolded

31

her legs. 'Let me show you around your new office.' Maggie got up and began tidying the coffee table, but Hilary took her arm. 'Leave it, you're not at home now.'

Maggie followed her down a carpeted corridor to the design department. There was a large well-lighted room with windows reaching practically to the ceiling. Two men and a woman looked up from their drawing boards to nod at Hilary. The men wore beards. One of them was completing a mock-up for the new Sylvia Goodwin picture. His composition was off, Maggie noticed. She longed to fix it.

Hilary half-dragged her out of the door and down the hall. 'One of the guy's gay, one's happily married, and the girl's an ambitious little thing. Reminds me of me. Ah, he's in.' They stood in the doorway of an office only slightly larger than Hilary's. 'Jim, this is the lady I told you about. Maggie Hollander, James Perry, our illustrious leader.'

Perry came around from behind his desk. He, too, was bearded. Perhaps it was a requirement for men working here, Maggie thought. The women had to be beautiful, the men hairy. Perhaps she ought to try growing a beard.

Perry had a kind young-old face – childlike expression and yet plenty of wrinkles in the forehead and around the eyes. He had probably suffered, but he was not embittered. His handclasp was warm and firm.

'I hear good things about you,' he said. 'I hope you'll be joining us.'

Maggie hoped her smile wasn't idiotic. Hilary walked her to the elevator.

'That's too much,' Maggie whispered. 'You didn't have to bother him.'

'We want you.'

'You don't even know what I can do.'

'Don't tell *me*. I'm paid to know what people can and can't do. It's you who doesn't know. You call me tomorrow.' It was a command. She gave Maggie a little shove into the elevator. On the way down, Maggie speculated as to why Hilary wasn't a more assertive bridge player. Perhaps if they tried playing in Hilary's elegant office where she felt most at home, there would be a marked improvement.

When Hilary had first showed up as a copy editor at *Woman's Companion*, Maggie had sensed the vine-covered walls and manicured lawns in her background. It turned out that the two women had been educated at neighbouring boarding schools and had almost certainly met on one another's lacrosse fields. They traded stories about the agonies of tea dances, the joy of tiffin, the mysterious forbidden attraction of 'townies'. One day when Maggie's parents arrived at the office to take her to lunch, Hilary pulled Maggie aside nearly exploding with suppressed laughter, to inform Maggie that their mothers owned the exact navy Lily Pulitzer wrap-around with the yellow daisy print. Before long, Maggie and Hilary called their parents identical pairs of 'BYWs', or Boring Yankee Wasps.

If these two had been watered in the same garden, how then, Maggie wondered, had their futures diverged so dramatically? Here was Hilary, a glittering success in her career, interviewed in *Time*, photographed for fashion magazines, with nothing but emptiness and discontent lurking one step outside her glamorous office. And for Maggie, there was the doling out of meals and comfort while her dreams of artistic creativity had shrivelled into a tiny painful knot in some obscure corner of her consciousness.

Back in her own kitchen massaging spices into the leg of lamb, Maggie thought about how it would be if she actually took the job. The idea seemed so radical, and yet women went back to work all the time. But the children still needed her. And Matthew, too. He was hopelessly disorganized outside his office. Of course, she could hire someone to do the errands. Still, nobody else could do them properly. Who else could have chosen the appropriate present for Fred's friend? Who else could select the exact colour of Matthew's shoelaces? What about groceries and menu-planning? It was so complicated, with Susan's allergies. By the time she finished explaining everything to a housekeeper, it would be easier to do it herself. And who wanted a stranger around the house? It was such an intrusion. No, she wouldn't take the job. Later, when the children were in college.

Besides, wasn't she supposed to be an artist, the kind who sits in a room by herself and creates things that do more than persuade people to buy things they can't afford? She always

33

meant to make art, not sales. On the other hand, she had never been convinced of the value of her vision. And CinemInc was so attractive. It had been a long time since she'd participated in the companionable activity of a busy office. And she was needed. Hilary had made that very clear. Oh, hell, maybe she'd just do it.

She changed her mind a dozen times before dinner. Finally, she resolved to let the ultimate decision rest with the reaction of her family. She would assess their response and act accordingly.

It was peculiar for Maggie to be the bearer of news. Normally, she listened while the others related the day's triumphs and defeats. Tonight would be different. She would wait and tell them at dinner when they were all sitting down together. She was eager to share it, and yet holding back for a little while was delicious, the way she had hoarded the confirmation of her pregnancy with Fred, lying on her bed and smiling at the ceiling for an hour before calling Matthew.

Finally, when everyone was seated, she handed the platter of roast lamb across the table to Matthew. Fred watched her.

'What's with you, Mom?' he asked.

Maggie reached out and touched her son's arm in appreciation. 'I've been offered a job.' There was so much music in the statement that it sounded like a chord played by a full orchestra, strings, woodwinds, brass and all. Everyone heard it differently.

'You don't sound very happy about it,' Susan said.

'She does, too,' Fred objected.

'What kind of job?' Matthew asked. 'Pass the butter, please, Frederick.'

'Assistant art director at CinemInc. I'd be doing the promotion posters.'

'Jeez, CinemInc,' Fred breathed. 'Maybe I could meet Harrison Ford.'

'Hilary got you into it?' Matthew asked.

Maggie nodded. 'She really put on the pressure. Even introduced me to James Perry. He's very nice.'

Matthew smiled indulgently. 'Jim Perry's a lot of things, but nice isn't one of them.'

'How would you feel if I took it?' Maggie asked.

'How you feel is more to the point.'

'What if your shirts aren't done on time? What about dinner? What about . . .'

He interrupted her. 'Get a go-fer. Hire somebody. It's just scutt work around here. I assume they'll pay you decently.'

Scutt work, Maggie said to herself. So that's what she'd been doing all these years.

'How *much*, Mom?' Susan persisted.

'Four hundred a week.'

'Take it,' Matthew said. 'It'll be good for you to do something useful.'

'Mom's useful,' Fred said. He was beginning to look anxious.

'Just like that, just take it,' Maggie said.

'Yup,' Matthew affirmed.

'You make it sound so easy.'

'Shouldn't be hard. It's nice of Hilary.'

'I don't know if she's being *nice* . . .' Maggie began. 'She seems to think I can do it.'

'Of course you can do it, but you don't have a track record in the field. She could choose anybody at all for an operation like CinemInc.'

Maggie sat in silence.

'Will you be home when we get out of school?' Fred wanted to know.

'I don't know. I guess not,' Maggie replied.

'I wouldn't like that. I'd live with it for the sake of art, though, I guess.'

'Art!' Susan sniffed. 'It's a big sellout if you ask me. Mom's work should be hanging in the Metropolitan, not the subway station. Boy, when I'm a writer, you won't catch me writing junk. If it's not good stuff, I won't write at all.'

'I thought you were going to be an actress,' Fred said. 'You're always blabbing away in that goony accent.'

'I'm just trying to stay in character,' she protested. As the lead in the school production of *Our Town*, Susan had adopted a decidedly New England inflection.

'You'll wind up writing TV scripts for *Dallas*,' Fred taunted.

'I'd die first.'

'Cool it,' Matthew said. 'I'll have another slice of that lamb.'

The decision is up to your mother. Let her struggle with it in peace.'

'It isn't only up to her, Daddy. We're her family,' Susan complained.

'Why do you talk about me as if I'm not here? I'm not "her", I'm "you".' Susan looked confused. 'Never mind,' Maggie said.

But Susan turned to address her directly. 'Okay, I'm saying that as my mother, you have a responsibility to be a role model and I don't think you're being a very good one.'

'Oh, listen to her . . .' Fred began in disgust, but Susan cut him off.

'No, really, she's this homebody type all the time and we all know what that means . . .'

Maggie wondered what it meant.

'. . . and now she's going to take this sucky job that just exploits her talent as a true artist, so then she'll be a failure as a woman *and* an artist. What kind of example is that for her children, especially me, since I'm the creative one?'

'That's the most ridiculous junk I ever heard,' Fred maintained.

Maggie sat looking at her plate. She was trying to hide the fact that she was crying but it was difficult because large drops kept splashing onto her vegetables. The others watched in horror as tiny thuds of tears hit her baked potato. Maggie never cried in front of the children.

'I think you'd better apologize to your mother, Susan,' Matthew said.

By this time, Susan was crying, too. 'I'm sorry, Mommy.'

But Maggie shoved her chair back and murmured, 'I think I'd better be excused.' She fled to the bedroom and shut the door.

Later as she and Matthew lay side by side in the dark, Maggie said, 'I think I might like to try sky-diving some day.'

'You're kidding me.'

'I don't know if I am.'

'Well, take it from me, it's not your style.' He rolled over and soon she could hear him breathing with the slow rhythm of sleep.

# Five

The buzzer sounded next to Matthew Hollander's elbow. He pushed a button. 'Send him in, Barbara.' Hollis Reardon's papers were ready, and Matthew was pleased. He had prised a reasonable deal out of International Films, a particularly gratifying outcome since Reardon had been screwed at least a dozen times over the years. It was pitiful how helpless creative people could be. In fact, their vulnerability was the reason Matthew had opted for entertainment law in the first place. Writers, performers, painters, it was all the same. Somebody had to protect their interests or they'd never survive.

The one exception was Maggie. She was the only artist Matthew had ever met with common sense. Joanne had the creative temperament in that family. Of course, Joanne was compelled to paint, and with Maggie, art was strictly part-time; though in his opinion, Maggie was more talented.

Hollis Reardon stepped into the office. Matthew rose to shake his hand. 'Glad to meet you in person after all those marathon phone calls,' Matthew said. Reardon was short, round and red-faced, not at all what Matthew had expected from the deep booming drawl.

'Some beautiful view,' Reardon said.

Matthew glanced out the window. His office was twenty storeys up over New York Harbour. The building, constructed in 1898, had long ago achieved landmark status. Matthew's mahogany-panelled office had been occupied by lawyers since the turn of the century. 'Thanks for reminding me,' he said. 'I don't think I've looked out of that window in three weeks. Have a seat.'

'I want to thank you for what you've done,' Reardon said. 'I really got my ass wiped with the last screenplay.'

Matthew smiled. Vulgarity seemed incongruous coming

37

from the rosebud mouth of this small man. Still, Reardon's writing was powerful, often even brutal. Matthew thought of Maggie's paintings. They shimmered with vitality, and yet she was a restrained person, rather formal, not the least bit flamboyant.

'We've built in some percentage points in case the picture does well,' Matthew said, 'but I think we've got the maximum up front. Once these guys get out of production and into the accountant's office, you end up with zero.'

Reardon nodded. 'I've been up that rat hole.'

They spent an hour poring over the papers for Reardon's contract. Then Matthew leaned back in his chair. A few years ago, he would have made sure his client was out of the door the moment they finished, but Matthew had put in plenty of pressure-cooker years. Now he was entitled to savour his triumphs. He snapped the stereo on to WQXR and was rewarded with Rubinstein's Chopin *Preludes*.

'You know what this contract means, besides for paying off the Mercedes?' Reardon asked. 'After I finish the film, I'm taking six months off to write poetry.'

'My mother was a poet for a while,' Matthew said. 'She even published a book. A small one.'

'That was in the days when people read poems, I guess,' Reardon said.

'She was damn good. It was a great disappointment to her that I didn't inherit any of her literary genes. Christ, she used to sit with me hour after hour doing "descriptions", she called them. I was supposed to describe things I saw or thought about or dreamed of. Hopeless. I couldn't even write a decent letter home from camp.'

Reardon's cherubic face looked so crestfallen that Matthew smiled. 'That's probably why I got into this business. I may not possess the sparks myself, but I can be the guardian of the flame.' Matthew looked at his watch. The gesture was not lost on Reardon. He rose and held out his hand.

Afterwards, Matthew sat and stared out of the window. The Statue of Liberty looked like a Staten Island housewife who had fallen into the water with her nightgown on. She rose out of the harbour with her hair in rollers. Helicopters flew past her head like gnats and she had raised a weary hand to swipe at them. Rubinstein switched to Brahms. The sound was complex, passionate and disturbing. Matthew felt eyes on him and turned to see Maggie's face regarding him from her portrait. It was his favourite picture of her, taken when they were first married. Her hair had been longer then, long enough to wear in stubby braids. She was sitting on the gunwale of a sailboat wearing white shorts, one of Matthew's t-shirts, and a wide grin. Come to think of it, he hadn't seen that grin in a long time.

Maybe he ought to take her on a vacation this summer when the kids went to camp. Up until now, there had been so many demands from the firm. Matthew had seen his opportunity to become indispensable. He had achieved that now, as much as anybody could realistically become indispensable. But he deserved a break, and the two of them hadn't been away alone together in several years. Maggie sometimes talked wistfully about London and Paris, but he failed to see the charm in clomping around a city when they lived in one. Maybe an adult tennis camp. Maggie enjoyed being active as much as he did. He'd check into it.

Funny how he couldn't seem to get into his work today. Ordinarily, he enjoyed his office. He was eager to plunge in every morning and reluctant to extract himself in the evening. Matthew performed countless juggling acts every day, keeping clients, adversaries, and other attorneys spinning in the air above his desk. For the most part, they returned to earth at Matthew's bidding to land on the appropriate spot. It had happened that way with Reardon, but there were two other challenging matters that required his immediate attention. However, rather than delve into the files with his customary ardour, he swung around in his chair again to avoid Maggie's stare. Home was intruding into his bastion today. Perhaps it was this morning's conference with Susan's teacher, where he was due in less than an hour.

This would be Matthew's first parent-teacher conference since Susan's nursery school years. During her first weeks, Matthew had walked her to the sunny brick building every morning on his way to work. She was so tiny that he could cup her chin with his hand as they strolled side-by-side along

Seventy-ninth Street. She had clung to him and cried when it was time for him to leave her. Matthew had expected this, but he was unprepared for his own pain.

In early October, there had been a crisis at the firm. Maggie took over walking Susan, and Matthew had never really participated in her education again. But he still remembered that when he kissed her good-bye outside her nursery schoolroom, she had smelled of bread and butter.

Matthew quickly became comfortable with Maggie's sovereignty in that area of their lives. He trusted her judgement with the children more than his own. What was more, he had come to dislike any trespass from home into the cerebral citadel of his profession. Today, however, Susan's teacher had particularly asked if both parents would be attending the conference. Maggie interpreted this to mean that Matthew's presence was expected. Susan had walked into the kitchen just as the topic arose. She had fixed her eyes on his face, and Matthew found there was no way to refuse.

He peered sideways at Maggie's photograph and could not help smiling. He remembered that they had just made love minutes before he snapped the picture. Christ, they'd been crazy about one another. In those days, Maggie could barely keep her hands off him. Even at the movies, she would have her hand hidden under his extra sweater or raincoat draped across his lap. It was the same with him. Her breasts were like small round magnets; even in public places, he was always managing a sly touch.

The first time he had got close to her, she was standing at the check-out counter in the Cambridge five-and-dime. Silently, he calculated that spot on his ribcage where her breasts would hit him. He liked the way she carried herself, proudly, like a beautiful woman. There was a cloaked quality of specialness about her that he found tantalizing, perhaps all the more because she was, at first glance, rather plain. Matthew was well aware of the bewilderment people like Helene Sargeant tried to mask when meeting Maggie for the first time. Matthew's reaction was inevitably one of smugness. Maggie was secret treasure. No one else knew her sensuality, her talent, her intelligence, her warmth.

He saw her work at the student gallery in May of their Junior Year. The energy of the compositions intrigued him. He thought about her, and her pictures, all summer, and at the first opportunity, which turned out to be that sparkling September day in Harvard Square, he had slipped his arm through hers.

He could still visualize her sitting across from him in the coffee shop. The flat surfaces of her face hid nothing, and yet she took such care in what she revealed with words. She had lightly-freckled skin and a wide smile that showed white teeth still grooved at the edges like a child's. There was a gap between the front two that created a slight lisp. Matthew found it enchanting. He could see the tip of her tongue as it appeared behind that space when she spoke.

Matthew was accustomed to being gazed at by faces that oozed adulation. Maggie's eyes, however, seemed to be measuring him. Their clear message said, *Look mister, I know you're supposed to be a hotshot, but I'm not impressed yet.* From the start, he was eager to earn her regard.

His clock bonged ten times. He would have to get a move on if he was going to make Susan's conference on time. Regretfully, he snapped off the radio.

Matthew was the only man wearing a suit in the subway car. At this hour, it was almost empty. Beside the uptown door slouched a heap of filthy rags with a pair of naked blackened feet protruding from the bottom and a rope of greasy hair on top twisted into a grotesque tiara. Two Puerto Rican men rode directly across from Matthew. They talked animatedly in Spanish with much gesticulation. One was angry, the other apologetic but calm. The louder the angry man became, the more silent his companion. Finally, at Fourteenth Street, the quiet man began speaking. He permitted no interruption and restrained the other man's speech by holding his hands down. By Thirty-third Street, he had finished. As the train pulled into the station, they stared at one another. Then the angry man, with tears on his cheeks, reached for his friend and they embraced. Both men's eyes were tight shut. After that, they sat next to one another without speaking until Fifty-ninth where they got off.

Since subway trips were normally for catching up on reading, Matthew was seldom aware of such interchanges. But something about the relationship between the two men captured his attention. Matthew had no close male friends. There were other lawyers to meet for lunch, men at the Harvard Club with whom he played an occasional game of squash, and there were the husbands of Maggie's friends, yet no one but Maggie was allowed access to his deepest feelings. Perhaps these men were brothers. Matthew was an only child, but he knew from watching Maggie and Joanne what passion siblings could rouse in one another.

Matthew had been born late to busy parents who often left him alone to fend for himself. He became accustomed to long hours on his own where companionship meant books or imaginative games with his stuffed bear. When Matthew was five, his father confiscated the bear and incinerated it, believing his son had become overly dependent upon it. It was the only time Matthew could remember raised voices in his home. Matthew's mother bought him another bear, but Matthew kept it on his shelf and did not play with it again.

He was always well-liked. He was elected president of his class every year. There were plenty of other boys around to study with or joke with in the locker room, but nobody ever really knew what Matthew was thinking or feeling. The boys he was drawn to were the loners, the types who baffled the popular group or were despised by them. Matthew admired the solitary boys' independence, their individuality, and he understood their loneliness. One's name was Bobby Hughes, he still remembered, a gawky, sheepish fellow with a genius for botany. Any attempt to become closer to such a boy, however, was ridiculed by the others or met with incredulity by the boy himself. Matthew kept himself busy with schoolwork, extracurricular activities, and finally girls, so that he rarely felt anything was missing. Anyway, Maggie was his best friend now.

The cool air tasted delicious after the sour heat of the subway. Matthew took deep breaths as he hurried along Eighty-sixth Street. Susan and Fred's school was in a handsome stone townhouse just off Fifth Avenue. Around the Central

Park Reservoir, joggers made splashes of colour like bright tropical birds as they flashed through the trees. What kind of work did those people do, that they could take a run in the middle of the day? Matthew wondered.

Maggie was waiting in the reception area. Matthew bent to kiss her, but they parted quickly when a trim young woman approached them with her hand outstretched. The teacher wore her hair pulled back into a pony tail tied with coloured yarn. Today the bow was hot pink.

'Miss Lennox. Good morning,' Matthew said, and shook her hand.

Miss Lennox drew them into a quiet room away from the reception desk's shrill telephone.

'Is Susan aware that you are here this morning?' Miss Lennox began. The woman never used contractions. Susan did a devastating imitation of her, which Maggie was trying hard to put out of her mind.

'Yes,' Matthew replied. 'She heard us making plans to come up. She didn't seem disturbed, just curious.'

'I think she is depressed,' Miss Lennox continued. 'There has been a decline in her work this term. She is doing all right, but not as well as she should be. Her demeanour has changed. She sits by herself sometimes in homeroom, and appears to be close to tears. I have checked with her other teachers, and they have all noticed the shift.'

'Maybe it's too much pressure from that play,' Maggie said.

Miss Lennox nodded. 'I did consider that, but then I realized that she only really seems like herself when she is discussing it. Her face lights up, she sits up straighter and so on. I wonder if perhaps it could still be her problem from last winter.'

'What problem?' Matthew asked.

'You know, Matthew,' Maggie said. 'When she started her period.'

Matthew looked stunned.

'It is harder for some girls,' Miss Lennox continued. 'It came late for her, which can be upsetting. And of course, Susan is very sensitive. She takes her womanhood seriously.'

'What can we do?' Maggie asked.

43

'I am not sure what is going on, as I said. Perhaps she will snap out of it over the summer. It is such a crazy age. I just hate to see her looking so down, you know? I am very fond of her. It's been a joy having her in my class.'

Maggie was thinking that this was the second time this week she'd heard the word 'down' used as an adjective, and also that Miss Lennox had ultimately surrendered to the contraction.

At the coffee shop on Eighty-sixth Street, Maggie stirred her black coffee with a spoon to cool it off.

'What's the matter with the way that woman talks?' Matthew asked.

'She's very formal.'

'I'll say.'

'What should we do about our daughter?'

Matthew took a gulp of his coffee. Maggie maintained that the inside of his mouth was lined with asbestos.

'Nothing,' he said. 'Typical adolescent *angst*. She'll be fine once she's in camp. When was it again she started menstruating?' he asked casually.

'You've forgotten about it altogether.'

'Weren't there a lot of false alarms, ever since she was, what, twelve, thirteen?'

'Don't you remember what a state she was in? Ashamed to go to school, everybody would know? How could you forget something like that?'

'February, wasn't it?'

Maggie's face was stony like an ancient sculpture with empty sockets where the eyes were supposed to be.

'I didn't forget,' he said.

'Please don't tell me you had a lot on your mind.'

'Okay.' He put his hand over hers. 'Mag, you want to take a vacation with me this summer? There's a really nice tennis camp in Vermont.'

'I don't know.'

'How come you don't know?'

'I don't know why I don't know. Let me think about it.'

'All right.' He glanced at his watch and rose. 'Gotta run, honey. You sit and enjoy your coffee.'

'What about dinner?'

'I'll call you later. I'll probably make it home.' He gave her a comradely slap on the back and disappeared out of the door.

Maggie took a sip of her coffee and gasped as it seared her tongue. Most likely he would forget to call, or call too late for her to organize dinner. She hated to phone him at the office. His voice always sounded like a tape-recorded message or else she was put on 'hold'. She was left with the usual choices: prepare dinner for the children at six-thirty or ask them to wait until their father came home, just in case he made it. Or feed them early, and either eat with them or try to wait until later. Or perhaps he would end up grabbing a sandwich at his desk after all. Phyllis Wheeler served dinner no later than 7 p.m. and thereafter declared the kitchen closed. But Maggie found she was incapable of doing that to Matthew when he worked such long hours and came home looking like he had been sucked dry.

Anyway, today was hardly a time to be looking for extra consideration from Matthew after he had trekked all the way uptown for the conference.

A twelve-year-old girl was looking through the coffee shop window, and Maggie imagined Susan's face chastizing her. Twelve years old was just about the time in her daughter's life when Maggie began to lose control, not in the sense of discipline but in her confidence that she was making valid decisions about Susan's life. Up until she was twelve, Susan had been deeply involved in art. Suddenly, however, Susan declared that she was finished making messes. She would become an actress or a writer. The art teacher spoke with Maggie about the sudden loss of interest, and Maggie had felt a strange sense of *déjà vu* listening to Susan's protestations that if she could not be great she didn't want to try any more. She had snatched a watercolour off her bulletin board, ripped it up, and then burst into tears. She slammed her door against Maggie's sympathy, and Maggie had gone into her own room to cry, for the destruction of a quite beautiful painting and for the pain of a young girl who could not tolerate her own talent.

Maggie wondered if psychiatry might help. Matthew would accuse her of overreacting, and yet she was at a loss as to how to help her daughter. Maggie envied Matthew his *laissez-faire* attitude towards the children, but she wished there was someone she could talk to about Susan. The only person who came to mind as a sensible, sympathetic listener was Fred – and of course, the thought was absurd.

Susan was propped up in bed, coming into the final pages of *Green Dolphin Street*. Maggie slipped in quietly and sat by her feet.

'What do you think of it?' Maggie asked.

'Pretty excellent.'

'Honey . . .' Maggie began. Susan's face was buried in the book. Maggie gently removed it, taking care to keep the place with her finger. 'You haven't asked about our conference with Miss Lennox.'

'Nope.'

'Aren't you curious?'

'I guess so.'

'She's a little concerned about your state of mind.'

'I am okay.' Susan began tracing the designs in her quilt.

'Don't mock her. I want to talk.'

'I didn't know I was.'

'Miss Lennox says you seem depressed.'

Susan shrugged.

'Is it your periods?'

'*That*.' Her voice was filled with disgust.

'Are you having trouble with it?'

'I'm getting it, isn't that trouble enough?' The reading light glinted off her braces.

'It shouldn't be trouble. It should be a joy.'

Susan burst out, 'A joy! That's rich!'

Maggie dipped her head and smiled. 'You're right. That sounded like something my ninety-year-old ex-gynaecologist would say. Let's call it a mixed blessing.'

'Well, I'd just as soon be a guy.'

'You seemed so happy when it first came, and then I don't know what happened to you.'

'Mom, it's different before,' Susan explained patiently. 'There's, like, this crazy idea that it's a magic event or something. Everything's going to be perfect when you get your period and it's practically all anybody ever talks about in Junior High. You'll be beautiful and, oh, womanly, or something. You wait and wait, and then, God.' She shuddered. 'Who knew it would just be gory and disgusting.'

Maggie fingered the soft tendrils that waved around her daughter's cheeks. 'It's not so bad being a woman.'

'Mom, I don't want to hurt your feelings . . .'

'But?'

'I don't know how to say this without . . .'

'Never mind. Just out with it.'

Susan dropped her eyes. 'I'd just rather not end up like you.'

Maggie sighed.

'If you're not miserable, you ought to be,' Susan declared.

'Why?'

'It's *nothing* here. You wait on everybody, do chores, tuck us all in, and I'm not saying I don't appreciate it. But Mom, *I* don't want to grow up and be everybody's nursemaid. I mean, God, Mom, you went to Radcliffe!' Susan's eyes had filled with tears. 'I want to be pretty,' she went on. 'I want to grow up and have babies. I love babies. I mean, when I'm baby-sitting and I hold Meredith, I pretend she's mine. But . . .' Her voice had deteriorated into a strangled choke. Tears spilled onto her nightshirt. Maggie held out her arms.

'I'm not saying it's easy,' Maggie said, rocking her. 'I guess I'm still looking for answers, too.'

Susan's voice was muffled against her shoulder. 'I don't want to learn with you, I want you to show me. I want you to know.'

'But those would be my answers, honey. You have to find your own.'

Susan sniffed. Maggie reached for the Kleenex box, handed it to her and sat back to watch her blow her nose. 'God, Mom, sometimes I'm so grim I can't stand myself.'

'That's your job. You're a teen-ager.'

'I just want to be happy.' She smiled wanly at Maggie. 'Tall order, huh?'

Maggie nodded. 'It'll require some effort.' She picked up

47

Susan's book and skimmed the last page. 'You're going to like the ending.'

'Don't tell me!'

Maggie gave the damp cheek a kiss. It tasted cool and salty. 'I'm nuts about you,' she said.

'Well, I'm just plain nuts,' Susan replied.

When Maggie crawled into bed later on, she realized that sometime since her conversation with Susan, she had decided to unearth her oils and her easel.

# Six

Phyllis Wheeler rolled over, propped herself up on an elbow and studied the young man lying next to her. She congratulated herself. He was beautiful. Blond and lean with none of the crude dark fuzz that matted Stephen's chest and back.

The bedroom was darkened by lined drapes closed against the noon sun. It was warm for mid-May, so Phyllis had closed the windows and switched on the air conditioning. Its level hum muffled the street sounds. She listened, imagining that they were on a ship in a deep turquoise sea, far from East Eighty-second Street.

Phyllis's love affairs were usually conducted during the daytime while Stephen was at work and Zachary in school. Always before, there had been hotel rooms or bachelor apartments. This was the first time she had permitted a lover into her own home.

She was perplexed at her voraciousness in making love just now. After all, she felt no particular affection for this young man. Perhaps it was danger that intensified the experience. Across the room, Stephen's bureau stood dark and disapproving against the wall. Its knobs were round eyes that had seen it all. There had been a stain on Stephen's tie this morning. He had snatched it off and it still lay draped across the foot of the bed, the very bed where his wife now lolled in naked depravity with another man. Stephen was everywhere. Phyllis put her hands between her legs where she was beginning to tingle again.

The last time she had played in her very own bed with a forbidden member of the opposite sex was nearly thirty years ago. It was in the bed of her childhood and the boy was her cousin Breen.

She leaned back against the pillow and closed her eyes.

Breen was five years older than Phyllis. She was eight when he came to Chicago for his first visit. He was taller and more developed than most boys his age, and Phyllis thought he was wonderful. Her uncle had married a wealthy non-Jewish heiress, and Breen had been raised on a horse ranch in Kentucky. To a city girl like Phyllis, Breen blazed with the allure of real cowboys, who were never Jewish. He even wore leather boots with pointed toes.

The first time Breen touched her between the legs she had been terrified. Their parents had gone out, leaving him in charge. He helped her into her nightgown – she remembered it was a long white one with a lilac ribbon at the neck – and began to talk about what horses did back home. He said that the boy horses would nuzzle the female horses like this, and he pressed his cheek against her flat little breast.

When Phyllis stiffened, Breen had asked her, softly, but with just the right amount of contempt. 'You're not scared, are you?' She had shaken her head and even tried to smile.

Phyllis knew nothing about horses then, but she soon learned: how the boy horse rubbed against the body of the female horse, how he licked and kissed between her legs, how the female horse would touch, sometimes with her mouth, the fearful swollen fascinating thing he had and she hadn't. Breen made her swear not to tell her parents, but it was not the sort of thing she would ever tell them anyway. The feelings Breen had aroused in her were too complex and powerful to entrust to her mother and father.

Morris Jacobson thought only of his business, a dry-goods store in Skokie that seemed always on the verge of bankruptcy, or so he would have them believe. Phyllis's mother was a woman of great emotional excess. Subtlety, nuance, even ambivalence were beyond her. She responded to the rare 'C' on Phyllis's report card with primitive despair, first wailing, then raging, and ultimately resorting to the supply of tranquillizers she kept in a dainty porcelain box in her handbag. How could Phyllis possibly explain to these two how she adored and despised her own cousin?

Breen's visits to Chicago became more frequent. At first, Phyllis would become ill just before. The vomiting always lasted until their first time alone together. After that, the sick feeling passed off. By the time she was ten, however, she had stopped dreading his appearances. In fact, she began to long for him. She could scarcely wait for the first weeks of summer vacation because she knew he would come. One time the two families took a trip to Canada together, and camped in a cabin on a mountain lake. Those were the best days of all. They would row across the water to a little island where they could take off one another's clothing without fear of discovery or interruption. Phyllis liked to pretend they were Adam and Eve, or that they were adrift on a ship far off in the middle of an exotic sea.

The 'horse games' continued until Phyllis was twelve and Breen seventeen. After that, he went off to college in California and by the time she saw him again two years later, the romance had become diluted for them both. Breen had his guitar-playing radical and Phyllis was enjoying her exploration of the junior varsity basketball team. She was not a pretty girl, but she was popular with the boys. They sensed she knew things the other girls did not have a clue about.

Looking back, two phenomena seemed remarkable about the adventures with Breen. First, that they had never been caught. Second, that the emotional aftermath resulted in a strange split for Phyllis. She developed a life-long terror of horses and a chronic addiction to sex. As she told her therapist, she considered herself lucky that it hadn't turned out the other way around.

The young man stirred in his sleep. He had claimed to be twenty-three, but Phyllis had her doubts. Lying there with his eyes closed, he could barely pass for eighteen. She ran her fingers lightly along the inside of his tanned thigh and watched with interest as his penis twitched and began to swell. Ah, youth, she thought. She knew from a mutual friend that he was bi-sexual. It seemed magnanimous of him not to deprive one entire gender of his stamina and expertise.

He turned to her and draped a shapely leg across her thigh.

'What do you want to be when you grow up?' she asked him.

'Kept,' he murmured.

'God, I wish I could afford you.' She cupped his genitals

reverently in her hand. 'You are a sensational fuck. Further-more, I've never done it in my own bedroom before.'

'Not even with your husband?'

'The one exception.'

The eyes opened finally. They were pale blue and ingenuous. 'Where is he?'

'Writing advertising copy on Madison Avenue. You know the one about putting zing in your mouthwash? That's my boy.'

'Oh, wow.' He was impressed.

'Stephen's hoping to make a name for himself with ads for douches that taste like brandy alexanders.'

'They can't do that on TV, can they?'

'Therein lies the challenge. Stephen always appreciates a challenge.'

'You don't seem to like him much.'

'Not a lot.'

'Why don't you get a divorce?'

'Because he's interesting. And very smart. He's the only person I ever met who got a perfect score on all his college boards. One of these days he'll set the world on fire, but it's taking him a while to gel.'

The young man glanced nervously at the bedroom door.

'Don't worry. It's lunch hour. He's probably at the Hyatt with his secretary.'

'Jesus. My parents wonder why I don't get married.'

'Marriage is fine as long as one has realistic goals,' Phyllis said. 'The object is to keep it from getting monotonous. When we get in a rut, somebody always livens things up.' She traced circles around his nipples. 'For instance today. Stephen's never had the nerve to bring anybody to the apartment. Now I'm one up on him.'

'I don't understand.'

'Well, but he would. He admires my sense of competition.'

'You're not going to tell him.'

'No, but *I'll* know, and he'll know there's something.'

She looked at the bedside clock and nestled down next to him. 'Let's have another round. I've got to kick you out at 2.30.' She kissed him. His back felt smooth under her palms, almost like a woman's. She wished she could persuade Maggie to try him out. It would do her a world of good.

The doorbell rang, twice in quick succession. Phyllis sat up abruptly. 'Oh, my God,' she whispered.

'Is it him?' The youth had pulled the sheet up to his neck.

'No, I think it's my son. It can't be . . . oh, Christ . . .'

The bell rang again, twice.

'That's his signal. Get out.' She yanked the bedclothes back. 'You'll have to hide in my closet.'

'Shit, I'm not hiding in anybody's closet.'

'Yes, you are.' She hauled him out of bed and shoved him towards the closet with his clothes. 'Don't come out of there until I come and get you. I swear to God, if he catches one glimpse, I'll kill you. I mean it.'

She slipped a robe on, shut the bedroom door and hurried through the living room. She peered through the peephole. A twelve-year-old, dark-haired boy stood outside. Phyllis's hands trembled as she unlatched the lock.

'Zach, I'm sorry, honey, I was napping. What are you doing home?'

'Mark has a fever so Mrs Johnson said I shouldn't stick around.' He smiled up at her. 'Aren't you going to let me in?'

Phyllis leapt aside. 'Of course. You hungry?'

Zachary gave her an odd look. 'You fed me lunch before I went down there, Mom.'

'Oh, right.'

'Are you okay?'

Phyllis ran her fingers through her hair and glanced down at her robe. She felt a sudden terror that there were semen stains across the front. 'I'm all disorientated. Serves me right for snoozing when I should be paying bills.'

Zachary was slight and willowy like Phyllis, but had his father's deep brown eyes. He was an imaginative child. Rather than submit himself to the rigours of rough-and-tumble playgrounds, he chose to stay at home and construct elaborate games from the vast laboratory of his active intellect. Sometimes Phyllis would call to him as she passed his room. 'Who're you talking to, Zach?'

'Formack, the Mighty,' he would say. Or perhaps it would be 'Zithgor' or the beautiful 'Rangillia'.

Phyllis thought the game-playing was healthy, but Stephen disagreed. There were fierce arguments about sending him to sports clubs after school to build up his slender body and encourage a competitive spirit.

'Can I watch TV, Mom?' he was asking her. From his expression, she gathered he had asked her at least once already. She gave him an affectionate swat on the back of the head.

'You know better.'

'Oh, come on, Mom. My head needs some zombie time. Like how can I really understand the genius of Samuel Clemens unless I get a good dose of *Happy Days* for contrast?'

Phyllis gave it some thought. The television was in the living room. If Zachary was absorbed enough, the young man could slip out of the door unseen.

'Okay,' she said. 'Just this once. But don't tell your father.'

'You're excellent, Mom. I thank you and my brain thanks you.'

The television was loud enough to drown out the sound of the front door closing. Afterwards, Phyllis went directly into the kitchen and swallowed ten milligrams of valium with a glass of wine.

Phyllis heard Stephen's key turn in the door. As always, the sound reverberated in her head like the gunshot at the start of a race. He was a medium-sized man of sturdy build, with a shadow of whiskers that no razor could ever erase. He stood with his shoulders hunched slightly forward, legs apart, lending him the faintly belligerent demeanour she still found exciting. He had lovely liquid brown eyes. They could look so tender, deceptive bastard.

'Dinner ready?' he asked, going immediately to the bar in the dining area to pour himself a drink.

'It's been ready since six-thirty.' Phyllis looked at her watch. 'Two more minutes and you would have been out of luck.'

'You wouldn't do that,' Stephen said with a grin.

'Try me. How come you're so full of *joie de vivre* tonight?'

Zachary slid into his seat at the table, gave his father a quick side-long glance, then kept his eyes averted.

'Because,' Stephen said heartily, 'today I pulled off a monumental coup. Zach, your dad scored a big one. Continental was absolutely wiped out by my new campaign.'

'That's nice,' Zachary said.

'Nice,' Stephen complained. 'Your enthusiasm is positively underwhelming.'

'He said it was nice,' Phyllis remarked.

'"Nice" is not terrific, "nice" is not compelling, "nice" is vanilla yoghurt and Julie Andrews and Mr Rogers.'

Zachary stared down at his dinner and watched it congeal on the plate.

Phyllis said quietly, 'If you wanted a twenty-one-gun salute, you came to the wrong place.'

'Christ!' Stephen exclaimed. 'I even brought the copy home to show you. It's fucking clever stuff.'

Zachary's eyes were filling with tears. 'I'd like to see it, Dad.'

'Oh, you would?' Stephen turned on him. 'I'll tell you what I don't need, mister, and that's your condescension. It's bad enough from your mother. I'm not F. Scott Fitzgerald. I will never be John Irving. Jerry Della Femina, just maybe, and that would be fine with me.'

Zachary got up from the table and left the room.

'Look at that,' Phyllis said.

'He's too damn sensitive,' Stephen answered.

'You're an egomaniac.'

'He'll be okay.' Stephen's voice was dubious.

'What makes you think so?'

'I guess I was pretty tough on him.' Stephen was bouncing his fork against the table edge like a drumstick on a snare drum.

'Unless we drop down on our knees every time you do well, you hear the voice of your dear old mother, may she rest in peace if it's not too much trouble. Just because she wanted you to write the great American novel doesn't mean we care one way or the other. It's called transference.'

'You think what I do is bullshit.'

'It pays the bills.'

'But you don't have the remotest idea about the creativity involved. You don't admire my creativity.'

'There are other things about you that I admire more.'

'Sometimes I think I'm just a hunk of sirloin to you.'

'Prime.'

He looked pleased.

'Now go talk to your kid.'

Stephen got up. 'Oh, shit, what am I going to say?'

'Say you're sorry you behaved like a troglodyte. And don't give him that lecture about advertising being the great art form of this century and all that crap about Toulouse Lautrec and his posters.'

When Phyllis peeked into Zachary's room later, she saw both dark heads bent over the bed. The ad campaign was spread across the quilt. Stephen gestured enthusiastically while Zachary nodded and tried to look interested.

When Stephen climbed out of the shower, Phyllis watched him towel himself dry. Water clung to the dark hairs on his chest and made damp ringlets. He was the hairiest man she had ever seen, a fact which simultaneously repulsed and excited her. He looked bestial, apelike, but then she knew how that matted chest felt against her breasts.

'That was a cute little scene, the two of you in Zach's room.'

'I told you he'd get over it.'

'It'd be nice, excuse the choice of word, if you would show the same interest in *his* work.'

'You show enough for both of us. He already thinks he's Albert Einstein.'

'On what do you base that observation?'

'Just the way he looks at me with pitying superiority.'

'Oh, for Christ's sake, Stephen. You know, you really ought to see a shrink.'

'I notice it's done you a lot of good.' He began sprinkling powder on his shoulders, but Phyllis took the container from him.

'Here. Let me do that.' She rubbed his back, and then his buttocks. 'You've been intimidated by Zach since he was old enough to count to twenty, as if it was some phenomenal mathematical feat.'

'He's the smartest kid I know. Hey, quit mauling me, will you?'

'Oh, excuse me,' Phyllis said, handing him the powder. 'And all along I thought I was being seductive.'

Stephen stared at his face in the mirror. He smoothed his eyebrows thoughtfully.

'Unless, of course,' Phyllis continued, 'you have no libido left. Been depleting the supply today?'

'Now who's paranoid?'

'Just realistic, darling. That little punk-rock secretary's been gone for three months now. I know you, Stephen. You can't manage much longer without something on the side.'

'My current secretary has a hairy chin, no ass and a wart on the bridge of her nose. I go cross-eyed every time I talk to her.'

'You'll think of some imaginative obscene way to turn her flaws into assets.'

'Got any suggestions? Christ, Phyllis, will you leave me alone?'

She had begun to stroke his back while he brushed his teeth, but she stopped abruptly now, left the bathroom and crawled into bed. She lay there marvelling at the intensity of her sex drive. But it often seemed that the more she had, the more she wanted. She felt now that she was no longer a person, simply a gaping aching hole, mouth open, legs spread. She would beg him if she had to. He would hold out on her until she began to cry, and finally her tears would arouse him and she would have him at last.

'What's this?' Stephen asked, as he slipped into bed beside her. He nudged at something with his foot.

'What?' Phyllis said. A roaring sound filled her head. She watched Stephen reach down beneath the sheet while she waited for her head to explode in midair. Stephen held up a white athletic sock and stared at it uncomprehendingly as if it were an animal whose species he could not identify. Then realization moved across his face and stained it the colour of red wine. He turned to her.

'You bitch,' he said.

She flattened herself against the headboard.

'In our own home. You bitch.'

'Stephen . . .' she pleaded.

'I suppose your son was in the next room while you fucked this jock.'

'It was . . . I don't know where that came from,' she protested.

'You're probably fucking one of Zach's little buddies. I wouldn't put it past you. Well, let me tell you something, bitch. You're right. I had myself something truly delicious today, something young and lively.' He straddled her now. She was pinned beneath his weight, helpless and naked. He struck her with the back of his hand.

'Stephen. Please,' she whispered.

'Why did you do it, then, if you didn't want this?' He struck her again, this time grazing her nipples. He grasped her arms and clasped them hard above her head, then kissed her roughly, bruising her mouth.

'What did he do to you? This? And this?'

She was sobbing now. 'He was nothing, nothing like you. Nobody's like you.'

After a few minutes, Zachary realized that tonight was going to be louder than usual. He reached for the knob on his stereo and turned the volume up until Beethoven drowned the sound of battle from the next room.

# Seven

Maggie telephoned Hilary in the morning and turned down the job.

'Why?' Hilary asked.

'I'm not ready for that yet. But Hil, I'm going to get back into it, my work. I don't think I would have if you hadn't prodded me.'

'What exactly are you going to do?'

'Enrol in a life class.'

'What's that?'

'Where you sketch a live model.'

Hilary sighed.

'I know it doesn't sound like much, but it scares me half to death.'

'Okay, love, but you tell me the minute you change your mind.'

They hung up and Maggie sat in the kitchen and tried to find the courage to take the next step.

It was as if over the past fifteen years she had given herself away piece by piece until there was practically nothing left. A week of all-nighters with a sick child guaranteed the depletion of creative energy. Paint brushes fell out of her hands from numbed fingers more times than she cared to remember. Or there would be a crucial dinner party for the partners in Matthew's firm. Making art and making *hors d'oeuvres* did not comfortably coexist. After Susan was born, Maggie had struggled to salvage at least half an hour a day with her paints, but then Fred arrived. He was beautiful and miraculous, just like Susan, and he required everything Maggie had left to give. Every now and then, there would be a moment when both children were napping and the house was in reasonable order. Maggie would sit at the kitchen table with her drawing pad and try to make some lines on the blank pages. But her compositions turned out tortured and stilted. After a while, Maggie found that a month would pass without any thought of her work. She told herself that one day it would be there for her again. Now the moment had arrived and she was terrified that it could all be gone.

She marched to her bedroom, dragged a metal box out from under the bed, and slipped open a manila file marked 'Art Classes'. Inside were clippings and articles she had squirrelled away over the years. Maggie reached for the item captioned 'Austin Presides at Life Classes on West Side' and went to the telephone. The summer semester had already begun, she was told. Maggie had missed only one session, however, and could join the class this evening.

The rest of the day was plagued with panic. It rose in her throat and lodged just behind her larynx. At three o'clock Matthew telephoned with an errand and remarked on the tone of her voice. 'You'll do great,' he said after she explained. 'It'll be like riding a bicycle, you'll see.'

Finally she ran a bath and sat in the tub with a glass of wine.

The studio was in an old grey building on Central Park West. Maggie arrived early; only the instructor and one other student were there. Eliza Austin was a tall, handsome woman in her sixties. Maggie remembered her work from an exhibit at the Winer Gallery ten years ago. The teacher held out a long, bony hand.

'They told me we had a new one. I'm glad to see you.' She gestured towards the man perched on the window seat. 'That's David Golden.' The man nodded. 'Perhaps David can fill you in on last week's class. This is Mrs Hollander.'

Eliza Austin began busying herself with easels. David Golden sat and stared at Maggie out of an angular face with fierce blue eyes. He could have been anywhere from thirty-five to fifty.

'How old are you?' Maggie asked, then blinked with surprise at herself. 'It's none of my business, of course.'

'Forty-nine,' he said.

'I'm thirty-eight,' Maggie said vaguely. The man was smiling.

'What are you doing here?' he asked.

'Trying to remember old times. And you?'

'I enjoy Eliza. I'm a sculptor, in fact. But I like to keep my hand in.'

Maggie wondered in exactly what way he enjoyed Eliza. It was outrageous to imagine him sleeping with her. Eliza was practically an old woman. Then again, perhaps it wasn't so outrageous. It was hard to guess about a man with such uncivilized eyes.

The class had filled up and the model had taken her place on a mat in the centre of the room. She was an Oriental girl, wrapped in a beach towel. Maggie and David Golden positioned themselves side by side at the two remaining easels. With a little shrug, the model undraped herself. She was slight, but had an exquisite body. Her breasts were perfectly round. Soft, shiny black hair fell to the middle of her spine. Maggie wondered if David Golden found the girl beautiful. Peripherally, she saw that he had already taken up his charcoal and had begun to make long, bold lines. There was intense concentration on his face but nothing else.

Maggie picked up her charcoal. She lifted her hand to draw and saw that her fingers were shaking so badly that it would be impossible to make even a crude line. Her face was hot, her throat constricted. Tears were building. She glanced to her right and saw David Golden watching her. In a second, he was standing behind her with his right hand around hers, guiding the charcoal along her paper.

'Sometimes it's just a matter of getting started,' he said. Then he returned to his easel and continued working. Her paralysis gone, Maggie watched her own hand gliding across the white surface, slowly at first, but with gathering confidence. Something nearly smothered inside her began to breathe. It felt so good, so good that she wanted to shout. Her hand looked to her like a small animal that had just been released from a trap. It swooped and dived and leapt across the paper. Maggie turned to David Golden, said 'Thank you' and began to laugh.

Once or twice during the next hour, she felt the old sensation of power, the heady invincibility, an impression of being suddenly surrounded with clear light. Then she became aware of David Golden standing beside her again. He was so close that she could feel his breath on her ear. He was exactly her height. If she were to turn her head, their mouths would be level. As if she could see out of the side of her head, she was acutely conscious of his jeans, his soft sweatshirt, his battered running shoes. He had the face of a prophet or a maniac, she could not decide which.

David reached towards her picture with a long blunt finger and ran it along the shoulder. Maggie had exaggerated the veil of hair.

'Nice. You're very good.'

His arm brushed Maggie's. She began to tremble. The finger moved along her drawing, down across the perfect breasts, down the soft line of the belly. Maggie was beginning to feel physically sick.

'Not so dark here,' David Golden said. His fingers gently brushed the shadow between the legs. Finally, the finger dropped, creating a small breeze. Maggie took a deep breath and tried to smile.

'Thanks. I see what you mean.'

'Now tell me what you think,' David said. He took her elbow and drew her over to his easel. He held her arm for a moment, then released it to point to the model's head on his drawing. 'I didn't see the hair your way. It's almost hidden.'

The picture did nothing to minimize the discomfort in Maggie's knees. It was powerful, sensuous, earthy. 'You must be a good sculptor,' Maggie murmured.

Eliza Austin joined them now. She said nothing about David's work, just touched the drawing near the feet. David nodded. The instructor's comments to Maggie were kind and respectful.

Matthew had not come home when Maggie arrived. Fred was asleep and Susan was reading in bed with her eyes at half mast. When the phone rang, Maggie assumed it was Matthew.

'Hi,' she said into the phone.

'Hello. This is David Golden.'

Stupefied, Maggie answered, 'Oh, hello!' in an overly hearty voice as if he were some dear friend who had materialized after a long absence.

'I neglected my responsibilities tonight. I was to fill you in on the first class. Can I see you?'

She struggled for words. At last she answered, 'You must think I'm very strange. I don't seem to know what to say to you.'

'Well, as I see it, you've got two choices. "Yes" or "no".'

'I appreciate the offer. It's very kind of you. But I think "no".' She hated the sound of her voice. She heard her mother telling the gardener he needn't come on Saturday.

'Okay. See you next week, then.' He did not say good-bye.

She sat by the phone and went over the conversation again and again. The way he had said 'Can I see you?' The request had seemed to hold some urgency. She was probably imagining it. He had a very soft voice with little modulation. She listened to it again: 'Can I see you?' An odd thing to say to her when he was supposedly calling to do her a favour. She jumped when the phone rang again, stared at it until the third ring, then picked it up.

'Hello?'

'Hi, Mags.' It was Matthew. Her heart stopped crashing around in her midriff. 'Be home in an hour.'

She was surprised at her disappointment, but then, she comforted herself, Matthew had not even remembered to ask her about class. He was well aware of her ferocious anxiety. When Matthew was worried about a problem in the office, Maggie always thought to ask how it all turned out, not necessarily from interest but at least to let him know she was concerned with his emotional comfort. Obviously, her preoccupations did not carry the same weight with Matthew.

He was very late getting home, by which time Maggie had fallen asleep.

She woke the next morning feeling angry. She glared at Matthew all during breakfast waiting for him to ask about her class. He was almost out of the kitchen door when Susan stomped in wearing her exercise sandals and enquired through a yawn, 'How'd it go last night, Mom?'

'Oh yes, how was it?' Matthew asked from the doorway. He looked a little guilty.

'It was fine,' Maggie answered, keeping her eyes on Susan.

'I expect to hear all about it tonight,' Matthew called on his way out.

'You expect,' Maggie echoed. Then she busied herself with the children's breakfasts and tried to stop hearing the words: *Can I see you?*

# Eight

Robin's apartment always made Phyllis feel claustrophobic. The place was festooned in crafts: needlepoint on the throw pillows, macramé hanging from the walls, hooked rugs on the floor, crocheted blankets on the sofa. Even the doorknobs wore little knit covers. Phyllis had trouble sewing on buttons and would rather throw out a skirt with an open seam than fix it. She reached for a cigarette. Being in Robin's living room was like being smothered to death by a wildly affectionate giant panda.

'I used to think you were supposed to douche standing up,' Robin was saying. 'I did it in the shower.'

'Oy yoy yoy,' Phyllis commented.

'Well, how was I supposed to know? Gynaecologists never tell you that kind of thing.'

'Mine informed me he thinks I should have no trouble maintaining a perfectly normal sex life,' Hilary said, arranging her cards.

'Hoping desperately for a few details,' Phyllis added.

'Exactly.'

'Are we ever going to play?' Maggie asked.

'Ah, the first words from Margaret Hollander this evening,' Phyllis said. Maggie looked odd tonight. Something was different. 'You pregnant?' Phyllis asked her.

Maggie laughed.

'I had a gynaecologist once,' Phyllis said, 'who had this god-awful stammer. He was okay when I was sitting in his office fully dressed, but once I put my legs in those stirrups, he started in. "I'm afraid you have a rather sig-ni-ni-ni-ficant p-p-p-polyp, Miss Jacobson."'

'Two hearts,' Maggie said.

'Two! She said two!' Robin cried with dismay.

'Yes, dear, I heard,' Phyllis said.

'Well, I pass, darn it,' Robin said.

'You'd better have points up the kazoo,' Hilary said.

'My kazoo is loaded,' Maggie answered. Phyllis gave her a sharp look. Maggie smiled benevolently.

'You sure you're not pregnant?' Phyllis asked again.

Maggie ended up in a small-slam contract. Phyllis's hand held no threat so she was free merely to follow suit and concentrate on watching her friends.

Maggie, for instance. Something was going on there. Phyllis had known Maggie so long she could predict an upset stomach for her former room-mate the day before it developed. Maggie seemed loose, sort of glowing and ripe. What's more, she had unbuttoned her blouse one rung lower than usual – which was still one button higher than Phyllis's. Perhaps Matthew was having a sexual renaissance, unlikely as that might seem. A decent guy, good-looking, but something essentially passionless about him, Phyllis had felt, even back at Radcliffe when all the co-eds were after him. Phyllis liked a man with some animal in him.

'What did you do to yourself, Phyl? Your neck . . .' Hilary was asking.

Unconsciously, Phyllis had been caressing her neck where there were two dark blotches parallel with the line of her jaw.

'My macho husband,' she explained with a broad smile. 'We got a little carried away over the weekend.'

'Don't tell me,' Hilary said with horror, but her eyes kept straying to the bruises.

'He was on top,' Phyllis continued, 'and I was struggling like crazy while . . .'

Hilary interrupted sharply. 'Stop it! I said I didn't want to hear it!'

'Okay, okay,' Phyllis smiled at her. God, she was beautiful, really the most beautiful woman Phyllis had ever known. Phyllis had been privileged enough to see Hilary naked just once. Unforgettable. She had gone home and described Hilary to Stephen, knowing it would drive him wild.

'Stephen's coming to pick me up tonight,' Phyllis said. 'He must have a tart in the neighbourhood.'

'Why the performance, Phyl?' Maggie asked.

'What *do* you mean?' Phyllis replied, but smiled to herself. Old Maggie, always on target. It was the Tuinol, probably. Tuinol made Phyllis feel erotic. She said abruptly, turning to Hilary, 'Do you remember your very first sexual experience?'

'You mean, like, when I was a kid?' Hilary asked.

'Whatever qualifies.'

Robin set her cards down on the table with a sigh. 'I don't think we should even bother playing bridge any more.'

'Well . . . it wasn't a relationship,' Hilary said. 'I don't know how to describe it, really. It was an assault, basically.'

Maggie took the final trick and swept the cards together into a pile. 'Are you sure you want to talk about it?' she asked Hilary.

'It'll be therapeutic,' Phyllis said.

'I don't mind,' Hilary said. She took a sip of wine. 'I was in Junior High, seventh grade, I think, at Greenwich Girls'. We came into the city, the whole class, for a museum trip. You know the kind of thing, three hours in the morning at the Whitney and three hours in the afternoon at the Met so you wind up hating art forever. Whew, I'm getting a headache . . .'

'Hil,' Maggie urged.

'No, it's good for me.' Phyllis was leaning forward intently. Hilary carefully ignored her, but Phyllis knew the story was being presented for her benefit. 'I went into the ladies' room at the Met and there was this woman there. I was, what, twelve, thirteen, but . . . well-developed. This woman was middle-aged, tall, very thin, wiry, strong. She looked sort of like Virginia Woolf. Except that she had this . . . smear . . . of bright red lipstick on her face. I still can't figure it out, maybe I let her in or something. But somehow she forced her way into the stall with me and locked us in. It happened very fast. She had her hands all over me. Up my skirt, she got my underpants off and she put her fingers up . . .' Hilary stopped again to take another drink. 'Finally I screamed and she left. She kissed me first, though. Got her lipstick all over my mouth. I scrubbed and scrubbed at that sink. The amazing thing was, nobody came in. All those thousands of art lovers milling around outside the door and not one of them had to take a leak.' She rubbed her forehead.

'God,' Robin said.

'What did you do?' Maggie asked softly.

Hilary shrugged. 'Nothing. What could I do?'

'Well, didn't you tell someone?'

'No.'

'Ever?' Robin asked.

'Not for a long time. Months. I finally told my best friend. But I thought about it a lot, I can tell you.'

It was not often that Phyllis was at a loss for words. Ordinarily, she was pretty clear about how she felt, but Hilary's narration had stirred her in too many ways. Conflict kept her silent.

'Not a great first experience in a welcoming sense,' Hilary went on. 'When I look back on it, the most amazing part was how guilty I felt. I was so ashamed of myself, as if I'd initiated the whole thing.'

Phyllis nodded and found her tongue. 'I know. Boy, do I know.' She rummaged in her handbag. 'Let's get you something for that headache.' She spilled a white tablet out from a pillbox, broke it in two, gave half to Hilary and took the other herself. 'Fix you right up.'

'What is it?' Hilary asked.

'Magic pain eraser.'

Hilary swallowed the pill with her wine and looked across the table at Maggie. 'Don't cry, Mag. It was a long time ago, all that. I've made an adjustment.'

'I'm not. I just wish I could hug you,' Maggie said.

'What about you?' Hilary asked Phyllis.

'Oh, God, I was doing it by the time I was eight,' Phyllis answered.

'I didn't think it was possible,' Robin said. 'Isn't a person too small down there?'

'I was in the beginning, but I got big enough pretty quick.' Phyllis's fingers were trembling slightly as she reached for her wineglass. 'My cousin Breen introduced me to the world of passion. God, I had such a crush on him. He was a whole five years older than me. One time my parents and his parents went out and left him in charge, and let me tell you, life was never quite the same.'

'Is there a full moon or something?' Robin asked Maggie. 'How did we get started on this? I don't think I like it.'

'It's *okay*, Robin. You don't have to tell us about you. But it's good to air these things, makes you feel better. Don't you feel better, Hilary?'

'Mm,' said Hilary.

'Anyway, Old Breen, he was from Kentucky and wore this Stetson hat so I figured he was a real live cowboy. He took me into my bedroom and locked the door and told me all about what horses do. He was huge for a thirteen-year-old, or at least that's how I remember him.' She was silent for a moment. 'We had a hell of a time getting the blood off the quilt.'

Nobody spoke.

'I've had this thing about horses ever since,' Phyllis said finally.

Hilary grasped the edge of the table as if it were about to tip over. 'What was it that pill?' she said thickly. 'I think I'm stoned.'

'Real good stuff. I'm getting there myself,' Phyllis said. 'Anybody else?'

'Let's call it quits for tonight,' Maggie suggested.

'We can't yet. Stephen's coming, my beautiful Stephen.' Phyllis's eyes felt as if they were wandering off in different directions. The buzzer sounded. Robin rose to get the door. 'That's him. He'll be in heaven. Four women all to himself.'

'The lights have the nicest rings around them,' Hilary said. 'Kind of like Van Gogh.'

Phyllis giggled. 'I wish we had time to strip before he gets up here. It'd be terrific, Stephen walking in here and us sitting here at the bridge table stark naked.'

Hilary snorted into her hand.

'You two are zonked,' Maggie said.

Robin let Stephen in. 'Am I early?' he asked, following Robin into the living room. 'It's pouring out there.' His hair glistened with rain.

'Right on time,' Phyllis said. She and Hilary started to giggle.

'Your wife is partially stoned and Hilary is completely beyond reach,' Maggie explained.

'So that's what you girls do every month,' Stephen said.

'I'm not really up to another hand,' Maggie said. 'Why don't you sit in for me?'

'It's been a long time,' Stephen said. 'Sure. I'll give it a whirl.' He took Maggie's seat across from Hilary. 'How's Matt?' he asked.

'Matt is superb,' Phyllis said. 'At the wheel. In command. Matthew is Stephen's hero, Mag, in case you didn't know. His idea of the successful American male.'

'Mine, too,' Maggie said lightly and drew up an extra chair.

Phyllis thought it was sickening how Stephen pandered to Matthew Hollander. The attorney's easy authority just reeked of success, and poor Stephen, despite all that ambition, never seemed to make it to the top rung. Phyllis couldn't figure it out.

'Who's ahead?' Stephen asked.

'We did true confessions tonight,' Phyllis said. 'Lots of sex and not much cards.'

'I'm sorry I missed it,' Stephen said. 'I don't remember any of the conventions. Let's see. One club.'

'Oh, you bid my suit,' Hilary said in a fuzzy voice, then began to laugh into her cards. 'Lordie, I don't know why I'm such a tit, I mean, nitwit. Sorry Stephen, but it's all your wife's fault.'

'One heart,' Robin said. She looked ill.

'Oh, dear, is that a short club, I wonder?' Hilary murmured. 'You got yourself a smashed partner, Stephen, but you can blame your wife. She's got terrific headache pills.' She gave him a provocative glance from under her lashes. 'Let's see, are you the short club type?'

'Nothing short about him,' Phyllis said.

'Three diamonds,' Hilary said.

'Four hearts,' Phyllis declared triumphantly. She felt so high. But then she had never popped Tuinol and Quaaludes together before. And she had to admit that the sight of Stephen and Hilary eyeing one another across the bridge table added to her intoxication.

'Four hearts from the walking pharmacy,' Stephen remarked. 'The hell with it. Pass.'

'Don't chicken out now,' Phyllis said. 'Faint heart never won fair lady. Or whatever.'

Stephen led a jack of diamonds. Phyllis covered with Robin's king from the board. Hilary played her ace and took the trick, led another diamond, which Stephen trumped with a low heart.

'Wow,' Hilary breathed appreciatively.

'I'd say we've got a damn good communication going here, partner,' Stephen said.

Hilary smiled at him. 'Maybe I'm not such a tit, I mean, *nit*. God, I must really be gone. What's this preoccupation with tits?'

'It's because you've got such nice ones,' Phyllis said. 'You'd just like Stephen to know.'

Robin got up with a red face. 'Excuse me. Ladies room.'

'Look, you got Robin all flustered,' Stephen said. But Phyllis knew he was amused.

'You still seeing that detective?' Stephen asked Hilary with his eyes on Robin's exposed cards. He threw a ten of hearts on the table. 'When in doubt, trump.'

'Now and then,' Hilary said.

The game ended with Phyllis down one. Stephen grinned at Hilary. 'That was fun.'

He made no move to rise, but Robin stood in the middle of the living room and announced in an impossibly cheery voice, 'Well, let's call it a night for this time.'

Phyllis laughed. 'We're being thrown out.'

'I'll get raincoats,' Maggie said from somewhere far away.

Stephen took Hilary's arm. 'I'd like to play again sometime.'

'Any time, dear,' Phyllis said. 'You liven up our little group.'

Hilary lurched and Stephen held her around the shoulders. 'How are you going to get home from here? Don't you live down in Soho?'

'Cab,' Hilary said. 'Whew, I think I'd almost rather have the headache.'

'What the hell'd you give her, Phyllis?' he snapped, helping Hilary into her raincoat. As Hilary arched her back to put her

71

arms into the sleeves, Phyllis saw Stephen's eyes fix on Hilary's breasts. Her nipples were clearly outlined in the sheer blouse. Phyllis felt herself rise another five thousand feet. It's dark up here in the stratosphere, she thought, but a dazzling, sparkling black. She and Hilary and Stephen were stars, hot and blazing.

'Coming, Mags?' Phyllis asked.

'No, I'll stick around a little while,' Maggie said. Phyllis grinned at the two morbid faces. Robin and Maggie were moons, cold, pasty, boring moons. Poor moons.

The door shut and they spun off into space together.

# Nine

Maggie sat on her bed and savoured the thought of art class where she was due in less than an hour. Her anticipation was so tangible it felt like a taste in her mouth, something delicious, a long-awaited treat that was sweet and satisfying after weeks of self-denial. Class could hardly live up to this, she thought, and she may as well enjoy her pleasure as long as possible. Maybe tonight she would find that she could not draw a convincing line after all. Maybe David Golden would not be there. She took a long, leisurely bath, then pulled on a pair of old corduroy jeans and a cotton sweater. No dressing up for David; he would see the real Maggie. She was late now. She grabbed her handbag, dashed to the front door and caught a glimpse of herself in the front-hall mirror. She laughed at the flushed, youthful woman she saw there.

Class was already in full swing and David was there. Maggie caught her breath with gratitude when she saw the empty easel beside him. She took her place and waited for him to say hello, but he only studied her quietly. His features were softer than she had remembered.

'I'm sorry I was such a fool on the telephone,' Maggie said. Then she laughed. 'Oh, God, I'm doing it again.' He just continued watching her with a half smile on his face. 'Help me out, will you?'

'How?'

'Say something.'

'All right.' He paused thoughtfully. 'I like the way you look.'

'That wasn't exactly the kind of thing I meant.'

Maggie glanced at the model sitting at the far end of the studio. She was a middle-aged, plump, coarse-looking woman. Her breasts were pendulous with large dark nipples and her

legs were tracked with varicose veins. But she had extraordinary hands. She held them in her lap tenderly as if they were
a pair of precious white birds. Maggie immediately thought of
the Stieglitz photographs of Georgia O'Keefe's hands. She
picked up her charcoal and began to sketch, losing herself in
this intriguing display of homeliness and beauty. After twenty
minutes, she stretched and stood back to look at what she had
done. David was standing beside her.

'Georgia O'Keefe,' he said. She stared at him. David went
back to work, but Maggie found it difficult to concentrate
after that. She imagined an invisible current transmitting her
thoughts to the silent figure standing a few feet away.

At the end of class, Eliza Austin inspected Maggie's work,
made a comment about tension and suggested some exercises
in quick line drawing to loosen her up. Maggie could see David
preparing to leave as Eliza spoke. He was going to get away
before she could speak with him. She could barely breathe
from panic, and here was Eliza Austin telling her to close her
eyes and let her hand 'sweep the page, sweep effortlessly,
no, quickly, don't stop . . .' Eliza was patient – endlessly
agonizingly patient. When Maggie opened her eyes again, the
model had dressed and David was gone. Panic turned to grief.

'You're very gifted,' Eliza said.

'Thank you,' Maggie replied, thinking wryly what those
words could have meant ordinarily. He must be out of the
building by now. Finally, Eliza said good night. Maggie tried
not to hurry as she left the room, but when she saw the crowd
at the elevator and noted that David was not among them, she
bolted for the exit sign at the end of the hall. She took the
stairs two at a time.

She saw him on Central Park West more than a block away.
He had a loose stride, legs slightly bowed, arms cocked and
swinging. Maggie took a few gasping breaths and started
running. A tiny voice in her head sang: *What are you doing?*
*What are you doing?* But it was easy to ignore under the rasping
noise of her respiration.

'David!' She caught him at Eighty-first Street, just north of
the Museum of Natural History. He spun around and reached
out to steady her with both hands on her arms. 'Let me buy

74

you coffee!' she shouted.

'All right,' he said.

'I'm a very reserved person,' she explained, panting.

They both laughed and began walking toward Columbus Avenue. After a moment he said, 'Your art's not reserved.'

'That's different.'

'Shouldn't be.'

'You're right,' she said. 'It shouldn't.'

It was dark now, but the soft summer dark that was still a little grey around the edges. In unison, they both said, 'You are what you paint.' They stopped in their tracks and gaped at one another.

Maggie whispered, almost dismayed, 'Does this often happen to you?'

'No.'

'With anybody?'

'No.'

'What's going on?'

He shook his head and drew her arm through his.

In the coffee shop, Maggie ordered a glass of juice. Her central nervous system was far too agitated to cope with caffeine.

'How long has it been since you worked?' David asked.

'Years. Close to ten, I guess.'

'I find that difficult to understand.'

'What's that accent?' Maggie asked.

'Leftover New Orleans.'

'New Orleans,' Maggie said. 'What a wonderful place to be from.'

'Not if you're a Jewish sculptor.'

'Do you have a family there?'

'Parents. A brother.'

'Tell me about them.'

'My father has a dry-goods store. He feels the same way about yard goods as I do about stone.'

'What does he think about what you do?'

'I suspect he's decided I'm homosexual.'

'Is that supposed to follow?'

'Artists, you know. But he's not unpleasant about it, just

regards me with a kind of bewildered disappointment.'

'And your brother?'

'Very upstanding. Plays golf on Sundays, drives a station wagon. He works with my dad, but they don't get on. Robert wants to bring in computers for inventory and my father would rather check things off on his yellow legal pad.'

'Does your mother work, too?'

David held up his hand with a smile.

'I'm grilling you. Sorry,' Maggie said.

'I'll tell you my entire life story if you can stand it. Sometime.'

Sometime, Maggie thought. That meant there would be another time. She felt the sudden sweet taste from before class in her mouth again. 'Were you always a sculptor?' Maggie blurted, then laughed at herself. But he was patient.

'I tried to be an artist at first. But I guess I always liked messing around with the materials more than making images. How about you? When did you begin?'

She sighed. 'Oh, God, I was making pictures before I had words. I think it was my way of being safe in a scary world.' She shifted her legs under the table and accidentally nudged his foot with hers. She wondered what his bare toes looked like. 'I used to have this dream,' she continued. 'There was a hideous monster, a massive shadowy thing with huge sharp teeth and claws. He would trap me in a room. I was terrified and desperate, but then I would put my finger on the wall and draw, no crayon or anything, just my finger. I would make this even scarier monster, even bigger, and it would come to life and destroy the one that was trying to kill me.' He was watching her over the rim of his cup. She shook her head and smiled. 'I haven't thought of that in such a long, long time. And it wasn't only fear. All kinds of feelings. Like anxiety. When my father had to go to the hospital for an operation, I built him a bed tray. I guess if I could build something, make something with my hands, I felt as though everything would be all right. I had some kind of control.'

'Then what's kept you safe these past ten years?'

Maggie had no answer. She looked away. There was a fly walking up the fake wood panelling beside David's left ear.

How simple to be a fly, she thought. Buzz, eat, an anonymous coupling now and again. A fly does not concern itself with the fly swatter, poised and vibrating, ready to slice through the air and obliterate.

'Carving is my adventure,' David was saying. 'A wild exploration. Pushing something past its limits, almost further than I think it can go.' It seemed to Maggie that he was also talking about them, their friendship, or whatever it was. 'There can be no preconceived notions about how it's going to come out,' he continued. 'That's a kind of death. Allowing the inconceivable to happen, that's the thing. Sometimes it means being very brave. Do you know what I mean?'

She nodded.

'Tell me about your husband.'

The fly did a little hopping dance on the sugar bowl, then veered off for the kitchen. 'He's a fine man. A lawyer. Good at what he does, very ethical. We have two wonderful children.' The sound of the word *we* reverberated in Maggie's head. *We, we, we . . . wee, wee, all the way home*. David was listening to it, too. She saw the sudden pain in his face. 'Do you know how long it's been since I wore these jeans?' Maggie asked suddenly.

'What do you usually wear?'

'Dresses, skirts, things to . . .' she trailed off.

'To what?'

'To get him to tell me I'm pretty,' she whispered. 'I'm such a fool.'

David took her hand, flattened her fingers against the table and traced them on the cool marble surface. 'I want you to model for me,' he said.

Maggie found she could not reply. She was imagining herself naked, with David's hands moving along her body as if she were stone. He stared at her with eyes that pierced her, bore straight through the centre of her brain and out the other side. 'I've got to go home,' she said.

'Please don't. Don't be afraid of me.'

'I'm not.'

'Let me see you tomorrow.'

'No. I don't know.' She wanted to kiss his mouth.

'Go ahead,' he said.

'I don't know how you do that. It's an invasion of privacy.'

'See me.'

'David, I'm so fucking respectable. I don't *ever* say fucking.'

'Let me call you.'

Maggie examined the check dropped on their table by a weary waiter long ago. She put some money beside her saucer and stood up. After a moment, David followed her out.

'Look, I'm getting into a cab,' she said outside in a trembling voice. 'God knows how I'll explain what my face looks like when I get home. Just walk away from me now. I can't even breathe. Please.'

He nodded, put his hand against her cheek for a moment and walked off. He turned to watch as a cab pulled up. The waiter inside the coffee shop also observed from the front window. He shook his head morosely. No money to be made off people like that. Lovers never eat much.

# Ten

'Mom, can I come in?' Fred looked pale and solemn outside the bedroom door.

'What's the matter, honey?' Maggie asked.

'I've got stage fright.'

Maggie smiled. 'Me, too.' She smoothed the collar of his blazer. 'You look marvellous.'

Fred sat down on the edge of the bed. 'What if she blows it?'

'She won't. She was great last time and she'll be great tonight.' *Our Town* had made such a hit in March that a special end-of-school performance had been scheduled.

'I think I'm gonna puke.'

'Maybe we ought to take air-sick bags.'

Matthew emerged from the bathroom wearing a towel around his waist. 'You've got two different colour socks on, Frederick.'

'Leave it to you to notice, Dad,' Fred said. The door clicked shut behind him.

'Just exercising my acute powers of observation. Maybe we should all go out somewhere afterwards to celebrate.' Matthew shed the towel and slipped into his underwear. His body appeared exactly as it had eighteen years ago, except perhaps his chest was slightly hairier.

'You're feeling festive.'

He grabbed Maggie by the shoulders and wrestled her to the bed. 'My daughter's a star. Shouldn't I feel festive?'

'Hey, cut it out, Matt, you're hurting me.'

He rolled her over on her stomach and pinned her arms behind her back. 'Gotcha,' he exulted.

For a man so trim, it was surprising how heavy his body felt. Maggie knew that no amount of struggling would free her

79

from the grip of those sinewy arms. She lay very still.

'No fight in the old girl tonight?'

'I've told you I don't like being manhandled,' Maggie murmured with her face pressed into the mattress.

Matthew whacked her rear end playfully and stood up. He sighed. 'I don't know. You used to be a good sport.'

Maggie rose slowly. The folds of her bathrobe fell open, revealing her bare breasts. She snatched it closed around her and belted it. Then while Matthew's back was turned, she plucked her clothes from the closet and slipped into the bathroom. It was still warm and steamy from Matthew's shower. Her slip stuck to her thighs but at least she was safe.

There was a time when Maggie was able to laugh at Matthew's rough-housing. Perhaps she had even enjoyed it. She tumbled and wrestled, never mind the bruises. But lately she had begun to feel like prey, never knowing when Matthew might spring from behind a closet door to lock her in a half-nelson or sneak up behind her in the kitchen and pinch her bottom. She thought of David Golden's hand, gentle against her cheek, and suddenly began to cry with deep twisting gasps. She turned the cold water on full blast, grabbed her towel off the rack and buried her head in it. But after a few moments, the sound of all that water being wasted induced such guilt that she quickly turned off the tap and pulled herself together.

When they reached the auditorium, Fred and Matthew found seats while Maggie went to deliver Susan's necklace, left behind in the last-minute rush. Years ago, Maggie had bought her a chain with a tiny gold shamrock. Susan swore it was insurance against forgetting her lines.

Backstage, costumed performers rushed about, their faces under heavy makeup hinting at features familiar to Maggie since Susan's kindergarten days. Maggie had fed them snacks, patched wounds with hand-decorated bandaids, comforted them on their first sleepovers and transported the pudgy actress playing Mrs Gibbs all the way across town at 2 a.m. when severe homesickness struck. The sweet smell of make-up was almost buried under the cloud of cigarette smoke that pursued the director everywhere like some hovering malodorous assistant.

Maggie edged her way through the circus to a long mirror where Susan sat applying final touches to her mouth. Like the others, the costume rendered her nearly unrecognizable, but Susan's transformation penetrated beneath the make-up and mascara. She gave Maggie a remote smile.

'Thanks, Mom. Can you put it on for me? My hands are all grease.' The New England accent had become expert.

Maggie closed the clasp around Susan's slim neck. 'You okay?'

'Yeah, I guess. But I can't talk now, you know?'

Maggie nodded, bent down for a quick kiss and left. On her way out, she heard the director admonishing some other interloper. 'No, you mustn't disturb Susan now, not before a performance.'

Maggie took her seat between Fred and Matthew and wondered where her child had disappeared to inside that quiet, contained figure at the mirror. 'I thought it would be easier this time,' she whispered to Matthew.

'She'll be fine,' he said.

'Fred, you all right?'

'Sure, I popped ten 'ludes in the boys' room.'

The houselights dimmed. Maggie's heart began to thunder. She grasped Fred's hand which was as cold and damp as her own. Susan appeared alone on stage, wearing a felt hat, pipe in hand. She walked slowly, comfortably, like a man taking a stroll on a Sunday evening.

'This play is called *Our Town*,' she began. 'It was written by Thornton Wilder . . .'

Maggie let out a long breath and settled down. The first time she had watched Susan perform as the Stage Manager, Maggie could barely concentrate on the play. Every stammer, every pause, sent trickles of sweat running down her sides. Tonight she was determined to absorb the performance. It was apparent that Susan was in full control. No matter that Mrs Gibbs shouted every line, that Emily Webb was saccharine, that poor George kept anticipating his cues. Susan maintained her composure. At one point, George Gibbs stood in panicked silence with eyes rolling wildly as if he might encounter his lines etched in the air somewhere above his head. Susan quietly folded her arms and fed him the words, *sotto voce*, but loud enough for Maggie to note that even when prompting a fellow actor, the New Hampshire accent remained intact. 'Mr Morgan, I'll have to go home . . .' Susan prodded George, the Morgan coming out 'Mawg'n'. Maggie glanced at Matthew, but he was scribbling on a small pad: *Ferris v. Smith, 1978*, followed by three question marks.

The first time Susan had performed in a play was in the third grade. She won the lead in an original musical written by the school drama teacher. For three weeks, the Hollanders endured her songs at breakfast and dinner. One of them Maggie still remembered was sung to the tune of *Don't Fence Me In*: 'Gimme smog, gimme dirt, gimme egg creams for dessert – New York's my town!'

On the day of her performance, Susan had stopped dead in front of the dry cleaner's on Madison and Eighty-fourth Street. Her confidence had dissolved into tears and sweaty hands.

'I think it's my appendix,' she said.

'Real nervous, huh?' Maggie asked.

'I've got a stomach ache. Well, it doesn't really ache, it's jumping all over.'

'That's called butterflies in the stomach.'

Susan smiled. 'That's good. Just what it feels like.' Then the smile turned to a grimace. 'Let's go home.'

'What is absolutely the worst thing you can imagine happening on that stage today?' Maggie asked.

'I'll fall down and forget my lines and mess up the songs and then I'll just die.'

'Will you really?'

'I'll wish I could.'

'And then what?'

'We'll go back to music class.' She thought a moment, then said, 'You know what, Mom? I think a few butterflies just flew out of my mouth.'

Maggie had given her a squeeze and they went on to school and triumph. Watching Susan now, Maggie imagined her surrounded by a cloud of butterflies, a delicate snowstorm on the stage. The image was so intense that Maggie felt her fingers twitch with the need to get it down on paper.

The Stage Manager was making a speech about marriage, about the natural urge to live life 'two-by-two'. But was it so natural? Maggie wondered. Here she sat next to this man who seemed at this moment no more related to her than the paunchy stranger across the aisle. Wasn't marriage an artificial alliance, and weddings an empty rite that bound two incompatible species together in something aptly termed wedlock?

Their wedding had been outdoors. A blue and white striped tent was erected on the Herricks' back lawn for refreshments and in the event of rain. But the early August day was bright. Maggie had lingered in bed thinking about how little she knew herself and how she knew Matthew Hollander even less. And yet pairing off this way had been going on for so long, there must be some merit in it. Even apes chose special mates, she had reassured herself, gazing at the white ruffled curtains that softened the morning light at her window. Then she had reached out to her bedside table for the worn Raggedy Ann she had inherited from Joanne and clung to it. No more little girl, no more daughter. She would be Matthew Hollander's wife. Who the hell was he? She sniffed, still clutching the doll, sat up on the edge of the bed and stared at his photograph. He was so handsome. Square face wearing the expression of a Viking warlord standing at the prow of his ship. But there wasn't a shred of vanity in him. He was direct to the point of brutality, so that when he said he loved her and thought her beautiful, she knew he meant it. He was the first person outside of an art class who truly appreciated her work, and the fact that the mere proximity of her body kept him in a continual state of arousal had its charm as well. But mainly she was marrying him because nothing bad could happen to somebody with those eyes. And as his wife, nothing bad could ever happen to her either. This man was as close to perfect as anyone she was ever likely to meet.

There was a tap at the door. Joanne poked her dark head inside. 'Nice day for a hanging,' she said with a grin. 'Are you ever getting up? Your presence is required downstairs in panicksville.'

'I'm up,' Maggie yawned.

'Think he's actually going to go through with it?'

'Who, Matthew? Maybe.' But Maggie knew he would.

Joanne came in and tugged at the doll under Maggie's arm. 'You still have this old thing?'

'I wish I could take her with me,' Maggie said.

'Old Matt wouldn't mind.' She put her hand briefly on Maggie's head. 'You're a good kid. All the best.' Then she fled.

After the triumphant curtain calls, they went to the *Summerhouse* restaurant on Madison Avenue. Susan asked to be seated by the front window beside the old painted wooden rocking horse. She was flushed and agitated. Her eyes were huge under dark splotches of make-up.

'Oh, God, did you hear old George Gibbs, I mean, Adam Newman? Oh, God, he was grotesque! Scared to death, just frozen solid, poor thing. I had to rescue him a million times. And I screwed up something rotten in Act Two with the wedding . . .'

'What would you like to eat, Stage Manager?' Matthew interrupted her.

'Oh, God, I couldn't eat a thing! Oh, well, maybe I'll try the *crème brulée*, it's so *élégante*. Oh, God, did you see how everybody cried when Emily passed into the great beyond? The place was absolutely awash!'

'Yeah, that must have been when Dad was making notes for tomorrow's meeting,' Fred said.

Susan's monologue stopped short as if someone had flipped the 'off' switch operating her tongue. Maggie stared at Fred. Susan stared at her father.

'You didn't watch,' she said.

'I did,' Matthew replied. 'M-most of it.' Maggie had never heard him stammer.

'Oh,' Susan said. 'Well, I guess since you'd already seen it before . . .'

Maggie looked away from the shame-faced Fred and gazed at Matthew. He was struggling with something. After a moment, he said, 'You forgot your line for a second and I couldn't stand it. I was too nervous.' He put his hand over Susan's. 'I'm sorry. I'm very proud of you.'

Maggie chided herself for ever harbouring uncharitable feelings towards Matthew. She knew how difficult it was for him to break through his natural emotional constraint. He loved his daughter. Maggie would never go to that art class again. David Golden was not reality. Matthew was reality. And these two beautiful children, one radiating triumph and the other struggling with envy, they were reality. It was enough. It ought to be enough.

# Eleven

The first twinge occurred at 6 a.m. Robin fell back to sleep and incorporated the mild discomfort into a dream about labour, like the last time when she had lost the baby at four months, only in her dream it was born fully grown, a man in a business suit with horned-rim glasses and a paisley handkerchief sticking out of his waistcoat pocket in three neat points. She heard the doctor, who looked like Jackson, say they had to wait for the placenta now, and while her child dusted himself off and sat perched on the edge of the delivery table, Robin felt another twinge, pushed, and out came a briefcase. 'You smell like death,' the doctor told Robin matter-of-factly.

She woke, turned to tell Jackson about the dream, and remembered that he was still in Chicago. Then another pain struck. It almost seemed to have a voice, like the type of person who delights in delivering bad news. She lay very still and calculated. She was a few days short of six months pregnant. They often saved babies born at this stage. If she could only hold on for another few weeks, even days. She spread her fingers across her belly and waited. Move in there, she implored. Just a little kick.

There was no rush about telephoning the doctor. She had been through this enough times to know the procedure. The important thing was to relax. She reached for the remote control. Channel Eleven was showing an antique Doris Day film which ought to dull the senses. Robin floated off again into a half sleep and thought about how much she detested Doris Day. Robin resembled the actress somewhat – freckled and wholesome, though Robin was smaller. Robin's idol was Katharine Hepburn, and here people were always telling her she looked just like Doris Day.

The huge sprawling family in the creaking house back in

Ohio had been a world where everything always came out all right in the end. Bad things happened, sure enough, like her father losing his job, but they all sat around the table, father, mother, grandma, Robin's three sisters and two brothers, and talked it over. Robin's brother, Gull, had carved initials all the way around on the edge of that old oak table: 'R' for 'Robin', 'G' for 'Gull' and so on. He caught hell for it, but Robin liked to sit in her seat and trace the 'R' with her finger. It made her feel that no matter what, her spot would always be there, permanent. As it turned out, Robin's father opened his own farm equipment company soon after he was laid off. It was a big success. Just like her mother said, everything always turns out for the best.

So, Mother, Robin wanted to know, what was the point of losing all those babies? More souls to populate heaven? God didn't need any more babies.

*Move*, she whispered to the curve under her fingers.

The major event in Robin's life to date had been New York City. When she was small, she used to watch *The Roaring Twenties* with her brothers. Gangsters seemed wildly romantic, but they certainly never trifled with places like Otis, Ohio. Films like that radiated street energy. A person could discover what she was made of in New York. Back home, with everybody protecting you and goading you every step of your life, it was impossible to know what was you and what was everybody else.

So after two years of the local college where she studied something loosely described as 'business administration', which meant typing, she announced her intention of leaving for New York. There was a summit conference at the table. Her sisters were shocked. Her brothers shouted. Mother said Robin would be killed in the train station the moment she arrived. Her father shook his head, saw there was no way to dissuade her, and gave her two hundred dollars. Robin put the money away in a zipper compartment in her suitcase intending not to use it, intending to present it untouched to her father when she had made it on her own, but of course she spent it the first week.

She had been crazy for New York the moment she disem-

87

barked in a cloud of steam at Grand Central Station. It was thrilling to think that of all those people scurrying beneath the vast vaulted ceiling, not one of them knew who she was. She was sorry she had agreed to room with her Auntie Jay.

Within two weeks, she had tumbled into Jackson Brody's lap at *Woman's Companion* and landed herself a job and a man. Jackson was so sad, so battered and disappointed, so hungry for the cheer she brought him. She settled into the crook of his protective arm before she had been away from Otis for a month. Robin had come to New York to find herself and found Jackson instead.

Doris Day was throwing another tantrum on the television set. This time her throaty voice skipped a few syllables altogether. Robin switched her off. She did not regret coming to New York. It proved that she was free, at least free enough to escape from home. And besides, New York meant more than Jackson. There were the others. Hilary was so beautiful, so chic, the quintessential New York woman executive. Phyllis, well, Robin had little use for Phyllis, truth to tell, though she would defend her to Jackson, of course. Phyllis's foul mouth made Robin uncomfortable despite the generous heart behind the acid tongue. Finally there was Maggie herself who was the closest thing to Katharine Hepburn this side of the silver screen. Sometimes in your life you run across people who wear just the right expression on their face. Who look you straight in the eye and say the perfect thing right off the bat. You figure you'll be friends for life. Maggie had been that way. The first day Robin came to work at *Companion*, Maggie had been assigned the job of showing her around. Robin was impressed with Maggie's simple navy linen dress, her poise, her no-nonsense face.

'How're you adjusting to the big city?' Maggie had asked.

'I love it,' Robin said. 'Mostly.'

'You must have claustrophobia,' Maggie said, ushering her into the production department.

'Yes,' Robin agreed eagerly. 'Saturday I went to the top of the Empire State Building to give my eyes a break. They needed some wide open spaces.'

'Our apartment has a fine view of the brick wall next door.

But it's amazing how soon you get used to it.' Maggie touched the elbow of a young woman with the longest, most scarlet fingernails Robin had ever seen. 'Phyllis, this is Robin Schultz. Phyllis Wheeler.'

'Do you play bridge?' Phyllis had asked.

Maggie and Robin went to lunch at Schrafft's on Madison Avenue. Over chicken sandwiches, Maggie became Robin's closest friend.

Jackson made Robin feel safe, but Maggie understood her. Maggie knew more about Robin's insides than any living person and could be trusted with the information, kind of like a safe deposit box. Robin made regular trips to Maggie to withdraw her special secrets and examine them. Maggie knew about Robin's ambivalence in marrying Jackson. Maggie was still the only person to hear complaints about him.

She snapped out of her doze as a sharp pain split her from navel to crotch. Sudden wet warmth oozed between her legs. She fought her panic while the word MOVE echoed in her head and bounced eerily like a voice shouted into a canyon. She reached for the bedside phone.

In seven minutes Maggie was at the door. Robin hobbled to meet her with a bath towel packed between her knees.

'I can't get it to stop.'

'Come on,' Maggie said, holding out her arms. 'The cab's waiting.'

'I can't go like this. Let me get something clean.'

'Screw that.' Maggie took off her cardigan and tied it around Robin to cover the blood-soaked cloth.

During the ride to the hospital, Robin leaned her head on Maggie's shoulder. Her eyes were closed, there was a film of sweat covering her face making the freckles glisten. Her arms, crossed under her belly, tensed with each jolt of the cab.

The emergency staff helped Robin onto a mobile stretcher. 'I'll take care of admitting,' Maggie said. She smoothed a lank piece of hair off Robin's forehead.

'It won't move,' Robin said.

'You'll be okay, honey,' Maggie said.

As the attendant started to wheel Robin towards the elevator, her eyes filled with tears. 'Don't leave me,' she whispered.

'I'll be right there,' Maggie said.

They wheeled Robin into a labour room. She could hear the cries and grunts from a cubicle next door as a woman worked hard to bear her baby. They don't call it labour for nothing, Robin thought. Except with me it's always been for nothing. Soon she could hear Maggie talking with the resident outside.

'Where's her husband?' he asked.

'Chicago.'

'Can he be reached?'

Something unintelligible, then, 'Is she miscarrying?'

More unintelligible sounds while pain hit as if a cement slab were slammed into her lower abdomen. It seemed incredible that the bed wasn't crushed from the impact. When she opened her eyes, Maggie was sitting beside her.

'Hi,' Maggie said.

'I love you,' Robin said. Maggie grasped Robin's hand and held tight.

After a while, Robin said, 'Don't let them throw it away until I've seen it.'

'Maybe it won't come to that,' Maggie whispered.

'It will.'

Robin began to cry softly. 'It's not the pain,' she explained.

'I know,' Maggie said. She laid her head next to Robin's on the pillow until the obstetrician came and asked her to leave.


After Fred and Susan went off to do their homework, Maggie told Matthew that Robin had lost the baby.

'I'm sorry. Is she all right?'

'Physically.'

'Damn shame. That's the second time, isn't it?' He snapped on the news: Roger Mudd reporting from Washington.

'Third,' Maggie said. She got up and went into the bedroom. Lying there mourning for Robin's baby, she remembered the births of her own children. Susan's arrival was obscured by the paralysing numbness of sodium pentothal. There was still pain. Maggie was aware of the hurt, but the person who hurt was somehow not exactly Maggie. The birth itself seemed depersonalized as well. About three days afterwards while her hormones were doing their wild dance, she became convinced for a few hours that Susan was not really her baby. When she found she was pregnant again, she decided that this time she would not be robbed of the experience.

She had been told that her second labour would no doubt be half the duration of the first. But Fred was a big baby. Maggie even wondered if a part of her were trying to hold him back inside, this final child. Matthew sat beside her labour bed and coached her through the various types of breathing. But her contractions were erratic. Just when she thought the peak had come and gone, another wave of twisting, wrenching agony would tear into her. It went on that way for twenty hours. Matthew, pale and frightened, pleaded with her to take a spinal block. But Maggie had not endured all of this only to relinquish her ultimate participation. Finally, the obstetrician announced that she could push. By this time, her abdomen was transformed into a solid block, no longer yielding and round, but squared like an immense fist. Everything in her lower body worked to urge the baby out. After several pushes, she could feel the foetus loosening, swimming down into the birth canal. The sensation elated her and gave her the energy to keep on. She was bringing this baby into the world. What joy to be giving life with her own courage, her own body.

In the delivery room, it took only three more pushes for the head to crown. There was such pressure that Maggie felt she would surely split up the middle, but the terrible pain had disappeared. The doctor performed an episiotomy which was also painless. Another push, out came the head, then one more giant shove and he was born. The thrill was almost sexual, like some spectacular orgasm.

Soon Fred began to howl, and turned from pale sickly blue to bright red. Maggie comforted him until he stopped yelping. He lay across her belly with solemn eyes wide open and his tiny fist crooked around Matthew's finger. After the umbilical cord was cut, they took him from Maggie.

'Where is he going?' she protested.

'Just to get weighed and have his feet printed. You don't want to take home the wrong baby, do you?'

'I couldn't. I know him now.'

When they gave him back, he was bundled in a soft white

blanket. He felt solid and warm. Both of them were transferred to a clean bed and pushed down the hall to the recovery room. Matthew brought champagne. Then Maggie and Fred drifted off to sleep with Fred nursing expertly at Maggie's breast.

Looking back on that golden day, Maggie wondered if sharing Fred's violently intimate beginning had influenced her feelings about him forever after. There was something direct and warm in her relationship with him that she missed with Susan. And yet the intensity between Maggie and Susan stimulated and challenged her. Oh, how she loved them, and how she grieved for Robin lying alone in her hospital bed with an empty womb.

# Twelve

After ten minutes in Zabar's, Maggie always found herself sailing off into a kind of trance. So much food, so many people. It was very pleasant. She had been lingering and swaying over the stuffed veal when she felt a hand on her bare arm. She turned and blinked into David Golden's face. He was grinning, the stark lines lifted in delight.

'I hate myself for blushing,' Maggie said.

'What are you doing over here?'

'My kids are going to camp tomorrow. I'm loading up on favourite things.'

'I'd like to see your kids.'

On the one hand, Maggie felt like whisking him home to meet Fred and Susan this instant. On the other, she wanted to bar him completely from her life on Seventy-ninth Street. But to protect whom? she wondered.

'I'll help you. Then come and see my place. You're only a couple of blocks away.'

'I can't.'

'Can't why?'

'I made this promise. It's too complicated to explain.'

'Try me.' They were jostled by a shopping cart. David held her around the waist as if they were dancing.

'You know those rash things you say in moments of severe stress . . . to whatever might be up there in the heavens?'

He smiled.

'A pregnant friend of mine was about to lose her baby. First I promised God that if He let her keep it, I would never see you again.'

'And what happened?'

Maggie shook her head.

'I'm sorry.'

93

'Then I had this feeling,' she continued, 'that she was being punished for *my* sins and I shouldn't see you anyway.'

'But you don't think that now.'

'No.' Too fast, Maggie thought. Altogether much too fast. 'Everything that happens these days is some kind of sign. If I wake up in the morning and it's raining, that means I should see you, or shouldn't see you. It's ridiculous.'

'I want you to look at my work.'

Maggie caught sight of her reflection in the meat-counter glass. A sensible face, rather haunted, not happy, getting older.

'All right.'

On their way down Broadway, David held one shopping bag and she the other. Their free arms were linked. Maggie thought briefly about being recognized and dismissed it. She was too giddy to care.

'I hope you appreciate my self control,' David was saying. 'I haven't called you.'

'I noticed.'

'I hoped you'd be pleased.'

'Disappointed. Grateful.'

Maggie could not identify what it was in David that made her so outrageously free, but she knew there was something in the sound of his voice that stirred her. He spoke softly with very little emphasis, yet she sensed strong feeling beneath the words. It tantalized her and was in no way frightening.

He lived in a once-elegant building on West End Avenue near Seventy-eighth Street. He followed her up the five flights of marble stairs. Her light summer dress swept against her legs with each step. She felt his eyes on them and wished he would touch her ankle and slide his hand up, up. Her breasts felt tight as if they were swollen. By the time they reached the top, she was gasping and glad for the long ascent to excuse her discomfiture. They stood in front of his door while Maggie's pulse thumped all the way to her toes. She could still turn and walk back down. But instead she watched David's hands unlocking the door – long brown muscular fingers. Where is my guilt? Maggie wondered desperately. But there was none. Not a scrap.

At last the key turned, the door opened, and he ushered her inside. The sun was high in the west over the Hudson. Light blasted in through tall windows that ran the length of one huge room. The floor was polished and gleaming. There was an unobstructed view of the narrow strip of green that was Riverside Park, the Seventy-ninth Street Boat Basin, and the river. New Jersey was a black shadow on the other side of the sunlight.

Part of the room was a living area. There was a chair and a reading light in one corner. Against the near wall was a small built-in kitchen, a table and chairs. Beyond the table, a mattress lay on the floor. Maggie averted her eyes, but not before she had seen that the bed was unmade. A pile of books stood on the floor next to the bed and there were bookshelves running all along the bottom quarter of the wall like wainscoting.

But the living quarters seemed incidental in the apartment, as if all the necessities of daily life had been only grudgingly alloted territory. Easily two-thirds of the room was given over to David's completed work. Stone shapes, marble, sandstone, alabaster. There were busts of faces here and there and one immense torso, but mainly the carvings were free form. They were forceful, multi-textured and pleaded to be touched. Maggie felt a lump in her throat. She turned to David who was watching her anxiously.

'Thanks,' he said.

'It would have made things a lot easier if I hadn't liked them,' Maggie said. 'May I take a closer look?'

They moved among the pieces while he introduced each one as if it were a friend.

'This,' he said, caressing the surface of a white lustrous piece, 'is very recent.'

Maggie understood that the work had something to do with her. She examined it curiously. It was smaller than many of his other sculptures, only about a foot high. It was pear-shaped with a voluptuous rounded bottom. Out of the top, the suggestion of a curved shaft appeared, then tapered and disappeared into space. Maggie suddenly wished she could sit down. Her knees felt as if they might give way.

'What's it made of?' she asked.

'Carrara marble. I did it after we had coffee. It was something about the way you got into that cab, those jeans . . .'

'Right now I'm going to kiss you,' Maggie said. She did. It

was a lingering, tender kiss. They remained that way for a long time, holding one another in the bright light with the dust motes dancing around them. Finally, she leaned back in his arms. 'I guess I don't have to tell you that I don't usually perform this way.'

'Why do you do that?'

'Do what?'

'Apologize.'

'I wasn't.'

'You really think this is a performance?'

'Oh,' Maggie said. 'No.' Looking into David's eyes was like falling into a gentle sea. She let the current wash over her, swayed with it, dreaming. 'This is just not possible,' she murmured.

'You can't be the artist you are and talk to me about impossibilities,' David said.

'Ah, David, you've got your work cut out for you,' she said. 'I think I've been living in negatives for a long time.' She disengaged herself. 'May I have a cup of tea or something?'

'Yes.' He tucked a piece of hair behind her ear. 'May I do your ears sometime?'

'I'm beginning to think you can do anything you please.' She laughed. 'It's as though part of me just took a step up on the evolutionary ladder and the rest hasn't caught up yet. Like I mean . . .' She laughed again. 'Oh, Lord, I sound just like my fifteen-year-old daughter.' She stopped, testing, but even the thought of Susan in that other cosmos did not sober her up. She sat at the table and watched him move around the tiny kitchen. He spooned loose tea into a tea ball and hung it inside a squat earthenware pot.

'Does a dormouse live in there?' she asked.

'Yes.'

'Margaret Herrick Hollander.'

He looked at her quizzically.

'That's me.' She shook her head. 'What *am* I doing here?'

'You don't sound unhappy about it.' He handed her a mug that had phases of the moon painted all around it.

'I'm thrilled with myself.' They both laughed.

'Are you looking for an explanation?' he asked, sitting down opposite her with his tea.

'Yes. All the time. Today it seems metaphysical. My friend Robin lost her baby and now I'm being born.'

'It's probably futile to analyse,' David said. 'It's just here, and we'd better figure out what to do with it.'

'Maybe it's physical attraction,' Maggie said.

'There's that, for sure.'

Maggie's stomach lurched. She put down her cup and tried to forget the unmade bed on the floor behind her back. 'I don't know you. Maybe you killed your mother and chopped her up into little pieces.'

'I'll admit to the fantasy.'

'I told you about my family. What about you? Any brothers or sisters?'

'A sister. An artist. She's the talented one.'

'Excuse me?'

'Oh, I have a gift, but Joanne would be a great artist if she'd discipline herself.'

'That the party line?'

Maggie looked startled. Then she began thoughtfully, 'I wonder if maybe a good girl can never be a great artist. Do you think? Maybe one has to be a maverick. Joanne's like that. Doesn't give a gamn about convention. God, she pretty miserable.'

'Does that go with it, too, the misery?'

'I don't know. I suppose there have to be some happy artists.'

'I know I've said this before, but it's hard for me to imagine you not working,' David said.

'It got edged out, I guess. There didn't seem to be time for it. I told myself it wasn't important, not like it would be for somebody like Joanne. Didn't you ever stop?'

He nodded. 'In the army.'

'You in the army? Heavens.'

'Yes, but they let me design things, garages, a recreation room. And it was good for me, being in the service. It made me feel lucky to be what I am. I always knew I'd get out and have control over my own life. There were so many others . . .'

'Did they cut off your hair?'

97

'Yes.'

She tried to imagine him in a crewcut. It seemed impossible. She needed to know what he looked like in every phase of his life. 'Do you have a photograph album?'

'No.' He was smiling.

'Some day when you're out I'm going to come up here and go through this place. I want to know what brand of socks you wear, what your chequebook looks like, whether you've got a fold-out umbrella or a long skinny black one . . . although come to think of it, I bet you don't own one at all.'

He laughed. 'I don't.' He poured some more tea from the brown pot. 'What kind of art does your sister make?'

'Representational. Portraits, mainly. She earns a lot of money when she works at it.'

'You like her paintings?'

Maggie thought for a moment. 'Not really. Everyone always has the same kind of sour expression. She's great with colour. Acrylics.'

'You don't approve?'

'For me, I can't stand them. They don't feel right or smell right. Oils are so delicious. I'd just as soon eat them as paint with them.'

'Let me get you some more tea.'

Maggie glanced at her watch and he winced. 'I've got to go.' They watched each other. Maggie had the oddest sensation that she was staring into a mirror. 'Do we look alike?' she asked. 'That might explain it.'

'A little narcissism?'

'Yes.'

He shook his head and rose with her. 'I want to wait on you. Do for you. Will you let me?'

'I'm not used to it.'

'Get used to it.' He held her by the shoulders. 'You'll be back here again.' She was silent. 'You're a very strong woman. You can handle it.'

'I don't feel strong.'

'Be strong enough. Don't shut the door on this.' He kissed her. She could feel the tension and power in his back, and yet he was so tender. He smelled of marble dust. 'Maggie, Maggie,' he whispered against her mouth.

98

She wrenched herself from him and imagined a beautiful rich tapestry tearing in two. At the top of the stairs, she turned to see him framed in the doorway, a clean form like the pieces of stone behind him, shimmering in the light like fanciful shapes at the bottom of a transparent sea.

Maggie stumbled out onto West End Avenue and stood blinking on the sidewalk, letting the heat wash over her. Then the roar of the Seventy-ninth Street bus reminded her that a cool, green apartment awaited her on the other side of the park. She walked the short block to the bus stop, stepped up onto the bus and took a seat in the back. She could not stop grinning. A trim woman who embarked at Broadway gave Maggie the brief suspicious glance New Yorkers reserve for lunatics. Maggie's smile became a furtive giggle. Poor woman. Poor everyone else. Maggie had experienced David Golden and life would never be the same. His connection to her was a fact of natural law, as absolute and basic as the principles that governed the solar system.

It was not until she got off the bus that she wondered what she would say to Matthew and the children. She was nearly forty-five minutes late already. She could say that she had run into someone from her art class, started talking and time had just flown away. It was not a lie; and it was a monumental lie. Maggie had always regarded herself as a truthful person, and yet David had made her realize that she had spent decades lying to herself. Denying herself was the worst kind of falsehood, the most pernicious betrayal.

In the elevator she imagined herself explaining, 'Well, children and Matthew, today I discovered that I have a Siamese twin. Remarkable, isn't it, that I never knew I had one? My parents kept it from us, and we just happened to bump into one another, this fellow and I. Separated at the heart when we were born, actually. In fact, we still share one . . .'

She put the key in the door and took a deep breath. It was Fred who scared her the most.

'I'm home!' she called.

''Bout time,' Susan yelled from her bedroom.

Maggie walked into the kitchen and began unpacking the shopping bags. Matthew appeared, looking rumpled as if he had been asleep. She felt a sudden rush of affection for him. She wanted to tell him. He was practically her oldest friend, after all. She turned the full radiance of her face on him and waited to see what would happen. Her heart was pounding crazily at the insides of her ears.

'Must still be hot out there,' he observed. 'You're all sweaty.'

'Yes,' she said. So easy.

During dinner, Fred asked her why she was so quiet.

'I'm thinking about you kids being away for eight weeks,' she lied.

'Well, you don't look very depressed about it,' he complained. 'I haven't seen you this happy since Nixon was impeached.'

At 6.30 a.m. on the corner of Forty-fifth Street and Vanderbilt Avenue, Matthew stood beside the Camp Poqomashee bus with his palms sweating. Maggie and the children were twenty feet away talking with the Wheelers, but there was such a crush that even if Matthew had felt sociable, he would have been hard put to join them. Instead, he distracted himself by counting fishing rods. So far, there were sixteen, each gripped in the small fist of a boy. This was a co-ed camp, and yet not a single girl carried a fishing pole. Biology will out, he supposed. Phyllis Wheeler's psychiatrist would say the rods were phallic symbols.

The camp director held up his arms as if he were about to make an important announcement. Nausea gathered in Matthew's stomach. Everyone else seemed so festive. Not one crying child. But of course they were all older. Matthew had been six when he spent his first summer at camp.

He remembered the bus trip. It had seemed a great adventure to climb up the steep steps, wave good-bye to his parents and set off for the Adirondack Mountains. The very name was exotic and thrilling. Upon arrival, he had gone swimming in the clear cold water that tasted sweet without a trace of either chlorine or ocean salt. He had even caught a bullfrog down by the waterfront. But after the campfire, after lights out, he had lain very still on the top bunk in the pitch black cabin and thought that it had been a very fine day, and tomorrow his mother could come and take him home. But she didn't come, not tomorrow or the next day or the next. In fact, his parents never made it to visiting day that first summer. Something came up, he couldn't remember what. Matthew had admired his counsellor, who always called him 'Sport'. Somehow Matthew felt obliged to live up to the nickname. A person named 'Sport' would certainly not call out for his mother in the dark.

But there came a time, finally, when Matthew began to look forward to spending his summers up in the mountains. He liked the rough cabins that were set back from the lake in a grove of pines. The fragrant pine needles cushioned his footsteps as he explored the woods imagining himself an Indian brave. He spent many hours sitting on his special rock beside the lake watching the surface of the water, how its depths reflected an endless variety of colours: turquoise, silver-white, blue, purple and black.

Because of his physical co-ordination and maturity, he was soon allowed to participate in overnight hikes with the older campers. The final trip of his fourth summer had been a three-day excursion up Mount Marcy. Near the summit on the second night, a violent electrical storm had struck. The campers clung together in the lean-to all night long, listening to the downpour and watching the lightning illuminate the forest like millions of exploding flashbulbs. That summer had been Matthew's introduction to the majesty of natural forces. His urban life seemed a long way from those early primitive communions with the woods, but even now on the rare occasion when he was wakeful at night, he would find himself remembering the lake and its moods. The memory comforted him still, so that finally with the sound of water lapping against the shore, he would drift into sleep.

He coughed as the bus started its engine and sent clouds of foul exhaust into the air.

'Daddy, we have to get on the bus now,' Susan was saying.

'Oh,' he answered. He wanted to tell her, No, not this summer. Stay home.

'Don't look so sad,' she said. 'In ten minutes, you'll be ecstatic we're gone. Think about it, just you and Mommy.'

'I guess so.' He hugged her. She was the oddest combination of sturdy and frail. His arm went all the way around her ribcage so easily. And yet the flesh that covered the bird-like bones was so firm. She wriggled free.

'Fred!' she called. 'Come and say good-bye to Daddy. He's having a breakdown.'

Fred and Maggie pushed through the crowd together. Fred extended his hand.

'Fat chance,' Matthew said, and pulled his son close for a bear hug. Here was a substantial person, not as pudgy as he looked. That bulk was mostly muscle.

Then Maggie held them both for a moment and they were away, up the steps and behind the tinted glass that turned all of the campers into identical silhouettes with raised fluttering hands. Matthew put his arm around Maggie.

'Shit,' he muttered.

Maggie looked up at him. 'You're crying,' she said, astonished.

'I'm going to miss them.'

'Yes,' she answered.

But that night when ordinarily she would have felt depressed and lonely in the aftermath of their departure, instead she lay in bed with a trembling sense of excitement. Susan and Fred were gone, they were safe, and she was free. David existed a mere half-mile on the other side of the park.

She searched for her guilt. It had to be there somewhere, lurking in the memories of her resplendent day like slugs clinging to the roots of a fabulous tropical flower. None. Matthew lay breathing softly, unaware that the wife beside him was no longer the wife of yesterday. Maggie's regret was that she could not rouse him gently, hold his hand in the dark and tell him about her happiness.

She dreamed that she was a mermaid with long streaming hair. She dived through the turquoise water, flipping her graceful tail, and when she sang in her soft sweet voice, tiny fish in many bright colours sprang from her mouth.

# Thirteen

While Maggie lay dreaming, David Golden was letting himself into his studio on Broadway and Ninety-fifth Street. At this hour, the ground floor stores were closed and heavily gated. There was a bakery, a small grocery store, a dry cleaner and a shoemaker. In the elevator to the fourth floor, however, David could hear the throb and thump of the latest rock band to rent space here. Among the other inhabitants were a psychotherapy centre which specialized in primal screams, an evangelical organization, and a dating service which matched singles of indeterminate sex. David rejoiced in his neighbours because they left him to himself. In fact, if there was one item in his life about which he felt ferociously possessive, it was this room. When David first arrived in New York, he had shared studio space with a group of artists. David was faster and stronger than the others and did things they told him were impossible. 'It won't balance,' they would warn him. Or 'Alabaster can't take that kind of abuse.' David ignored them, but he longed for privacy. Finally, when he began to sell his pieces, he scraped together enough money to rent his own place.

The first studio was spacious, but it was a three-floor walkup. After a year of hauling four-hundred-pound blocks of rock up and down the stairs, David began looking again. An apologetic real-estate broker had finally brought him here. The place had everything: a large freight elevator; a window for ventilation; floors sturdy enough to support several tons of rock; twenty-four-hour access. Even now, five years later, David felt gratitude when he slipped his key into the door.

He stood blinking in the bright fluorescent light, breathing the rich musty smell of stone dust. Despite David's efforts to protect the shelves with plastic and canvas drapes, the fine grey film had seeped into everything. Even the inner crevices of his supply manuals were grainy with it. Pompeii had probably looked like this, David thought, as he gazed at his shrouded statuary.

David walked to the window and snapped on the powerful fan. It would suck out clouds of powdered stone which thereafter sifted down onto the two stunted bushes in a courtyard below. Every few weeks, his conscience needled him into trekking down with a watering can to clean off their encrusted leaves.

A massive piece of raw white stone stood on his work table. David walked around it, feeling his excitement grow. Normally, he ordered his material directly from a quarry in Italy. But last week, he had spotted this five-hundred-pound slab of Bianco marble at his favourite supply store on Nineteenth Street. It was expensive, almost six hundred dollars. David had gone to battle with himself. His pneumatic air drill was broken and required a costly new part. His toaster had expired and he was getting tired of toasting bread in the oven. Besides, this difficult stone demanded a brand new set of carbide tools. It took about half a minute to decide. Maggie Hollander was in that rough marble somewhere and David was going to find her.

He had never carved a woman's torso before. A man's once, as an exercise. Women had always somehow become abstracted into free forms that later seemed cerebral and cold to him. David caressed the rough surface of the rock and wrestled it over onto its side. He picked out a toothed chisel and the hammer that was so perfectly weighted it seemed more an extension of his arm than a tool. He slipped a safety mask over his face and started taking down the stone, beginning with the shoulders and working back. Five or six shots, then rest. Five or six, then rest. The first few bites into rock always hurt him, as if he were piercing flesh, but soon he began to feel that he was working with the stone, that they were creating something together. This marble was even more lovely than he had anticipated. It was webbed with pale grey lines like the translucent veins in a woman's skin. He thought about the underside of Maggie Hollander's arm as she had reached behind her head to smooth her hair.

He remembered the sight of her standing in the doorway of Eliza's studio illumined by tangerine light. There was an extraordinary tension emanating from her slender body. She was clearly afraid, yet seemed determined to master her fear. The light flickered off the hollows and curves of her face as she spoke with Eliza. David wished she would stand still so that he could sketch her.

Maggie had walked towards him like a dancer, head high, back straight, yet somehow liquid. As she shifted her shoulder to shrug off the strap from her handbag, he could see the shape of her breasts under the cotton sweater. Her stomach would be a long curve slipping into the shadow between her legs.

Close up, her face was almost severe. But when she spoke, her mouth was soft and curled up at the corners in a child's smile. She was hesitant, self-conscious, and brave. David decided she was unaware of her own courage. But he found it immensely moving.

When class began, David watched Maggie freeze. Suddenly she was a George Segal sculpture, lifelike in all respects except for the dead eyes staring at the easel. At once, he understood. Every artist experiences that particular numbing horror. That it is gone. Whatever the mysterious impulse that makes it possible to create something out of nothing, whatever the elusive power that connects an artist to his environment through his mind, his eyes, his hands, that it has vanished forever. David went to Maggie at once, took her hand and warmed the terror out of her fingers.

Once loosened, how they flew, darting, diving, trailing bold streaks of charcoal. There was nothing tentative about this woman's art, no restraint, no apology. She had already forgotten him, absorbed in a kind of ecstasy as intimate and intense as making love. David felt he should shield such naked joy from the others.

She had escaped from him that night. He had looked for her in the groups of people on the street outside, by the bus stop, in front of the museum that stood ghostly and secretive in the dark. His pulse was crashing in his head, his mouth was dry, his knees trembling. In one evening, Maggie had engaged every crucial part of him: his creativity, his intellect, his sexuality. He could not forget the startled, pleased look on her face as hidden feelings flew out of her mouth unbidden.

Finally he walked home and telephoned every Hollander in the book until he heard her voice. He lay in bed that night thinking of her, and just before falling asleep, heard his grandfather's voice with its thick Eastern European accent saying, 'Davidel, you're a dead pigeon.'

The rough approximation of shoulders began to emerge from the stone. David was sweating heavily now and he could feel the dust collecting in the back of his throat. It was curious that he had never asked Sharon to model for him. Eight years of living together, and the notion had never occurred to him. Perhaps it was because in some essential way, Sharon had remained outside his art. He remembered how she would wander among his sculptures in the apartment, touching them cautiously, her small face bewildered. Her questions irritated him. 'What does this bulge here mean? Does it represent something real?' She had never asked him why he needed to carve, but the issue hovered in her eyes. David was continually on the defensive. Either he found himself defending Sharon to his carvings, making excuses for her obtuseness, or he would apologize to her for their ubiquity and even occasionally talk of getting rid of them. Such discussions always left him feeling sick at himself.

When Sharon moved out, the silence she left behind seemed sunny and clean. He felt unaccountably elated. For the first time in eight years he was alone with his most intimate friends – his carvings. But after a few weeks, desolation settled in. David began to miss her so profoundly that the inside surfaces of his arms tingled with the need to hold her. He could not sleep. He wadded his quilt up into a ball and hugged it in a futile attempt to fool himself into unconsciousness. He struggled with himself about asking her to move back in. He knew she would come. He also knew that ultimately he would want to cast her adrift again.

In that first decade after David's arrival in New York, the only apartment he could afford had been a roach-infested hole in the East Village. Congregations of junkies murmured and nodded in front of abandoned tenements while David hurried past trying to avert his eyes from the incessant assault of ugliness. He missed the intimate, drowsy atmosphere of New Orleans, the scents of tropical flowers, sweat, decaying garbage, strong coffee. But once he entered the artist's world, he believed he would never settle anywhere else but New York.

It began with the chaotic shop on Nineteenth Street where David bought his supplies. The owner, Ben Ginsburg, was a hulking lumberjack of a man. He took David on a tour and watched carefully as the young sculptor watered down particular stones and ran his fingers over their surfaces. Afterwards, Ben invited David into his office, which was a wild collage of invoices, chequebook stubs, tax forms, calendars and bills – here and there disciplined into piles by paperweights that were carvings made by Ben's many friends. Ben pressed a buzzer on a half-buried telephone, asked to be left alone for an hour, and he and David talked, about art and whose work David should see, about New York, and loneliness, the philosophy of work versus leisure, and Chinese restaurants.

Finally, Ben had stood up, held out a huge paw for David to take, and said, 'Hey. There's a bunch of folks show up here on Saturday nights. Carvers mostly, but a few painters, too. We put away a sixpack or three and sort out the world. Come along if you feel like it.'

David had left, feeling as if he had passed some important test. Over the years, he watched Ben measure other newcomers, and the fact was, each person Ben introduced to the inner circle had some contribution to make to the group. Someone with an abrasive personality would turn out to produce work of such monumental genius that the brash package no longer mattered. And Ben was always there to extend advice and credit. 'Pay when you sell something,' he'd say, which could be never. He had even found David his teaching job at the West Village School for the Arts. In those early years, David rarely missed a Saturday night at Ben's. David had gravitated hungrily towards the gifted. Artists with special vision electrified him, and he felt the influence upon his own work in a new intensity and willingness to experiment.

Maggie Hollander's breasts had appeared under the steady blows of David's chisel. The need to possess her was so powerful that it frightened him. If there had been no white stone waiting for him here in the studio, he wondered if he could have controlled himself with her this afternoon in the apartment. He thought of that soft skirt brushing Maggie's legs as she climbed his stairs. An erection pulsed against the stiff fabric of his work pants. He imagined wetting down the stone with his own semen. The hammer struck, beating rhythmically, tiny bits of rock flew about him, and he was past happiness into a kind of rapture.

It was dawn when David finished blocking out the torso. He was aching and covered with dust. The insides of his mouth and nose were thick with it and his eyes burned. But he liked what had emerged under his hands. The torso rested on its hip and curved upward with breasts pressed forward, shoulders back. There was energy and powerful sensuality in the rough stone. David was too exhausted to clean up. He snapped off the fan and the lights, stretched out on the gritty floor where he could see the outline of Maggie's body ghostly through the soft dust clouds and slept.

# Fourteen

Matthew loaded the car early Friday morning in anticipation of holiday traffic. The Fourth of July was traditionally spent with Maggie's parents, in part because Maggie's birthday fell on the third. It used to be a hectic affair, transporting the two children. Maggie had not yet accustomed herself to the simplicity of travelling as a couple. She was used to refereeing disputes that began somewhere west of Bridgeport and continued all the way to Stafford. Nevertheless, Maggie always enjoyed long trips in the car, particularly when she was not required to drive. She liked to look out of the window and let the colours blur together. She would play tricks on her vision, first narrowing her eyes, then quickly widening them. Telephone poles, woods, houses alongside the road, leapt and squatted and contorted themselves into fantastic shapes.

Today the interior of the car seemed hushed. But the inside of Maggie's head was whispering, shouting, chortling, arguing and carrying on lengthy discussions with itself. What if she were actually to embark on an affair with David? The word 'affair' seemed so crude, so ordinary. Entering a relationship with him would be to plunge into a mysterious wonderful world. A few short hours with him and already she had begun to discover hidden pieces of herself as if she were a diver upending encrusted old rocks to reveal the sunken treasure beneath. She imagined them submerged together, twisting, arching, curling in the shining light, coming together to embrace with long slick limbs, kissing and slowly rising to the surface.

Matthew slammed on the brakes as a battered station wagon veered suddenly into their lane. Maggie stared at him. His reflexes, as always, were quick and sure. How well she knew him. Matthew would have made a perfect pioneer. Bounding into the fray, dispatching outlaws or hostile Indians, persevering through harrowing adversities, that was Matthew. Admiration ought to be sufficient in her marriage. Why did her heart keep on stretching to accommodate David Golden?

Matthew glanced at her. 'What's up?'

'Nothing, why?'

'Do I need a haircut or something?'

'No, you look just fine.'

'Phooey, I bet you say that to all the guys.'

My Matthew, she thought. Her mouth moved; she almost said it: *Matt, there's a man named David Golden. He thinks I'm beautiful. Isn't that something?* Instead, she said 'La *la*.'

Matthew grimaced. 'What was that?'

'I'm singing,' Maggie said. 'La la *la*.'

'You can't sing. You're tone deaf.'

'Doe, a deer, a female deer . . .'

'Spare me,' Matthew said. But he smiled at her.

I won't do it, Maggie thought.


Her lightheartedness began to falter as they got off the highway and drove through the Stafford town square. It was a neat village, like an eighteenth century New England town fabricated by Walt Disney Productions. The fringe of grass along the sidewalks was perfectly trimmed. The little gazebo that sat on the green was freshly painted. No litter, no sprawling drunks. Even the old shade trees appeared to have been pruned. There was not a dead limb or drooping branch to be seen.

They passed the high school, a pristine Georgian structure with white columns. The scent of cut grass struck the car like a soft green wave.

'Far cry from PS 102?' Maggie said, thinking of the graffiti and broken windows that blemished the junior high on Seventy-fifth Street. Matthew turned off onto Barnstable Road.

'Oh, dear,' Maggie sighed.

The Herrick home was set far back off the road. The groomed lawn was untroubled by rocks or patches of garden. Two maple trees of nearly equal height loomed one to each side of the brick walk. The house itself was a handsome white colonial. It stood unperturbed and cool in the sun, as permanent and unyielding as some great gleaming boulder deposited by the glaciers twelve thousand years ago.

Norma Herrick came down the front steps to greet them. Her kiss felt bony. She was nearly six feet tall. There was nothing soft about this woman, no excess flesh to pillow the no-nonsense architecture of her frame. Standing near her mother always made Maggie feel insignificant. It was an illusion that Maggie had to stand on tiptoe to kiss her, but it felt true enough.

'Hello, children,' Norma said. Maggie shrank another inch. 'Good trip?'

'Yup,' Matthew said. He and Norma did not kiss. Matthew had gone straight to the trunk to unload.

'Your father's at the airport picking up Joanne. They should be here any minute. We're barbecuing, so as soon as you're settled in, come down to the yard.'

'Ah, the scene of the crime,' Matthew said. Maggie knew he meant their wedding. Maggie grabbed her overnight bag and went into the house. She paused in the living room doorway. Sure enough, her mother had redecorated again. Every two or three years, Norma reupholstered the sofa, the side chairs, and bought new curtains. This time, the colours were predominantly peach and green.

'What do you think?' Norma asked next to Maggie's elbow.

'Very pretty. The nicest, I think.'

'Oh, I don't know. I'm not sure it does what I hoped it would do.'

'Well, Mother, you never give up anyway.' Maggie understood that Norma was trying to achieve some measure of warmth. But the immaculate room with its perfectly restored antiques and polished floors spoke with a cool voice. Maggie thought of Robin Brody's apartment and smiled. Robin's place was so warm it made Maggie sweat; her mother's house gave her the chills. Maggie supposed she was hypersensitive to her environment the same way she was also acutely aware of the height of whomever she happened to be standing beside. Next to Robin, Maggie was a hypothyroid freak; next to her mother, she was a dwarf. Suddenly it struck her that other people may not measure themselves this way, by using the rest of the world as a yardstick. It seemed like a revelation. She wished David were here. It was the kind of observation that would interest him.

'How was it for you, being tall, when you were growing up?' she asked her mother.

'In what way, dear?' Norma asked.

'Being the tallest girl. You must have been, straight along.'

'Oh, yes.' Maggie watched her mother's face as it went on a long unaccustomed journey into the past. After a moment, Norma said, 'I made it a point never to slouch.'

There was a tray of drinks and mixers on the table in the back yard. Matthew was showering, Norma was in the kitchen, so Maggie poured herself a gin and tonic and lay down in the lawn chair. Unlike the front of the house, the back yard was wild with the sight and scent of flowers, as if it were important to keep this excessive display of colour and aroma hidden behind an austere façade. The rhododendron bushes made Maggie think of Phyllis who had once announced that she thought of her friends in botanical terms: Robin a buttercup; Hilary a calla lily; Maggie a rhododendron. Maggie had enquired how she classified herself, and Phyllis replied without hesitation, 'Venus fly trap.' Maggie was impressed by Phyllis's poetic notion, Phyllis who understood them all so thoroughly. How outrageous to have David Golden billowing like sea grass just beneath the surface of her life and Phyllis knowing nothing of him.

Maggie and Joanne's Snow Tree still stood beneath Maggie's bedroom window. One Sunday morning in early May there had been a freak blizzard. Maggie woke to see two inches of snow like vanilla frosting on the lilac bushes, the daffodils, the tulips. Below her, the little cherry tree glistened. Among its dazzling branches sat a pair of cardinals, some sparrows, a blue jay and a finch. Maggie ran to fetch Joanne and together they gazed at the magical tree with its bright chattering decorations.

Maggie let her eyelids droop. Soon her father would arrive

with Joanne and there would be no peace. She let her thoughts drift like the dandelion fluffs floating above the lawn. Her very first memory of life emerged on a day like this. Maggie remembered being on her back and looking out through golden pillars at something soft and green. She had felt comfortable and happy, and yet tantalized by the greenness beyond her grasp. She theorized now that she must have been in her playpen gazing out at the wooded area past the toolshed.

She took another sip of her drink and heard the dreamy buzz of ladies' voices, the clink of ice in glasses, laughter. Norma used to hold her bridge club parties out here in the early summer. Maggie liked to help set up the chairs and place the decks of cards on each table with their scorepads and stubby pencils. There was always the picnic table with goodies on it, too: cool drinks, limes, lemons, and little cakes. Maggie enjoyed the sight of the bright-coloured summer frocks, even sometimes broad sunhats with ribbons. One day Maggie was reading in her room upstairs when she heard great hilarity explode on the lawn below her window. She leaned her arms on the windowsill and looked down to investigate. Her mother seemed to be the focus. She had paper in her hands, lots of white squares which she was passing around. Suddenly Maggie felt her face burning. Norma had found her drawings, her secret collection of cartoons that were hidden on the top shelf of her closet behind the shoeboxes. There were drawings of her parents, of Joanne, of her teachers, even of some of the women present. Most of them were unflattering, but they were her diary, her method of releasing outrage, irony, sometimes even adoration. There was a cartoon of her favourite teacher in that collection, her beloved Miss McAdams. It hurt Maggie the most to imagine those women laughing and pawing at her movie-star rendition of that kind young lady.

She felt like screaming at them: *How could you?* But instead she pulled down the shade and threw herself on the bed and sobbed. The collection reappeared in its nest that evening. Maggie took each drawing out and ripped it into tiny pieces. Then she flushed them all down the toilet. Norma never mentioned the empty hole on the shelf.

Maggie sat up and took a deep swallow of her drink as her mother came through the back door with a trayful of crackers and cheese.

'Having a nice sunbath, dear?' she asked.

Maggie felt the click as she switched herself into the present tense. 'Lovely. I didn't check the barbecue. Should I have?'

'No, let's wait to see the whites of their eyes.'

Norma stood looking down at her. Maggie tried to shade her eyes against the bright sunlight but her mother's features were blackened and dazzled with multicoloured dots.

'Have you been going to exercise class?' Norma asked.

'No. Good Lord, no,' Maggie answered. 'Why?'

'You look, I don't know, Margaret. Different. Rather glowy.'

'Well, you know how fast I tan,' Maggie said, but she was pleased. Norma was rarely complimentary. She was always rearranging Maggie's collar, tucking in a blouse, checking her stockings for runs.

Matthew, Collin Herrick and Joanne trooped out of the back door one at a time with enough space between exits for the stiff spring to slam the screen each time with a loud snap. Here they come, Maggie thought. Husband: SNAP! Father: SNAP! Sister: SNAP! There was a ritual quality about their arrival that seemed appropriate. Maggie stood up and swayed from the sudden elevation.

'Hello, Dad, you're dapper as always.' She kissed him on the cheek, but was suddenly nearly toppled over by a hug from Joanne who had grabbed her around the middle. 'Whoa!' Maggie yelped. The sisters did a little dance until Maggie regained her balance. Then she held Joanne away from her and took a good look. Joanne was medium height, but her pudginess made her seem shorter. She had full breasts, but never wore a bra so that she sagged and bobbled with every movement. Her hair was wild, wiry and black with reddish-brown frizzled ends so that she looked as if her head might recently have been set afire. She had a pouty child's face and bit her nails.

'You look smashing,' Joanne said.

'Thanks. So do you,' Maggie replied.

Joanne shook her head impatiently. 'I don't, but that's all right. You look *really* smashing. Are you pregnant?'

Matthew hooted. 'She'd better not be.'

Joanne disengaged herself and made a futile effort to smooth her hair. 'Well, y'all're doing something right.' Maggie noticed the Southern accent. Wherever she alit, Joanne quickly adopted the local intonations.

'Where did you fly in from this time, Jo?'

'New Orleans.' Maggie's heart lurched.

'Where's Hob?' At the time of her child's birth, Joanne was reading *The Lord of the Rings*, hence the name 'Hobbit' for her baby.

'With his father for two weeks. He'll come back all freaked out,' she said with a shrug, 'but it's nice to be free.'

Maggie had never noticed that Hob in any way cramped his mother's style. He went along in a backpack when he was small enough to carry – to peace marches, all-night parties, gallery openings. Later on, he got left at home along with the telephone number of some reliable neighbour to keep him company. Maggie kept waiting for the dire effects of Hob's haphazard upbringing to surface, but the last she had seen of him, he appeared well-adjusted enough, if prone to a somewhat unorthodox diet. Maggie had once watched him eat Mallomars and *sushi* for breakfast.

'Drinks, anyone?' Collin asked. His face was round and pink, but the softness was deceptive. He had been sufficiently shrewd and tough to make a success of his investment firm amid the established Connecticut financiers.

'I'll have a vodka, straight up, Daddy,' Joanne said. 'A little more, fine, that'll do just fine.' Maggie noticed that the drawl was becoming more pronounced. Joanne plunked herself down at the foot of Maggie's lawn chair. 'Now let's hear what y'all've been up to,' she said.

Matthew shot Maggie a look of amusement at the same time that Norma and Collin exchanged glances of faint disgust. Then all four looked at Maggie. She had a wild thought. What would happen to those four pairs of expectant eyes if she were to say, 'Hey, listen, I've met a wonderful man and I want to sleep with him, but it goes against everything I've ever thought

I believed in. What do you think I should do?' Instead, she said the next best thing.

'I'm getting involved in art again.' Maggie waited for some shock waves, or at least a few ripples.

'Lucky you,' Joanne said. 'I think I've just burnt myself right out. Nothing's happening any more.'

'I thought you'd just finished an exhibition in Santa Fe,' Norma said.

'Yeah, yeah, but nothing sold. Nobody wants representational stuff any more, especially portraits. Unless they're somebody's kid or favourite aunt.'

All right, Maggie thought. She would try again. 'I'm taking a life class with Eliza Austin,' she said, rather loudly.

'Didn't I see her work in an exhibit on Newbury Street in Boston once?' Collin asked.

'Yes, you probably did, back in the sixties.'

'I'm not wild about her stuff,' Joanne said.

Norma turned to Maggie. 'Maybe you know some people in New York who might be interested in Joanne's work. If you're involved in the art world these days.'

'I'll look into it,' Maggie said quietly. She looked down at her hands. Perhaps she could have brought up David Golden after all. No doubt Joanne would respond that she had once had such a lover, or that she had not had one and wished she had. The conversation continued about the sad state of Joanne's finances while Maggie imagined herself standing up and calmly stripping off her clothes. No one would notice unless somebody needed something. Then all eyes would turn to Maggie. Even then, they would see what they expected to see. Maggie visualized herself as a vending machine. Each little window displayed a particular body part: an ear for listening to tales of woe; a selection of mouths – one for kissing bruises, one for deep sexual kisses, one for advice; a hand for performing the necessary tasks like drying the dishes or writing cheques; a foot for walking to the dry cleaners and the grocery store; two breasts, one lactating, one not. She began to get very excited. Her fingers were tingling in the old way. She stood up abruptly, spilling her drink on the arm Joanne had draped across her knee.

'Excuse me,' she said. 'Bathroom.'

There was a moment's pause in the conversation, but by the time Maggie had taken a few steps towards the house she heard her mother talking to Joanne again. It was the tone Norma reserved for addressing people who were very young, very old, or handicapped. For the first time, Maggie began to wonder which of Norma's children was better off. Perhaps in this household it was preferable to be ignored rather than the object of all that stultifying condescending attention.

Maggie went up to her old room and rummaged through the desk for paper and a pencil. Quickly, she began sketching her vending machine. Maggie liked the profusion of shapes that was emerging; there was an intriguing balance of curves and sharp edges. If she pushed the idea just a little further, perhaps it could really mean something. She was working very fast now, trying out various combinations as they occurred to her. She sketched the ear towards the centre, but somehow that destroyed her focus. She realized with surprise that there was no eye here, but then she understood the significance of the omission. This was a blind machine.

Finally, she achieved a drawing that pleased her. And yet something was missing. She stared at the strong black marks on the white paper and was struck with a tremendous sense of excitement. Scissors! That was it! She wrenched open the drawer and hunted down a pair of child's blunt scissors. Then she began cutting out the drawing, but not exactly conforming to its edges, here and there slicing across the sketch itself. She was so elated that she did not hear Matthew come in.

'What the hell are you doing? I thought you were sick or something,' he said.

'I . . . wanted to do this. It was the scissors I needed . . .' Maggie stammered. She felt jarred as if she had been awakened from a delicious dream by being shoved out of bed onto the floor.

Matthew leaned over her shoulder and peered at the cutouts. He made no comment about them, just told her that dinner was ready and left the room.

'I hope this is still your favourite birthday dinner, Margaret,' Norma said. Maggie watched her mother's reflection in the dining-room mirror as she dipped into the mixed salad and portioned it out onto five salad plates.

'Wonderful,' Maggie said. 'But I've still got a few more hours of being thirty-eight.'

'Five to be exact,' Matthew said. 'Then you'll be starting your fortieth year.'

'Lordie, my sister almost forty years old,' Joanne said. 'That must mean I'm a grown-up, too. How revolting.'

Collin arrived from the back yard with a huge steak still smoking and sizzling from the grill. 'I'm sorry we couldn't celebrate on the actual day,' he said. 'It's this affair at the club. With my being president and all, I couldn't really.'

'You don't worry about being grown up, do you, Joanne?' Norma asked with a smile, or the facsimile of one. Maggie supposed the intention was to dilute the effect of any words that might offend. Norma almost always smiled when she spoke. In fact, Maggie had noticed the same tendency in many women. They could say the most appalling things with a bright smile stretched across their faces. Maggie had listened to the mother of one of Fred's classmates describe her husband's affair with the baby-sitter. The woman grinned throughout the entire narration. Maggie had found it difficult not to respond with a ghoulish smile of her own. She had begun to catch herself at it now and then. Good sport at all costs, she thought. Watch us smile as our souls splinter.

Collin had risen and was holding his wine glass up in a toast. His pleasant face became uncustomarily solemn. 'To my daughter, Margaret, on her thirty-ninth birthday. May she taste the sweetest fruits life has to offer.' He drained his glass and sat down. Maggie searched his face and thought she discerned sadness there.

Joanne spoke first, into the hush. 'Hear, hear,' she said. 'But Daddy, what are the sweetest fruits?' Maggie noticed that her mother was looking down at her plate.

'That depends on Maggie,' Collin answered. He speared a slice of streak. 'Medium or medium rare, Margaret?'

Maggie thought of David's voice, David's face. Forbidden fruit, and surely sweet.

Norma had embarked on a monologue about vandalism at the golf course. 'Perhaps there's malice in it,' she was saying. 'They drive their cars straight across the greens and dig these great yawning chasms with their treads. I rather think it's more casual than malicious. Children are no longer being endowed with consciences. It's the parents' fault.'

Maggie noticed that her father maintained a habitual glazed countenance when Norma was talking. He held his head tilted towards her in apparent attentiveness but the eyes were operating in a different sphere altogether. Maggie resolved to appraise her mother's face once Collin began to speak.

'There's some pretty conscienceless people in your generation, too, Mother, after all,' Joanne said. 'Look at Nixon and that tribe. No wonder kids behave like delinquents.'

'Oh, Nixon again,' Norma sighed.

'I have a young man in my office,' Collin began. 'A Negro fellow, or black, I should say. He came to us through one of those programmes that encourage businesses to hire ex-convicts . . .'

Maggie quickly glanced at her mother. Norma was rapt. Maggie imagined her mother's ears vibrating with the effort to capture every syllable Collin Herrick uttered. Maggie recognized herself in the intent posture of her mother's body as she leaned towards him. Maggie pictured Matthew reciting passages from a bicycle repair manual and she, Maggie, kneeling at his feet, gazing up at him with total concentration. We are children, Maggie thought. My mother is still a little girl and so am I. It suddenly became clear to Maggie why she felt so utterly confused about David. She could not ask Matthew to make this decision for her.

A large box was placed under Maggie's nose. She had entirely missed Collin's story about the ex-convict.

'Happy birthday, Margaret, from your father and me,' Norma said. Her gift packages were legendary. Norma claimed that her giftwrapping talent was her sole contribution to the artistic ability of her children. This present was decorated with sprigs of flowers from the yard, and it smelled as good as it looked.

Inside the box was a dark grey cashmere sweater, V-neck cardigan with pockets on the sides. 'It's very . . . practical,' Maggie said. She failed to track down an appropriate facial expression, so she smiled.

'I thought it was handsome,' Norma said. 'I should think you'd get a lot of wear out of it.'

Maggie glanced at her father. This was not a sweater in which to taste the sweet fruits of life. Maggie remembered her pink ruffled dress, the most treasured item in her second-grade wardrobe. It had been a gift from Maggie's grandmother.

'I can't imagine Mother sending you a ridiculous piece of fluff like that,' Norma had said.

But Maggie loved it. When her ninth birthday arrived a few days later, she put it on.

'You're not going to wear that to your party,' Norma said.

'But I like it,' Maggie protested.

'Take it off,' Norma said, and began undoing the buttons at the back.

Maggie wrenched herself away. 'No! It's pretty! I never get to wear anything pretty!'

'Margaret!' Norma had shouted. 'What in the world has gotten into you? You get ahold of yourself this instant if you want your party, and take off that ridiculous dress. Look at your legs sticking out under those flounces. You look like an ostrich.' Norma withdrew with a white face leaving Maggie to stare at herself in the mirror. Her legs *were* long and skinny. So were her arms. What was more, her face was funny looking. Silently, she unbuttoned the pink dress and put on the paisley jumper and white blouse with the Peter Pan collar.

'I've got something for you, Mags,' Matthew said. 'I was going to wait until tomorrow, but . . .' He handed her an envelope embossed with the name of his law firm: *Berwick, Saunders & Ross*. It was certainly not the new Georgia O'Keeffe book Maggie had hinted about and then finally asked for outright. Somehow she had not wanted to buy it for herself; she wanted it to be given to her. She opened the envelope. It

120

was a cheque for five hundred dollars. She noticed that the five had been changed from a three.

'Thank you, Matt. You're very extravagant.'

'I didn't think a book was quite enough,' Matthew said.

'I didn't have a chance to shop in New Orleans,' Joanne was saying. 'I'll find you something fabulous. I promise.'

There was silence. The words It's okay were hurling themselves against Maggie's clenched teeth, fighting to get free. But Maggie knew that Joanne would forget, or would send some totally inappropriate item, like the plastic lizard pin that arrived two weeks after Christmas, complete with a jewel in its mouth and instructions as to how it was to be worn on one's shoulder. And then there was this awful sweater, and Matthew's hastily-produced cheque. They were all staring at her.

'You know what?' she said to Joanne. 'Don't bother.'

'Excuse me?' Joanne said. Her speech was clipped, with no reference to the deep south.

'Don't send a gift. It wouldn't have anything to do with me.'

'Margaret,' Norma said.

'No, Mother, don't get nervous. I'm just speaking my mind.' She turned to her sister. 'You didn't remember, Jo. Well, that's not so terrible, though it would have been nice since I always remember yours and Hob's.'

'But I almost always do eventually,' Joanne protested. 'I just sent Matthew's birthday present.'

'Yes, two months later. And six silk cravats?'

'Maggie, I don't mind,' Matthew said.

'I don't care if you mind,' Maggie went on. 'Matt, you wouldn't wear a cravat if God himself ordered you to.'

Maggie had a sudden sensation of cool air surrounding her, as if the air conditioning had been switched on. She began again, softly, to Joanne. 'I'm just asking you to think a little. That's what being thoughtful means, being full of thought for another person. It's just that I'm always doing it for everybody else. Couldn't you do it for me now and then?'

'All right, Mags.' Joanne's eyes were damp. Maggie reached across the table and squeezed her sister's hand. Then she got up. 'If we're all done, I'm going to go and ring the children.'

In bed, Matthew asked, 'What was that all about at the table?'

'It seemed immoral somehow to let it go on and on.'

'They were horrified.'

'So were you.'

'I'm not used to your doing that sort of thing.'

'Well, I don't suppose it'll happen very often.'

'A blessing.'

'Why is it a blessing to let Joanne get away with behaving like a self-centred child forever?'

'I just think you're better off saving the moral indignation for the really important stuff.'

'Oh,' Maggie said. He had the most uncanny knack for making her feel trivial. It was so much simpler just to release the easy words: *It's okay. Don't worry about it. No problem. Maggie doesn't mind.*

She woke up sometime in the middle of the night. The illuminated bedside clock said 1.25 a.m. The room felt alive with another presence, someone vital and greedy and hot. Well, David Golden, she thought, I'm thirty-nine. One more year and I'm forty.

# Fifteen

The telephone rang at eight-thirty on Wednesday morning. Matthew grabbed the receiver off the wall on his way out of the kitchen, said 'Hello' and then stood poised in the doorway for a moment. Maggie could tell from the way he was listening that the caller's voice was unfamiliar. He held the phone out to her.

'For you. Who's David Golden?' But he did not wait for her to tell him, just set the telephone on the counter and started off down the hall. Maggie sat still and stared at the white object that held David's voice. Then she picked it up gingerly, and rested it against her shoulder a while before answering. Finally she said hello.

'It's David. I want to see you.'

'Class,' Maggie said. 'Tonight. Isn't it?' She was trying to squeeze the syllables out through paralysed lips.

'I mean before. Come to dinner. I'll fix you something here.'

'God.'

'It'll be all right.'

'Oh,' she said.

'Are you okay?'

'No,' she said.

'What is it?'

'Monosyllabic. Just fear.'

'You're not afraid of me, are you?'

'No, it's not you.'

'Will you come?'

'All right.'

'Five-thirty. See you then.' He did not even say good-bye.

Matthew was calling from the hallway. 'See you!'

'Okay,' she answered, then 'Wait!' She wondered what would come out of her mouth when she reached Matthew

123

looking all slick and pressed and self-contained by the front door.

'I won't be here for dinner. Are you coming home early?'

'No. About ten.'

'Fine.'

'Got a hot date?' he grinned.

'A few of us are getting together before class.'

'Well, have fun.' He kissed her and was gone.

Maggie leaned against the wall and slid slowly to the floor. She wanted to laugh and yet was not so sure it was laughter that was caught in her throat. She sat on the hard parquet in her bathrobe and took stock.

David, this man she had kissed, had spoken on the telephone to Matthew, her husband of eighteen years. Absolutely nothing had happened. Not only had the telephone not exploded, but Matthew appeared to be completely without suspicion, or even curiosity. Next, Maggie had told Matthew she would be out without even checking to see if he needed her at home to cook dinner. And finally, she had lied. 'A few of us . . .' she had said, and it slipped out so easily. Lies were ugly, odious. So why then did she not feel corrupt? Why instead did she feel almost proud? There was revolution on East Seventy-ninth Street and it was only 8.45 in the morning.

'But I'm not a morning person,' Maggie protested aloud and then laughed. What kept billowing up through the questions and confusion was one fact: she would see David. Alone. Soon.

She was supposed to meet Phyllis for lunch, but the idea seemed impossible now. First of all, Phyllis would surely notice Maggie's excitement. Secondly, Maggie felt a profound need to be alone with her happiness. She wanted to be the miser who locks his doors, pulls his shades and gloats over his golden treasure in peace.

'Up, Margaret,' she said to herself, aloud, and then giggled. 'Losing it, I must be losing it.' Other than the occasional blasphemy after stubbing her toe, Maggie could not remember ever talking to herself. 'Probably because I simply had nothing to say,' she murmured on her way to the kitchen. 'Oh, shut up,' she told herself, and stood by the telephone trying to figure out what to tell Phyllis.

'Matt needs me at his office,' Maggie said. 'I'm sorry. Can we make it next week?'

'You sure everything's all right? You sound odd,' Phyllis told her.

'Yup. Fine.'

'Yup?'

Maggie coughed. 'Got a frog in my throat this morning.'

'What's he want you for?'

'Oh, uh, something with a client. I'm not really sure, but it's rather urgent.'

'You going down there to get laid?'

Maggie coughed again. 'Nope,' she said in a strangled voice.

Phyllis was silent. Maggie could almost hear gears clicking and meshing through the receiver. 'Okay, hon. Let's talk Monday and we'll set something up.'

'Thanks. Talk to you soon. Sorry. Bye.' Maggie hung up and told herself she would have to do better than this. Phyllis had antennae that could pick up the sexual impulses of a gnat. At the last bridge game, Phyllis had asked twice if Maggie was pregnant. The notion had seemed absurd at the time, but this morning, pregnancy seemed the closest status to describing how Maggie felt: full up, swelling with something beautiful, wonderful, mysterious. Special, as if she were the only woman in the world to be so blessed.

At five o'clock, she changed into her white sundress with the spaghetti straps and dropped a bottle of wine into her straw bag. Out front, a doorman was hosing down the sidewalk in the sunshine. Maggie said good evening, and as she stepped across the puddles, wondered why the water did not instantly turn to steam around her feet. She was high voltage, crackling, sparking. Everything tingled, nipples, between her legs, and her underpants were soaked. In the cab across town, she told herself she was not ready for an affair. Danger, she said. Danger! Yet there was nothing menacing in the memory of David's face. It promised excitement, yes, but shelter and comfort as well. Certainly something mysterious awaited her on the far side of Central Park. The future lay trembling and full of colour, just out of reach.

Each time David looked at her, he grinned as if the sight of her were a thoroughly unexpected surprise. He had led her to a chair at the round table and seated her almost formally.

'Here, sit while I unpack this stuff.' There were two grocery bags on the counter. 'I was out all day.' He turned to smile at her again. 'I was afraid you might call and back out so I stayed in the studio and worked.'

'I didn't call.'

'How about a glass of wine?'

'How about the entire bottle?' But the truth was, she felt relaxed. The sun streaked in the window at the company of statues which made fantastic shadows across the floor. Maggie could see every hair on David's hand as he uncorked the wine and poured them each a glass.

'Sit with me a minute,' she said. 'We've got plenty of time to eat before class.'

He sat opposite her. His feet were bare, and he captured her ankles between them under the table.

'Tell me about your trip,' he said. 'I thought about you.' Then he laughed as if to say he would have thought about her all the time anyway.

'Oh, my parents . . .' Maggie sighed. 'My first great unrequited love.'

'That bad.'

'Have you ever been to the Museum of Holography down in Soho?' He nodded. 'It was a little like that. I felt as if I could walk around them all right, view them from all sides. They have three dimensions. And yet, well, they're not solid somehow. There's no reality to them. I could stick my hand out and it would pass right through them without encountering anything.'

'And Matthew?'

She dropped her eyes.

'You don't like me to mention him.'

'You talked to him this morning.'

'Yes.'

'Did it feel odd?'

'Not the way you think,' he answered. 'I didn't feel guilty.'

'I guess that's what I meant.'

'No,' he said. 'Angry. Jealous.'

Maggie looked at him incredulously.

'He's got you and I haven't,' David explained.

'I don't know if that's exactly true.'

They stared at one another for a moment. Then Maggie said, 'I never plan on talking to you this way. How come we always seem to get right into it?'

'What should we talk about?' he asked.

'Oh . . . art, I guess.'

David got up abruptly. 'I've got something for you.' He opened his bureau drawer and removed a package.

'I don't remember telling you I had a birthday,' Maggie said.

'No. This is just something I think you should have, if you don't already. Call it a birthday present.'

Maggie opened the gift and caught her breath. It was the Georgia O'Keeffe studio book. She covered her face with her hands and began to sob. David knelt beside her and stroked her hair.

'What is it?'

'I'm happy. I can't even tell you,' she choked. 'Oh, David, I feel so lucky.' She kissed him on the mouth, a long full kiss. 'How hungry are you?' she whispered.

'Very,' he said hoarsely.

They kissed again. His hands followed the line of her body from either side of her neck down her bare shoulders and arms. She wanted to be stripped bare with him, wanted to show herself to him naked. He slipped the straps off her shoulders and unzipped the front of her dress. He pushed the fabric aside gently, releasing her breasts. Maggie felt his name catch in her throat as he kissed her nipples. So gentle, his mouth and hands were like butterflies against her skin. She felt the heat rising from a part of her that had long been cold and dark. He was a magician, drawing fire with the lightest touch.

All resolve to go slowly gave way to greed as they undressed one another, frenzied now, with frantic kisses and hands searching. Finally David was inside her. Maggie cried out, a moan, a sob, a kind of deep laughter against his mouth. And soon they lay together, two long naked bodies clasped like a companion piece for the other stone figures, serene and complete in the sun.

'David, I'm so happy I don't care if I die this second.' They were on his bed on the floor now, exhausted and glistening with sweat.

'Please don't.'

'Now I know why I've always been afraid of death. I never knew what it was like to be . . . to have *joy*. How terrible to die without ever experiencing it.' She was silent a moment. 'What if we hadn't signed up for that class, David?' she went on. 'What if only one of us had? God . . .'

'I would have found you anyway, by the smoked salmon at Zabar's.'

'You don't really believe in fate.'

'I never did, but I have to tell you I've been giving it some thought lately.'

'You make me want to work,' Maggie said, watching their fingers twine together on his chest. 'What do other people do when they feel something so strongly, *so* strongly that it won't stay inside their bodies? When there's not enough room to contain it.'

'I don't know how many people feel things that way,' David replied.

'It can't only be creative people. Children do, I think.'

There were patterns on the ceiling now, the windows' outlines stretched into long rectangles. 'You see that?' David asked, taking her fingers and pointing at the shapes. 'That's the very first thing I remember in this life. Patterns on the ceiling above my bed, or crib, I guess. There were leaves and slats from the blinds, all moving. Beautiful.'

'Any colour?'

'Greys, I suppose.'

'Funny . . .' Maggie began, then stopped.

'What's funny?'

'No, it's just that something's happening. I'm not sure what. With making art, I mean. The shapes. I've never been involved much with that . . . more with colour. Form, too, but . . . I can't explain. It's almost as if suddenly I'm more interested in the margins around the pictures than the picture itself. I did something at my parents' house, not like anything I've done before. With scissors and glue.' She laughed. 'Like a child with cutouts. Only it was so exciting. I can't stop thinking about it.'

'You'd better explore it.'

'I guess I'd better.'

They lay quietly for a while. Finally Maggie said, 'David, I'm in love with you.'

'I know.'

'Are you going to make me dinner?'

'All right.'

She stood up and held out a hand to help him. 'But let's not get dressed. We should always be naked.'

'Wait 'til January and my landlord turns off the heat.'

They stared at one another, both wondering where they would be in January. 'When I was talking about holograms –' Maggie said, 'my parents?'

David nodded.

'That used to be me, too. But not any more.'

He reached for her and held her for a long time.

# Sixteen

❧

Hilary held a thick clump of hair off her neck and gazed around her with satisfaction. She was sweating and breathing hard, but today even the July heat failed to daunt her energy. While summer crouched outside, seething and casting white blistering squares onto her floor through the skylight, Hilary had scrubbed, dusted, arranged flower pots, and made numerous trips for ice cubes and provisions which had to be hauled up six flights of stairs in an ancient clattering elevator. Tonight, a full three years after buying the apartment, she would celebrate this ultimate evidence of her independence: a place of her own.

Everyone had wondered at Hilary's choice; a loft on Prince Street was an unconventional habitat for a successful female executive. But Hilary was attracted by the contrast Soho offered to the bland efficiency of her midtown office. The area simmered with the kind of creative excitement that had once existed in Greenwich Village. There were artists of integrity here, people who took risks, not the play-it-safe types who surrounded her every day at work. The 'bottom line crowd', she called them, those so-called creative people who dominated the movie industry. Not that she didn't play the game herself. Hilary liked money. Power was intoxicating, liberating. But once she had wound up the day's meetings, it was pleasant to slip back into this strange world of experiment and naïveté. Hilary adjusted a vase of Peruvian lilies and smiled to herself. In all honesty, buying this place had offered the additional bonus of horrifying her parents.

They had arrived that first Sunday afternoon and stood with Hilary at the dreary entrance to her building. Elizabeth Vonderhyde confronted her daughter with wounded eyes that said: *I came all the way in from Greenwich for this?* And Martin announced that he would wait in the car. 'Look around, why don't you?' Hilary had suggested. 'There's a lot to see down here.' But Martin was cautious rather than curious, and preferred to sit in the Mercedes to ensure that none of the outrageous creatures parading past would snap off the bonnet ornament.

Elizabeth Vonderhyde marched into the elevator wearing her usual expression of brave suffering. It was ninety degrees at street level and probably over a hundred six floors up, but Hilary's mother stood at the threshold without so much as a drop of perspiration on her face. *Horses sweat, women perspire, and ladies are all aglow.* Here was a woman who took her aphorisms seriously.

Back then, the place had been a single sprawling barn-like room. Hilary had split the space by erecting walls and half-walls to designate kitchen and sleeping areas while still maintaining the extraordinary sensation of light and openness. She painted the walls white, polished the floors to a high gloss, replaced the shattered skylight and set about collecting furniture that appealed to her instinct for elegance. She bought an overstuffed couch and upholstered it in deep blue brocade. Oriental rugs of various sizes and shapes gratified the eye with splashes of warmth. A pair of antique English chairs faced the couch, and a massive mahogany sideboard displayed an eclectic assortment of china and pottery acquired from local shops. Ordinarily, Hilary was too busy or too distracted to appreciate her dazzling aerie, but recently she had felt an unaccountable urgency to celebrate it, or perhaps to celebrate herself. She crossed the sunny living room and leaned on her windowsill.

Prince Street was a crazy circus beneath her. Women sported layers of colourful rags, oversized unmatched earrings, fishnet stockings and spangled high heels. Men wore tight leather shorts, patterned socks and combat boots. A noisy crowd of young people with predominantly hot pink hairdos had gathered in front of the gallery opposite Hilary's building. This week's exhibit consisted of twisted neon shapes displayed against black velvet draperies. Next door to the gallery, a store called 'Huge' had hung a giant green comb and brush in its window. Out front, from the back seat of a sports car, poked two crayons the size of nuclear warheads. The shape of the crayons made her think of men, which made her think of Stephen Wheeler, which made her think of Phyllis. A ball of excitement formed in her stomach, like a fist unfurling and wriggling its fingers. These past weeks, Hilary had felt herself stepping ever closer to some great discovery. It had begun with bridge at Robin's when Phyllis and Stephen's provocative behaviour had touched her like many caressing insistent hands that would not be denied. At first she had thought it was the drug Phyllis had administered for her headache. The next morning, her headache had disappeared along with the giddiness, but the sensation of living inside a diaphanous cocoon of highly stimulated skin remained. Her face glowed, her body tingled, and she had been forced to wear a bra to conceal nipples that were constantly erect. Ever since that night, she had been making the long climb up a ladder, and now she stood poised at the edge of the diving board, raised on tiptoes, arms outstretched, body arched, ready to plunge into the depths below.

There was danger, of course, but Hilary was exhilarated rather than frightened. The pair of swimmers waited below with upturned faces and bodies white beneath the transparent surface, ready to guide her exploration of a glistening exotic world.

She knew that tonight's party marked the culmination of that long climb. She was celebrating her expectations at the same time that she commemorated what was now to become a part of her past.

The evening had cooled enough so that with the large windows open there was no need for air conditioning. Since it seemed appropriate to shed her customary style, Hilary slipped into a new pale silver dress and pulled her hair into a knot at her neck. She made a slow turn in front of her mirror and watched her body shimmer in the luminous fabric. Soon the buzzer rang and she heard the elevator cables squawk and complain. She stood at the door, kissing cheeks and enjoying the shock in each pair of eyes as her glamorous appearance made its impact.

Phyllis and Stephen arrived with the Hollanders. Phyllis wore a strapless black summer jersey that showed off her tan.

Hilary let her fingers rest on the bare flesh for a moment, but Stephen quickly intercepted by grasping Hilary around the waist and kissing her full on the mouth. After that, Hilary could barely muster the equanimity to greet Maggie and Matthew.

'Drinks,' she gasped, waving towards the long array of bottles on the kitchen counter. 'Help yourself to whatever.'

Hilary's boss, Jim Perry, arrived next with his new administrative assistant in tow. Jim had stunned Hilary this week by showing up in the office without his beard. After twenty-five years, he had decided to see what his face looked like. Hilary wondered if there was some universal force in operation that was causing personal revolutions lately. Jim's assistant was a California golden girl with an irritating habit of punctuating her speech with repetitive catch phrases: 'I can well understand your gist' followed directly on the heels of 'Oh yeah right'. Hilary heard her tell Maggie that she was from Boston, which was true strictly speaking, though Hilary knew from the job résumé that she had moved to Los Angeles when she was eighteen months old. The young woman had soon backed Matthew into a corner near the stereo and blinked up at him while his face grew grimmer and grimmer. Hilary watched his attention habitually gravitate to Maggie and Jim Perry. Maggie looked attractive tonight, Hilary thought. Not exactly herself, not exactly wholesome, even a trace mysterious.

Stephen appeared by her elbow, carrying two tall drinks. He handed her one, but Hilary raised her Perrier and shook her head.

'No, thanks. I'm all set. Are you meeting people?'

'I'm watching you,' Stephen said. He had a low voice with very little colour in it. Despite his declaration, he was not looking at her, even as he spoke. His eyes moved restlessly about the room, settling briefly on each attractive woman like flies on perishables at a picnic. Hilary imagined herself parading naked in front of him to capture his attention. He slipped away, leaving her with a pleasant tingling sensation behind her ear where his breath had stroked her.

Most of the guests had arrived. There was the satisfying full-bodied chorus of conversation and laughter that signalled a successful party. Though she stood in the midst of it, Hilary felt removed from the crush. Everyone faded like drab splotches except Phyllis and Stephen. No matter where they got to, their bodies seemed outlined in phosphorescent paint. Hilary was always aware of them, her eyes drawn to their light, her ears catching fragments of their conversation despite the noise. She was suddenly gripped with an almost unbearable impatience to get rid of everyone else. She held her glass to her forehead and forced herself to focus on the others. The apartment had heated up with the crowd so that perspiration stains began to appear on the back of the men's shirts along their spines. There was Maggie still talking with Jim Perry, joined now by Matthew who seemed a lot happier standing beside his wife.

'Sorry to butt in,' Hilary said, 'but I want to borrow Maggie for a minute.' She pulled Maggie off to the side. 'What's the story with Robin?'

'Isn't she here?' Maggie asked.

Hilary shook her head. 'She called with some phony story about not feeling well.'

'I don't know,' Maggie said. 'You think there's trouble?'

'Maybe it's the baby business. She was so disappointed about not adopting.'

'You know something, Hil?' Maggie said. 'The older I get, the less I think I can figure anybody out.'

Hilary grinned.

'Oh, my, and what's going on with you?' Maggie asked.

'Why do you ask?' Hilary's eyes involuntarily flickered to Phyllis who was standing near the window with one hip cocked against a bookcase.

'You look like the Cheshire cat, that's why. There's somebody new, isn't there?'

'I think so,' Hilary said. Maggie's face was so full of affectionate delight that Hilary grabbed her in a hug. 'I'm happy, Mag, isn't that a gas? Or at least I'm pretty damn sure I'm going to be.'

Sometime around midnight, Hilary managed to corner Phyllis in the kitchen. 'Having fun?' she asked.

'I like your boss,' Phyllis said. She ran her fingers through the short cropped hair in the impatient gesture Hilary had watched for years.

'Let me do that,' Hilary said.

'What?'

Hilary reached out and touched Phyllis's hair, then pulled her hand back.

'It's all right,' Phyllis said softly.

'You think so?'

'I know so.'

Jim Perry strode into the kitchen with a plate of stuffed mushrooms for Phyllis. Hilary stood back, jarred by the collision of two different worlds in her life. 'I, uh, wanted to check about Zach,' she said to Phyllis.

'Who's Zach?' Perry asked.

'My son,' Phyllis said. 'Hilary's baby sitting tomorrow.'

'Some baby,' Hilary laughed. 'He's thirteen. I only borrow him. He's at the Hollanders overnight, yes?'

'How come he's not at camp like every other New York kid I know?' Jim asked Phyllis.

'His buddy had to come home for a day to get his braces adjusted, so Zach developed a severe case of mononucleosis. He had a remarkable recovery on the Triborough Bridge, so he'll probably show up here about eleven tomorrow.'

'And you two can stay out late and play,' Hilary said.

'That's right, old friend,' Phyllis answered, and turned her smiling face to Jim Perry.

About 5 a.m., Stephen and Phyllis fell asleep. Hilary, who had never felt more wide-awake in her life, slid out of bed, pulled on her robe and went into the bathroom. She was studying her face in the mirror when Phyllis tapped on the door and let herself in.

'What are you doing?' she asked.

'Wondering if I've changed,' Hilary answered.

'And?'

'Nothing that shows.'

Phyllis sat down on the edge of the tub while Hilary dropped down cross-legged on the bathmat. There was a dark smear on the inside of her right knee. 'What's this?'

Phyllis touched the spot lightly. 'Blood, darling.' Hilary looked at her in alarm. 'Things got a little rough there for a while.'

'There was a scratch on . . . his face.' Hilary found it impossible to articulate Stephen's name.

Phyllis nodded.

'Did *I* do that?'

Phyllis nodded again.

'Jesus.'

'I'm sure he loved it.'

They were both silent for a moment. Then Hilary said, 'I suppose we're Lesbians.'

'I don't know.'

'What does your shrink say about you?'

'That everybody's sexuality is multi-dimensional.'

'So we're all gay, heterosexual, exhibitionistic transvestites.'

'Right.'

Phyllis's body was tanned a deep brown except for white patches at her breasts and crotch. Hilary held out her finger and gently touched a nipple. 'We've been friends for such a long time. Don't you think it's very strange?'

'No.'

'Have you thought about me this way all these years?'

'Sometimes.'

'I dreamt about you once, a long time ago,' Hilary said. 'You were standing on my parents' lawn beside the porch and I ran to you and we embraced and kissed, a real kiss. It scared the wits out of me at the time, you know. It was one of those very vivid dreams.'

'It's nice that we've been friends,' Phyllis said. 'I've never had a lover who was my friend.'

Hilary reached out again and let her hand move along Phyllis's hip. Phyllis leaned forward and pushed Hilary's robe apart. 'So beautiful,' she whispered. Her eyes were filled with tears.

The sun woke Hilary in the morning. She was tangled in the sheets and baking like a potato wrapped in tin foil. She wriggled herself free and lay still in the sunshine with her eyes closed. Once she tried to get up, she was sure her muscles would ache, but for the moment, her body felt deliciously warm and supple.

She had astonished herself last night. Somehow she had

expected to need a great deal of prodding. But in the end, it had been Hilary who made the first move for the bedroom, and Hilary who had stripped herself, shaken out the knot in her hair, and lay open on the bed. Stephen's body was muscular and unyielding. He was thrilling and basic. She remembered imagining herself a naked child clinging to the strong hard branches of a tree. But looking back, it was the few moments alone with Phyllis that resonated, like the sweet hum of chamber music from a nearby room.

The skylight looked like a large square eye staring down – the dispassionate gaze of a lepidopterist scrutinizing the lovely butterfly trapped in the sheets below. Hilary supposed she was an aberrant specimen, the freak butterfly who shuns the lamplight and is forever drawn into the shadows. But there had to be reasons.

There was the incident in the museum toilet, of course, but that was an isolated moment in which her assailant's gender hardly seemed relevant. There were ten-year-old games with her best friend when they took turns rubbing one another's backs with lotion. Once Peggy had flipped Hilary over and massaged her chest. The sensations aroused in both little girls were so terrifying that the lotion was put away for good. There were the pyjama parties at Peggy's house where six girls had practised kissing with open mouths, like in the movies. Hilary's attempts to touch tongues with Rosemary were met with hilarity and shouts of 'Eeeyew!' There had been no little boys in Hilary's early years, not so far as she could remember. Her mother had told her there would be time for all that when she was grown.

Elizabeth Vonderhyde was very pretty, in a small-featured, fragile way. She 'dithered' a lot, by which her husband meant that she worried aloud about inconsequential things that could not be altered: the couple who moved in down the street had too many children and spoke with an obscure foreign accent; the president of Martin's company – Peggy's father, as it happened – patronized Martin at the country club; Hilary was growing too tall and showed no gift for music. All of these futile protestations were presented at the dinner table in a soft frantic little voice that produced two lines of irritation down the centre of Martin Vonderhyde's forehead.

It was not long before Hilary absorbed some of her father's contempt for these empty babblings, and began to examine him for clues as to how a reasonable person might cope with the vast incomprehensible adult world. But Hilary was encouraged to identify with the young ladies in Victorian novels who called their fathers 'Papa' with the accent on the last syllable and who tiptoed when he was in the house. Conversations between Hilary and her father were rare and stilted. While Martin appeared to take some interest in her mathematical achievements, Hilary only assumed this by the fact that he occasionally questioned her about it at the dinner table. He displayed no curiosity about any other area of her life. Once Hilary announced that she had been chosen to represent her school on a trip to Washington, DC. Elizabeth Vonderhyde had said, 'Well, that's fine, dear. Isn't that fine, Martin?'

Martin had not responded, other than to pour himself the second of the four glasses of water he consumed over the course of his meals (to keep himself from becoming constipated, Elizabeth explained to Hilary). After he had finished his coffee and left the dining room, Hilary tearfully flung out at her mother, 'Why did you ever have me anyway?'

Elizabeth had replied, 'We wanted a child. Everyone wants children.'

'*He* doesn't. You should have bought a dog or another car or something, not me!'

Then the summer before Hilary left for Miss Curtis's School, Peggy reported that Hilary's father was having an affair with his secretary.

Hilary had laughed out loud.

'No,' Peggy insisted. 'Everybody knows about it. Mom saw them in the city coming out of a hotel. She was on the phone with my aunt and she said, and I quote, "I saw Martin Vonderhyde and his secretary in front of the Biltmore again" and then she went on a whole tirade about how indiscreet he is and how this is the third one she knows about and God knows how many others there have been and shouldn't something be said. God, Hil, isn't it exciting? Who would ever have thought that *your father*, I mean, he's so incredibly stuffy looking. Well, I guess there's hope for everybody.'

Hilary had been glad to go away to Miss Curtis's. She and Peggy gradually drifted apart.

Hilary never resented boarding school the way so many other girls did. After the archaic rigidity of her parents' home, she was grateful for the din of young voices, the bustle and clatter, the bright colours. After twenty years, Hilary could even remember the smells. Home-made biscuits for breakfast, sugar cookies for Tiffin, that split-second break between classes at ten-thirty every morning. The dorm was always thick with the (pleasant, Hilary thought) odour of sweaty feet.

There had been the usual boarding-school crush, the object of Hilary's infatuation being her geometry teacher. Hilary sat through her classes in a kind of trance, gazing at the sturdy athletic body of Miss Franklin as she scratched parallelograms onto the blackboard. The highlight of this romance had been Miss Franklin's gift to Hilary of a paperback book called 'Puzzles for the Math Genius'. Miss Franklin's hand had touched hers as the present was transmitted. But Hilary realized even then that most of the other girls entertained similar crushes, so that there was no sense of being abnormal. Rarely did the intense ardour of these relationships blossom into actual affairs, and when they did, the couples were discussed in scandalized whispers. One was supposed to worship from afar, always with the tragic understanding that consummation was out of the question, even undesirable. Not that there was ever a clear notion about how one went about the physical expression of such a love other than the vague idea that there would be some kind of touching.

By her junior year, a fervid obsession with boys replaced all interest in poor Miss Franklin, who, it was now noted, sometimes had perspiration circles under her arms. Tea dances began to take on a tantalizing dimension once Hilary discovered that it was possible to lure a young man into the dark recesses of the senior smoking room for a session of heavy necking. Hilary particularly enjoyed her sense of omnipotence as an erection throbbed against her thigh.

By the time Hilary reached Wellesley, she had begun to recognize a certain dichotomy in her character. Intellectually, she excelled. Her grades were always in the top fifth of her class. She was inevitably elected President of the student government. And yet, her social life was a shambles. The self-possessed girl who could delegate responsibilities with skill and tact, address crowds of people unflinchingly, act as liaison between students and faculty and demonstrate all the qualities of leadership one would expect in a born executive would, on the other hand, arrive back at the dorm on a Saturday night and cling, weeping, to her date who was indisputably the biggest cad at Yale, Harvard, Brown or Dartmouth. Hilary worked her way through them all, each time falling hopelessly in love and each time being dragged through the thorny underbrush of masochism.

Until last night, the pattern had remained the same. She had always mistrusted her impulses enough to refrain from marrying any of the men who paraded through her life. But the union with Phyllis and Stephen seemed like marriage. There was a sense of symmetry and commitment that had struck all three of them, she believed. Hilary was convinced that as of today, Stephen and Phyllis would no longer feel drawn into promiscuity. And whereas Phyllis alone had been powerless to help Stephen discover the tenderness that surely lay beneath the veneer of bitterness and rage, with Hilary as an ally, he would change. As for Zachary, they would protect him from a full understanding of the unorthodox arrangement. Hilary had watched the boy suffer in an atmosphere of discontent. He, more than anyone, would benefit from a new stability.

Hilary yawned into the pillow that was still scented with Phyllis's perfume. She glanced at the heavy marble clock beside her bed. There was still time for another hour of sleep before Zachary was due. She curled herself into a ball around the wadded bedclothes and drifted off into a sleep without dreams.

Zachary Wheeler arrived at eleven precisely. Hilary hauled herself out of bed at the sound of the buzzer and greeted him with frazzled hair.

'Some party,' Zachary observed.

There were dirty ashtrays and unwashed dishes scattered everywhere.

'It's not so bad when you don't drink. I can even face this

mess. Why don't you find something to do while I take a quick shower and then we'll go and have brunch.' She glanced up at the skylight. 'Looks like a great day.'

'Yeah, the cab went past the park and the trees smell real good, you know, from the rain.'

'Did it rain?'

'Yeah, last night, but just one of those quick steambaths that make it feel like you're in a jungle.'

Hilary smiled. 'Sometimes I think you're going to wind up being a writer like your Dad.'

Zachary looked away. 'Nah, I don't think so.'

'There's TV,' Hilary said quickly, 'and magazines under the couch. I hid them from the hordes. Help yourself to juice. I'll be out in a minute.'

Hilary showered, threw on a pale-blue sweatshirt and went into the living room to find Zachary picking celery sticks from between the cracks in the couch. The ashtrays had all been cleaned and stacked on the cocktail table, the trays of food scraped and set beside the sink ready for washing.

'Oh, Zach,' Hilary said.

'I just felt like moving around.'

'Well, come on, now. Let's go and eat. You've earned it.'

West Broadway was nearly deserted. Soho never really began to crank up until afternoon. The residents, mainly artists, slept late, leaving the streets to tourists. Hilary kept her arm around Zachary's shoulders. They passed a patrolman who smiled and said good morning.

'I bet he thinks you're my son home from boarding school for the weekend,' Hilary said.

Zachary looked pleased. Hilary steered him into a restaurant called *Central Falls*. They took a table next to the window. Zachary studied the poster behind Hilary which advertised a show for Norris Church Mailer. 'It's okay down here,' he said. 'Nicer than uptown.'

'In what way?' Hilary asked.

'People don't look as . . . I don't know . . . phony, I guess.'

'I think they're probably just as phony in their own way, but I have to agree that at least they seem more interesting.' A young woman passed the window wearing a t-shirt with holes cut out at her breasts. Her bright silver bra poked through and flashed in the sun like headlights.

'I'll say,' Zachary remarked, and they both laughed. After they had ordered, Hilary sipped her coffee and studied the boy. There was a tremor in his left eye she had not noticed before, a quick rhythmic crinkling at the outside corner. Now and then he rubbed at it with the palm of his hand like a sleepy child.

'How're the Hollanders?' she asked.

'Okay.'

'Is Fred your best friend these days?'

'He's mine but I'm not his.'

'He wouldn't hang out with you if he didn't like you.'

'Nah, his mother makes him. But I help him out with his essays so it's worth it to him.'

Hilary searched his face for signs of self-pity but there were none. These were merely facts.

Zachary buttered a hard roll and took a bite, sending a spray of crumbs onto the table. 'Mrs Hollander's okay, too,' he mumbled, swiping at the debris. 'She does real nice art. She let me see her new stuff last night, all these, like, cut-outs.'

'Oh? I thought she was into representational things, realistic paintings.'

'Nope, collages,' he said, proud to be telling Hilary something she did not already know. 'Mr Hollander says it's gimmicky, but I liked it. One of them reminded me of this old brownstone they're renovating across the street from us. She was real happy when I told her that.'

'Would you like to see some galleries today?'

'Sure, why not?'

'There's some really kinky work around.'

'Excellent. I'm into kinky.'

Hilary thought of Zachary's parents and was silent.

When the food arrived, the boy bit into his bacon cheeseburger while Hilary picked at her omelette. 'How'd you get the name "Zachary"?'

His face darkened as if someone had passed by outside the window and cast a shadow across his cheeks. Hilary glanced out at the sidewalk but there was no one.

'Old family name from Mom's side.'

'You don't like it.'

'My father says it's a faggot name.'

Hilary noticed that Phyllis was always referred to as 'Mom' while Stephen was invariably 'my father'. She set her fork down. 'What about our president Zachary Taylor, Old Rough and Ready? He was pretty tough.'

Zachary looked at Hilary with his mother's piercing intensity. 'Do you think a name can make you . . . can make a person into what . . . well, say your name is . . . uh, Mike or Jack or something, like, strong. You think that has an effect on you so you end up being like your name? Say I had a name like Chad Stallion or maybe like that guy John Wayne? His name could have made him a tough guy, I bet.'

Hilary thought for a moment. 'First of all,' she said, 'I don't imagine John Wayne's real name was John Wayne. It was probably Percy Higginbottom.'

Zachary laughed. The sound was light and clear.

'I suppose it would have an effect if you let it,' she went on. 'But after all, a name is only an arbitrary label. You can change it any time you like.'

'Nah, Mom loves it. It was the name of about the only relative she didn't hate.'

'Well, then maybe you could compromise. Keep Zachary for your middle name, for instance.'

Hilary watched him think this over. He rubbed his eye.

'What name would you choose if you changed?'

'John,' he said without hesitation.

'John Wheeler,' Hilary said, 'John Zachary Wheeler. It's nice.'

Zachary topped off his brunch with a double chocolate mocha sundae. Then Hilary paid the bill and said, 'Okay, John, let's go and get some culture.'

He laughed again. Hilary was struck with the sudden bizarre fantasy of quitting her job to spend her lifetime provoking that joyful expression on Zachary Wheeler's shadowed face.

# Seventeen

Fred's small room was the perfect size for a studio. Maggie liked being confined while she worked; that way her ideas hung close around her in the air and could not escape beyond her reach. Her old accomplices had disappeared. The tortured tubes of oils were heaped in a cardboard box in the closet. No brushes stood in cans on the window-sill. The stinging scent of turpentine had been replaced by the sweeter aroma of glue. Her easel stood neglected against the wall like a reproachful spectator. Maggie sat at Fred's desk surrounded by a wild array of coloured paper: tissue, cardboard, newspaper, ribbon, tags from new clothes, dry-cleaner receipts, the chopstick wrapper from a Chinese restaurant. It was mid-morning, but she was still in her nightgown. The breakfast dishes were unwashed, the newspaper unread, even the mug of coffee beside her had turned cold as she snipped, pasted, arranged and rearranged.

Last week, Maggie had stood in David's apartment and watched a flock of birds over the Hudson River. Those near the surface circled relentlessly, as if caught in the funnel of a tornado or a waterspout. But high in the sky with the sun setting behind them were three who had broken free. They sailed and dipped and dived in a sea of salmon-pink light, as if they had exploded upward, out of the merciless pattern of the others. The beauty of their swirling freedom had moved Maggie. And now she sat staring down at a square of deep rose-pink Christmas wrap. The paper was a glossy foil whose reflective qualities suggested to her the brilliancy of a sunset over the river. She had cut white triangles out of various types of paper and had arranged them so that the heavier shapes were near the bottom of the shiny square. Those near the top were sheer tissue which she wrinkled slightly as she

144

pasted them down. She imagined becoming so light, so diaphanous, that the wind could lift her effortlessly and send her spinning into the air in a wild, free dance.

The telephone rang. At first, she ignored it, remaining suspended like the birds. But soon the sound began to tug at her. She was to see David this afternoon. What if he were calling to cancel their appointment? She let it ring again. What if it were the camp in Vermont reporting an accident? She leapt up and dashed to reach the telephone before it stopped.

'I knew you were there,' Phyllis said.

Maggie was too breathless to respond.

'I want to know why you won't see me,' Phyllis said. 'It's okay, you can catch your breath. But I'm not hanging up until I have an explanation.'

'I've been, ah, busy, you know, I'm working again,' Maggie began. 'I mean, not a job, of course, but making art . . .'

Phyllis interrupted. 'The kids are in camp, Matthew's at the office, you can't possibly create masterpieces every minute of every day. What the hell is going on? I haven't seen you since bridge at Robin's and neither has anybody else.'

'I saw you at the party.'

'Two seconds in the middle of a mob.'

Maggie felt as if the telephone receiver had melted and stuck to her ear, that no matter how hard she tried to pry it loose, it would hang there forever on the side of her head like a grotesque appendage.

'I don't know,' she said. 'I didn't realize.'

'Listen, room-mate, if you don't have lunch with me today you can kiss me right off. Are you my friend or not?'

Maggie was to see David at two o'clock. But Phyllis's voice, despite the upbeat banter, could not disguise a thread of urgency. 'Okay, Phyl. An early one, twelve at *Mortimer's*?'

'Fine. See you then.'

When Maggie arrived, flushed and panting, Phyllis was waiting at the bar on a tall stool.

'You're late,' Phyllis commented.

'Sorry.' Maggie glanced at her watch. 'Only seven minutes.'

'The table's not ready anyway. What do you want to drink?'

'White wine.'

'Well, at least that hasn't changed.'

But the maître d' was able to seat them immediately, allowing Maggie the chance to compose herself by consulting the menu she already knew by heart. Once they had ordered, however, there was nowhere to hide. In the bright light of the table overlooking Lexington Avenue, Maggie felt as if she were on display to Phyllis and the rest of Manhattan.

'So how are you, Phyl?' Maggie asked, leaning forward on her elbows. A good defence is a strong offense, Matthew always said.

'Oh, no, you don't,' Phyllis replied. 'You can't get away with it, Hollander.'

Maggie tried to look bewildered.

'Don't insult my penetrating intelligence. The subject of today's luncheon meeting is Margaret, not Phyllis.'

Maggie sat back and drained her glass. She knew it was no use. 'All right,' she admitted. 'I know I've been sort of unavailable lately.'

Phyllis hooted and signalled to the waiter for two more glasses of wine. Then she looked at Maggie for a long time with a smile on her face. 'Listen, Mag,' she said when Maggie had begun to squirm. 'I know you're having an affair.'

Maggie's mouth opened and closed but no sound came out.

'No, it's all right, you don't have to talk about it if you don't want to. I'm not going to harass you about it.'

'What on earth makes you think such a thing?' Maggie asked.

'Don't get clutched. I'm sure nobody else has any idea. It's only because I've known you such a long time. And besides, I can usually tell. There are signs.' She looked around at the noisy fashionable crowd. There was a sprinkling of famous faces at the choice tables. 'Some people can spot a nose job or a face lift,' she went on. 'I'm an expert at who's screwing around.'

Maggie winced.

'Oh, every once in a while I get muddled between pregnancy and adultery. Pregnancy lends a similar voluptuous look to people sometimes, in the beginning, a smugness. I know you're not pregnant, and you're positively oozing sexuality. I bet you've got men following you on the street like dogs these days.'

Maggie was concentrating very hard on maintaining eye contact. If she looked away, it was capitulation. But Phyllis was right. In the space of five blocks between her apartment and *Mortimer's* she had been whistled at twice and saluted with an awful sucking noise by a van driver on Seventy-sixth Street.

'I don't suppose there's any point in denying it,' Maggie said finally. 'You really want to believe this.'

Phyllis smiled and shook her head. Then she reached out and covered Maggie's fingers. 'Honey,' she said softly, 'I don't mean to torture you. I only wanted you to know I knew, so you wouldn't hide from me any more. I've missed you. Besides, it can be pretty rough sometimes. If you ever need to talk or if there's anything I can do . . .'

When their salads arrived they ate hungrily.

Infuriatingly, Maggie's eyes brimmed. At the sight of Maggie's tears, Phyllis's eyes grew damp as well, and the two women began to laugh.

Phyllis lit a cigarette and took a long drag. 'So what do you hear from the kids?'

'Fred hates the food and he says Sue's turned into a Nazi now that she's a Counsellor-in-Training.'

'Zach's always complaining about the food. What do you suppose they feed them?'

'Minced toad *en croûte*,' Maggie said. She was feeling very light-headed.

'Did you get your room assignments from the lodge for parents' weekend?'

'Yes,' Maggie replied. 'Can Hilary make it this time?'

Phyllis's eyes narrowed as she exhaled a billow of smoke. 'Uh huh. She's right down the hall from Stephen and me. Any luck with Robin?'

'As far as I know, they'll be there.'

'It's the first time we'll all be together,' Phyllis said.

'Yes.' But Maggie was thinking that there would be someone missing. She glanced at her watch. One-thirty already. 'I think I'll skip dessert and coffee today.'

Phyllis gave her a suspicious look, then sighed. 'Me, too. I love their home-made ice cream but it just melts right onto my thighs and sits there. Let's get the check. I can see you're about to have an anxiety attack.'

Outside on the street, it had begun to rain. 'Oh, look at this,' Maggie cried in dismay. 'Wouldn't you know it would rain? I didn't bring my umbrella, and God, the traffic.' A siren wailed. Looking up Lexington Avenue, which was jammed with cars, Maggie could see the flashing lights of an ambulance. Unexpectedly, it pushed south past the entrance to Lenox Hill Hospital. As the emergency vehicle reached Seventy-fifth Street where Phyllis and Maggie stood, the light changed. Traffic began to move across town, ignoring the scream of the ambulance.

'Jesus, Phyl,' Maggie said. 'They don't even let it through.'

'New York,' Phyllis said.

'God damn it!' Maggie stepped off the curb into the intersection and held up her hand. 'Stop, you creep!' she cried at a taxi driver. The startled cabbie slammed on his brakes and hung out of the window to shout at her. But in the meantime, the ambulance managed to squeeze behind Maggie and move on down the avenue.

Back on the sidewalk, Phyllis gaped at her and shook her head. 'Well, I'll be goddamned,' she said softly.

Maggie was to meet David at the West Village School of Art where he taught sculpture three afternoons a week. In the cab, she was struck by a powerful ambivalence. She was so eager to be included in this other mysterious sector of his life, just as she longed to spend a day sifting through his apartment, examining his clothing, searching his wallet for photographs or membership cards, anything that would enrich the texture of him so that she would know him inside and out, inch by inch. But on the other hand, what if David were a dreadful teacher, inarticulate or nervous or foolish? What if they were both embarrassed? Well, what of it, she decided. That would be another factor to absorb, and she had to know David Golden, warts and all.

The school was in a small brownstone on West Thirteenth Street. She followed the sound of chisels tapping against stone, and slipped into a large fluorescent-lit studio containing David and six women. David was leaning over the shoulder of a middle-aged lady with blue-white hair. The discussion was intense, Maggie could see, with the woman shaking her head in bewilderment and David being insistent. Finally he stood up. He looked in Maggie's direction but did not appear to have seen her.

'Hold it a minute!' he shouted over the din. As he spoke, he paced back and forth, back and forth. 'Mrs Ridgeway here has a problem. It's a familiar dilemma for sculptors and I'd like to throw it out to you.' He paused. Everyone gazed at him respectfully and Maggie relaxed. He was obviously in full control. 'Sometimes you'll get a stubborn stone. Maybe there's an imperfection in the marble or maybe it's some elusiveness in your own vision. You have to come to an agreement with your material. It's enough that you gouge it, beat it, scrape it. You're the one who has to make the adjustment. It takes patience sometimes. I've had stones stare at me for months before I figured out what I'm supposed to be doing. You must be flexible but don't compromise. Adjust. Can you understand the difference?'

There were a few slow nods, but not from Mrs Ridgeway. She seemed close to tears.

'A word about polishing,' David said, 'since some of you are at that point now.'

'Thank God,' said a stringy young woman near the window.

David smiled. 'Yes, it means, really, that your struggles are over, it's all been resolved. I regard polishing as my way of apologizing to the stone for all that abuse. It should be a bit like making love. Your carving will reward you with a wonderful soft glow.' He shot Maggie a tiny smile. So he had seen her after all.

'That's it for today. Make sure everything is put away in the proper slot. No points with chisels, please. See you Friday, and please stay for a moment, Mrs Ridgeway.'

After the others had left, Maggie stood uncertainly in the doorway. But David had drawn the woman over to the window and was already deep into conversation with her. She was crying openly now, and David held her hand, all the time speaking urgently in a low voice. After a while Mrs Ridgeway got up heavily, blew her nose and left, passing Maggie wordlessly. David waved at her to join him.

'My goodness,' Maggie said.

'I told her it was no use,' David explained.

'Oh,' Maggie said.

'The woman has absolutely no ability. Look at that.' He swept his hand towards the sandstone lump that represented several weeks of Mrs Ridgeway's attention. 'She was all set to sign up for another semester.'

'Maybe she just enjoys it.'

'Oh, she does. I don't know why. She was with me last term and she did another couple of awful things. But it's criminal.'

'What's criminal? Her spending money on the class?'

'No, her producing these ugly hunks.' David seemed surprised at the question.

'But what's the harm, David, if she gets pleasure out of it? Nobody has to look at it except her.'

'But Maggie, it's what she's doing to those beautiful pieces of rock. It's like child abuse. I've even had nightmares about it.'

'You're an uncompromising man.'

'Do you think she was devastated?'

'Yes. But it was nice of you to hold her hand.'

'I wasn't aware that I was.'

'I hope you don't ever feel that way about me,' Maggie said fervently.

'How could I? You're a wonderful artist.'

'No, I mean that you wouldn't know if you were touching me.'

'Not likely.'

He took her hand and kissed the palm.

'I liked that part about making love to the stone.'

'I was thinking about you at the time. And trying to figure out the fastest way to get uptown.'

'I'll treat you to a cab.'

'A deal.'

They lay on David's mattress in the grey light listening to the rain sweep across the windows in deep sighs like waves breaking. They no longer waited to make love by lingering over mugs of tea or teasing themselves with preliminary talk. They were too greedy now. David's body was always ready for her before she had reached the top of his stairs.

'What is it that's so wonderful about summer rain?' Maggie murmured sleepily.

'Makes things grow.'

'Like this.' Maggie held his penis, miraculously soft and yielding, stone transformed to flower. 'How frightening to carry all these important things on the outside. I'm glad mine is hidden away in the dark.'

'Not all of it,' David said. A gentle throbbing had begun in response to Maggie's curious fingers.

'It curves,' Maggie said, watching him grow erect in her hand. 'Is it because you're Jewish that it curves this way?'

David laughed and pulled her over on top of him. The wind sent another spray of raindrops against the windows. 'Like making love beside the sea.'

'And I'm riding a dolphin,' Maggie said, bending down to kiss him.


They stood naked looking out over the Hudson River. Sometimes the clouds were grey and impenetrable, sometimes they were wispy enough to permit a glimpse of a ghostly high-rise on the New Jersey side. David had opened the window so that the mist could cool their bodies. 'Just the two of us, alone in Atlantis,' he said.

Maggie leaned her head against him. 'You're the only person I know who could turn Fort Lee, New Jersey, into an underwater utopia. You know what I've been wondering about? Sharon. Do you mind talking about her?'

'No.'

'I'd like to know more.'

'She was . . . small. A small person who made little rustling noises, like a mouse in the breadbox.'

'You don't make her sound terribly significant.'

'She wasn't.'

'But all those years.'

'Maggie, I didn't know you. It was another life. When I met

151

you in class that night, it was like entering a new dimension, like it was when I discovered art. All the definitions changed. Nothing will ever be the same.'

Maggie thought about Matthew. He had been the earth and she a satellite spinning around him, governed totally by his field of gravity. And now he was a shadow who moved in and out of her world. She fed him, spoke to him, but he no longer had substance or vitality. 'I'm getting cold,' she said.

He draped a sheet around her, then stood back to take a look.

'A David Golden original,' Maggie said. 'Elegant in its simplicity.' She watched his eyes move over her body with the cool obsessive scrutiny of the artist. 'All right, I'll do it,' she sighed, understanding that he would want her to pose for him this way. 'Sometime. But I get to do you nude.'

He grinned at her. He hated sitting still for her sketches. 'Bargain. Come on, I'll make you some tea.'

Maggie sat wrapped in her sheet while he filled the kettle. He wore an old-fashioned tank-style undershirt. There was barely enough flesh on him to cover muscle and bone. While his back and shoulders rippled as he busied himself in the kitchen, Maggie gazed into the essence of him. She could see ligaments twisting as he reached over his head for the sugar bowl. His lungs swelled and shrank rhythmically, his blood marched through his veins in short pulsing steps, the bones in his long fingers flexed and straightened as he poured boiling water into the tea pot.

He looked up at her suddenly. 'What are you thinking?'

'Why?'

'You look so intense. I feel like I'm being X-rayed.'

Maggie laughed. David's uncanny perceptions no longer stunned her, but there was always delight when he availed himself of his direct route into her thoughts. He poured the tea out into mugs, taking care to give Maggie her favourite with the moon design. They sat quietly for a while, enjoying the warmth of hot tea and intimacy.

'Know where these flowers come from?' David asked her finally, indicating the red carnations Maggie had brought him this afternoon.

'Holland,' Maggie guessed.

He shook his head. 'The Andes. They grow very high up.' It's desolate, nothing green at all, just scrubby brown villages here and there in the mountains, and then suddenly these brilliant patches of colour, field after field of carnations in rose, pink, white. They're shipped off to the States by the ton.'

Maggie imagined the barren peaks adorned with blossoms, like bony old ladies whose necks were draped with jewels. 'That's what I want to do with my work,' she said.

'You mean the surprise?'

'Yes, that, and also the beauty. I don't want to make ugly art. I don't see the point. Life is grim enough as it is.'

'You want to celebrate the good stuff.'

'Yes.' She glanced at David's sculptures. 'You, too.'

'We're propagandists, I suppose,' David said.

'Yes, but aren't all artists trying to make people see things the way they do?'

'That's part of it, sure,' David replied. 'But for me most of the impulse comes from trying to work something out for myself. It's more self-discovery than getting a message across.'

Maggie thought about her new fascination with constructions. It was an adventure in building rather than copying out what she saw. If nobody ever saw her work, she would still be driven to do it, and yet there was an effort to communicate as well. She had never questioned herself about her creativity, but the long-dormant part of her was demanding attention now. She wished she understood it better.

'David, what were you doing in the Andes?'

'Peace Corps.'

She shook her head. Facts about David kept rising to the surface and popping in her face like bubbles. 'The Peace Corps *and* the army?'

'I'm a patriot.' He drew his chair next to hers so that they were sitting thigh to thigh. 'Besides, I could never figure out what to do about a job.'

'You put your face very close to people when you talk to them,' Maggie said. 'Is that Southern?'

'I only do it with you.' His mouth was two inches from hers. 'No, you do it to everybody. There was that poor lady in

153

Zabar's when you were telling her where to get bagels. She looked so alarmed, but you kept closing in on her until she was stuck right up against the Russian coffee cake.'

'I'll have to watch it.'

'It's very sexy.' She kissed him.

He drew his hand through her hair. 'Maggie.'

'What?'

'Move in with me.'

She stared at him.

'I didn't mean to say that. I'm sorry. I'll take it back if I can.'

'But you can't.'

He held her hands between his. 'Do you have any idea what it's like for me when you've gone?'

'Yes.'

'I drift around like an empty husk and every minute I'm thinking about the next time.'

'It's the same for me, David.'

'Then please.'

'Oh, God.'

David stood up. His chair scraped harshly across the wood floor. 'I wasn't ever going to do this.'

'You have the right.'

'I'm not the one with a family. This is my family.' He gestured angrily towards the carvings. 'I don't even know what it means to be part of something like that. I'm jealous of it, Maggie.' His face was anguished. 'I want too much. I want everything, and I'm pressuring you. I'm sorry.'

'Don't you know I think about it all the time, too?' Maggie said. 'It's so easy now, with the kids away. I imagine just packing my bags.'

'Do it.'

'And send the children a postcard with a pretty picture of the West Side explaining that Mommy has left them?'

David turned away from her to stare out the window. 'What about you, Maggie? When are you ever going to start thinking about you?'

'But I am thinking about me. Thinking about them *is* thinking about me.' He was silent. She put her arms around his waist from behind and leaned her head against his back. 'Sometimes I believe I'm losing track of reality.'

He spun around. 'Reality is you and me.' He took her hand and touched it to his mouth, his heart, his crotch. 'And this, and this, and this.' She began to look frightened. 'Ah, Maggie,' he went on softly. 'I must be a man of extremes. I never cared for a woman before, and now I want you with me every second.' He held her quietly for a moment. 'But if we had to go on like this for the rest of our lives, it would be enough. I could handle it.'

'Things don't stand still like that.'

'They will if we make them, if we want it badly enough.'

She shook her head. 'David, I'm such a conventional person, really.'

'You're not as conventional as you think.'

Maggie eased back in his arms. Sometimes it seemed to her that his face was just two immense burning eyes. 'What do I give you, David?'

He looked surprised. 'You know me. No one else on this earth knows me except you. You live inside my head, my guts, sometimes I don't know where you leave off and I begin or who thought what. We recognized one another that first night, remember? It didn't take more than a couple of minutes and I knew who you were, what you could mean.' He shook her gently. 'Shit, Maggie, maybe there's some other language that has words for it.'

Maggie knew without looking at her watch that it was nearly time for her to go. 'I want to work together,' she said, grasping for something they could both look forward to. 'If you're just polishing now, couldn't I be there at your desk?'

'I'd like that. But when is it going to be?'

Now came the excruciating part. Matthew's mother was due this evening. It would be difficult to get away. 'I don't think I can come again until a week from tomorrow.'

'Oh.'

'It's my mother-in-law. Sometimes she hovers and sometimes she ignores me totally. I can never predict which it's going to be.'

'Will you call me if you can come before?'

'Yes. David, I hate this more than anything.'

'I know.'

On the way across town, Maggie put her hands to her face and took a deep breath. After she had been with David, her fingers always had the clean dry scent of stone dust.


'Hello, my darling!' Rhoda Hollander threw her arms around Matthew's neck. Maggie watched him flinch. The older woman pulled back and examined her son's face. 'But a trifle peaked, *n'est-ce pas*?'

Matthew reached behind him to unhook the veined fingers that were crusted with rings. 'I'm fine, Mother. How was the trip?'

'I've just been telling Margarita. Ghastly. Stuck on that hideous bus in the Lincoln tunnel with all those noxious fumes. The State of New Jersey has finally invented the supreme method of torturing its mature citizens. Denying us the right to drive.' She flung herself dramatically onto the sofa with a sigh.

Matthew took his drink from Maggie with a grateful smile. 'Only those mature citizens who drive over eighty miles an hour on the Garden State Parkway,' he reminded his mother.

Rhoda pointed a painted fingernail at him and shook it. 'Don't nitpick with me, Matthew. If I'd been eighteen years old, they would have marked a few points on my licence and sent me on my way. Don't you agree, Margarita?'

Rhoda Hollander had always called Maggie everything but 'Maggie', which she claimed was a name that smacked of Tennessee Williams and corruption. Sometimes it was 'Meghan', sometimes 'Marguerite', even 'Peggy'. A clue to Rhoda's current affinity for Margarita could be found in today's Mexican attire – multi-coloured cotton skirt and heavily-embroidered blouse. But even at seventy-three, Rhoda was authoritative enough to carry off such costumes. She travelled incessantly – restlessly, Maggie thought – and inevitably arrived home sporting the native dress of whichever country she had just visited. Maggie secretly explained Rhoda's aversion to Japan by the fact that nowhere in Tokyo was there a single pair of *Kutsu* size ten triple A.

Maggie was always struck by the similarity between Matthew's face and his mother's. There was the same square shape, same bold nose and widely-set eyes. On Matthew, the features were handsome, on his mother, formidable. When Rhoda made her infrequent appearances, Maggie always found herself searching Matthew's face for intimations of his father who was known to her only through photographs from which he peered with vague kindliness. Edward Hollander had been an administrator in a small prestigious hospital in Princeton. Rhoda always referred to him as 'poor Edward', presumably in reference to his early death from emphysema.

At the dinner table, Maggie watched the two identical faces chew broiled chicken with jaws moving in unison and decided that Rhoda's genes had been far too intimidating to permit the contribution of hereditary characteristics from 'poor Edward' or anyone else. In the engendering of Matthew, his father had been as close to unnecessary as was scientifically feasible.

Rhoda regaled them with the travelogue of her trip to Mexico, although as always, the narrative tended to feature greater detail about her travel companions than the exotic landscape.

'What I appreciate about Marion,' she said, 'is her decadence. One sits on a tour bus beside this tidy little old lady with her hair in a bun, just like Helen Hayes, you know, and suddenly she's talking about fellatio. It's quite refreshing.'

Maggie had often expressed admiration to Matthew regarding his mother's extravagance, conversational and otherwise. Her own parents seemed so ordinary. But Rhoda was an original. She often said aloud the things Maggie was too constrained to express. 'I wonder what I would have been like if your mother had been my mother,' she had said to him.

'God forbid,' he replied.

'Well, I think she's wonderful. Irritating, maybe, but she's never dull.'

'Jesus, Mag, it was like having Auntie Mame for a mother. Freshman Week at college she showed up with a handbag full of joints and sat around the dorm smoking grass with my classmates.'

Maggie laughed.

'That was her anti-alcohol phase. She figured we were bound

to get high once in a while, and marijuana was preferable to booze.'

'It was a protective impulse anyway,' Maggie said. Ever since that conversation, Maggie had wondered if Matthew had married her because she was his mother's opposite: repressed, conventional, withdrawn, and colourless.

'I disapprove of summer camp,' Rhoda was saying. 'Get me some Sweet 'n Low, won't you dear?' she asked Matthew.

'Mother, you just swallowed seven hundred and fifty calories worth of pecan pie.'

'All the more reason for the Sweet 'n Low.'

He got up and Rhoda turned her attention to Maggie. 'Unless it's a music camp or one of these ethics places where they teach potting and acid-rain testing, that sort of thing. Those dreadful sports factories ruin American children, just turn them into mindless robots who wind up watching Monday night football every week and never read a book.'

Matthew returned with the Sweet 'n Low. 'Thank you, dear,' she said, and emptied three packets of the fine powder into her coffee. A pale cloud rose around her fingers. With a sense of shock, Maggie noticed that Rhoda's hand trembled as she reached for her spoon. The woman had always seemed magnificently impervious to the cruelties of time. This first evidence of vulnerability filled Maggie with sadness.

'Though I suppose camp is somewhere to acquire friends,' Rhoda went on. 'You don't realize until you're an old wreck how valuable companionship is, except that everyone's continually dying on you.' She turned to Matthew. 'Myrna Billings keeled over last week in Shop-Rite beside the produce counter. Humiliating to go out that way, clutching a head of lettuce.'

'I'm sure she doesn't care.'

'You think not? I wonder.' For a moment, Rhoda was silent. The next words out of her mouth were unexpectedly tentative. 'I've been thinking. About death, I mean.' She paused again. 'One does, at my age. Obviously.' She waved her hand as if with impatience at her own weakness. 'I was remembering poor Edward only last night. I don't know how long it's been since I thought about him.' Her eyes met Matthew's briefly, but he quickly looked away. 'Sometimes I wake up in the night and turn towards that side of the bed . . .' She waved her hand again. 'Silly after all this time. I hope I'm not getting Alzheimer's. Promise me you'll put me in a home if I ever lose it.' The staunch shoulders hunched forward, leaving a hollow between breastbone and gay frilled blouse. 'I understand you're back at work again,' she said in a voice so abruptly brisk that Maggie nearly jumped.

'Yes. I've been trying . . .'

Rhoda scraped her chair back and stood. 'Well, come on. Let's see what you've been up to.' She followed Maggie into Fred's room. 'Criminal to allow such talent to flounder. Matthew never permitted his gifts to emerge. I can't think why.'

'I don't have any gifts,' Matthew said in a tired voice.

'Let's not get into that again,' Rhoda said, picking up the sunset collage.

'I think I'll catch the news,' Matthew said.

Rhoda inspected the work from all angles. 'Interesting, Margarita. But don't you think a touch primitive?'

'It's Maggie.'

'I beg your pardon?' Rhoda said.

'My name. It's Maggie. I'd appreciate it.'

For the remainder of her visit, Rhoda never addressed Maggie by name. She just pursed her lips resentfully, leaving spaces where Maggie's name should go, and looked deprived. She left two days early, and as soon as the door shut behind her, Maggie was on the telephone to David.

'How was your mother-in-law?' he asked, holding her at the top of his stairs.

'She makes me think of the Colosseum.'

'Why's that?'

'I think because she's a beautiful old ruin but it's important to keep in mind that terrible things happened to the lions and the Christians in there.'

'Poor Matthew.'

'Yes. Come to bed.'

# Eighteen

At a certain moment while she was packing for the trip to Vermont, Maggie plucked the old madras dress out of her closet and stuffed it in the waste basket. The rush of elation that followed made her so giddy that when Matthew came into the room, she was tossing his rolled-up socks into the suitcase from across the bed.

'How many points for a foul shot?' she asked.

Matthew appeared not to have heard her. He strode directly into the bathroom. She could hear him removing his shaving things from the medicine cabinet. There had been a few seconds when she had feared that he might notice the discarded dress. But then, he had always teased her about her reluctance to throw it away, and besides, he was obviously preoccupied. He could be stone deaf when he was involved in an interesting case.

When they had crossed the Connecticut border, Maggie thought about the dress again. There was such satisfaction in tossing the old relic away, freedom and a titillating sensation of nakedness.

'How do you suppose snakes feel when they shed their skins?' she asked Matthew.

'I don't think they feel anything much, do they?'

'They look so shiny when they crawl out of those dry old husks. I would think they'd have to feel something. Fresh, unburdened, clean, something.'

But he was away again, concentrating on the traffic which had thickened as they approached the turn-off heading north. Though Maggie drove well, Matthew always preferred to take the wheel. She could not remember his ever having relinquished the driver's seat, even on their three-week honeymoon across the country.

It was uncanny what had happened to her, she thought. She had become two entirely separate women. There was the David-Maggie – sensuous, confident, spontaneous. Today she was Matthew-Maggie, who was the cautious, withdrawn, efficient mother-of-two. She imagined Matthew-Maggie as the freeze-dried version of herself. When she crossed the park to the West Side a magic transformation took place: just add David and stir. Presto! The essential Maggie Hollander, full-bodied and steaming, emerged again and again.

There was a place where both Maggies co-existed. In Fred's room, her little studio, all the ingredients blended into a rich stew. Everything poured out into her constructions: the longing for David, the deep attachment to her children, the turbulent feelings for Matthew, the need for creative isolation and the contrasting magnetism of family and friends. Ambivalence and conflict thrived in that room. Sometimes the atmosphere became so thick that she was forced to the window for air. But she was never frightened there. Her scissors and glue and odd fragments of paper made her omnipotent. It was venturing outside that filled her with dread. She understood that the two Maggies must not mingle beyond this sanctuary. Keeping them balanced, precarious but separate, was the only insurance against loss. An integrated Maggie meant choice, and choice was unthinkable. Her heart had begun to beat very fast. She watched the oncoming cars with terror, certain that one of them would surely leap the barrier and smash into them head on. What if there was an accident and Matthew was killed? The thought surfaced like the snout of some hideous swamp creature coming up for a breath of fetid air. If Matthew were dead and she survived . . . Maggie pressed the monster back into the dark waters where it belonged and thought about how much she missed David. If they could just hold out until the children were in college, Maggie thought. There'd be a divorce and the children could come home to David and her . . . But her mind veered from the concept. Somehow David and her children seemed mutually exclusive. Fred and Susan adored their father. David had not shared the years of anxiety and pleasure that accompanied the parenting of these two particular fledgling human beings. Maggie tried to imagine

Susan and Fred cavorting among David's sculptures, or sprawled on the floor watching the television that would have to be imported since David had none. No, instead the young people would sit stiffly at the round oak table staring accusingly at Maggie and David.

Her head began to ache. She inched closer to the window to let the breeze cool her face.

'You know, I really can't stand my mother,' Matthew was saying.

'What?' Maggie was not sure she heard him correctly.

'I hate her,' he said, then looked at Maggie with a triumphant grin on his face. 'Whoa, that was terrific.'

'What do you suppose inspired that?'

'I don't know. I was just remembering the way she puts on her lipstick with that kind of kissing action at the end and I wanted to strangle her.' He shook his head wonderingly. 'If this is what going to a shrink does, maybe I ought to try it. I must have been saving that up for forty years.'

'Well, I hate Joanne,' Maggie blurted. Then they both began to laugh.

'Oh, Christ,' he moaned. 'I'd better pull off or we'll wind up in the ditch.'

The laughter brought Maggie dangerously close to sobbing. Matthew was not permitted to indulge in sudden insights or make emotional declarations. These were David's province. She took the tissue Matthew offered, wiped her eyes, and took a sidelong glance at him. But he was peering ahead already, lost in thought. If she spoke to him, she knew he would not answer her.

Their resort was carefully scattered among the trees along the top of a ridge called Frenchman's Notch. There were tennis courts, racquet-ball courts, indoor and outdoor pools, saunas, even a small indoor ice-skating rink. Maggie liked the place because the architects had left its wild surroundings intact. Even the parking lot had been constructed with deference to the shade trees that prevailed over the macadam here and there. There were very few spots available when they pulled in. Parents' weekend always jammed the hotel to its limit.

'I wonder if the others are here yet,' Maggie said. She looked around the lot for other New York licence plates. There were several.

'It's touch and go with the Brodys, isn't it?' Matthew said, hauling the suitcases from the trunk.

'Last I knew, they were coming.'

Matthew handed her the overnight bag and they headed through an opening in the tall hedges for the entrance. 'They'll be all right,' he said. 'Robin's just doing some crazy hormonal dance from the last pregnancy.'

But when they checked in, there was a message at the front desk for Maggie to telephone Robin in New York.

'Have the Wheelers arrived yet?' Matthew asked the clerk.

The young man punched some keys on his computer. 'Yes, sir. Party of three.'

As soon as the door shut behind the bellhop, Maggie sat down on the edge of the bed and called Robin.

'It's me. Why aren't you here?'

'I'm sorry,' Robin answered. 'I kept trying to hold out until after the weekend, but I just couldn't. And then yesterday this apartment came up, and I went over there this morning and signed a lease.'

Maggie was stunned to silence.

'I'm moving out this weekend.'

'I didn't realize things had gone that far.'

'I hated to put a damper on things, but there's no way we could have faked it. If you want to make up a story for the others until you get home . . .'

'I don't think I could do that.'

'I'm sorry, Mags. Don't let it ruin everybody's fun.'

'Robin, whatever made you . . .'

'Let's talk about it face to face, okay? I'm fine. Jackson's okay, too. I'll see you next week.'

'All right,' Maggie said. But she had suffered another shock. People were not behaving the way they were supposed to behave. First Matthew, and now Robin, sweet Robin, who was so intimidated by Jackson that she did not own a single pair of slacks because he disliked how she looked in them.

'Are you all right?' Matthew asked. He was staring down at her as she sat motionless on the edge of the bed with her hand resting on the telephone.

'She's moving out,' Maggie said.

Matthew laughed. 'That's ridiculous. She would never leave him.'

'She signed a lease. She's moving this weekend.'

Matthew headed for the closet with an armful of clothes from the suitcase. 'I'm sure she's just trying to give him a scare, that's all. But why she'd want to make Jackson miserable is beyond me. He's a terrific guy.'

Maggie did not reply. When he returned for another batch of clothes, he ruffled her hair. 'Don't take it so seriously, Mag. They'll be back together in no time.'

'Jesus Christ!' Phyllis exclaimed. Her voice travelled in the muted elegance of the hotel dining room. 'It's like Santa and Mrs Claus getting divorced.'

'Nobody said anything about divorce,' Maggie protested.

'Did you have any notion this was coming?' Hilary asked.

Maggie shook her head.

'She's just trying to throw a scare into him,' Matthew said.

'Because he won't adopt?' Hilary asked.

'I don't suppose it's as simple as that,' Maggie said.

'Well,' Phyllis remarked, 'I must say I'm impressed. She really has an apartment?'

'That's what she said,' Maggie replied.

'And I always thought she was your basic lap dog,' Phyllis mused.

'You sound as if she deserves the Nobel Peace Prize,' Stephen said. Gingerly, he touched a scratch on his forehead.

'I think of it more in terms of the Boston Tea Party or the Slave Rebellion,' Phyllis answered. 'I propose a toast.' She raised her glass. 'To Robin Brody. The worm turns.'

Matthew's jaw muscles were clamped tight shut and Stephen's face looked murderous.

'Forget it, Phyl,' Hilary said. 'Nobody shares your elation.'

For the remainder of the meal, there were long pauses during which everyone looked thoughtful except for Phyllis whose attempts to conceal her smug delight were a total failure.

Later Matthew turned to Maggie in the dark in their king-size bed, placed a hand over her breast and said, 'You think that could happen to us?'

'What?' Maggie asked. She was nearly asleep. She had mistaken Matthew's fingers for David's, and his voice had jarred her.

'Robin and Jackson.'

'You're the one who keeps saying it'll be all right.'

Matthew was quiet for a while. Then he stared in the direction of the ceiling, 'I guess I don't say it very often. I figure you know it without my saying so. But I do love you.'

Maggie's throat tightened. He was waiting, she knew, for her to respond in kind. 'I love you, too,' she whispered finally. It was true in a way, she told herself. They had lived together for a long time. You can't share that many years without loving, in a way. But as Matthew's caresses grew more insistent, she thought of David with shame. I'm doing this because I have to, she told David silently. As Matthew drew his body across her and nudged her legs apart with his knee, she thought with sickening irony of the guilt she felt in allowing her own husband to make love to her.


'Fred's gonna get best boy camper this year,' Susan proclaimed from the back seat.

'I won't,' Fred protested.

'You will.' Susan spoke with the profound authority of her new position as Counsellor-in-Training.

'Mom, can't you move the seat up? I'm all tangled back here.' Fred seemed to have grown four inches since June. He was thinner. For the first time, Maggie thought she saw a resemblance to Matthew.

'Zachary Wheeler may make *worst* camper,' Susan said. 'If he doesn't get thrown out.'

'Oh, dear, why?' Maggie asked.

'The kid's a walking disaster, Mom,' Fred replied.

'I thought you liked him,' Matthew said, swerving to pass a tractor carrying a load of hay.

'I do,' Fred said. 'But he's probably gonna get busted for smoking dope and messing around with Freda Gross.'

Matthew shot Maggie an alarmed look. He had a dread of drugs anywhere near the children. 'How could he get hold of anything way up here?'

'Oh, Daddy,' Susan said. 'Don't be so naïve.'

'He never does it around me,' Fred said. 'And anyhow, he's been warned, so maybe he'll watch it now. They already threw one kid out, and that scared Zach. They told us he had appendicitis and had to go home.'

'Reuben Marshall had appendicitis,' Sue said in her capacity as a spokesperson for the camp.

'That must be why he was popping all those little blue capsules,' Fred said. 'To kill the pain.'

'My God,' Matthew said.

'Don't worry about us,' Fred assured him. 'We don't do drugs, Sue and me. We're much too well adjusted.'

'Remember camp, Matthew?' Maggie asked. 'Roasting marshmallows over the campfire, hikes in the fresh air, square dances?'

'Actually we got drunk in the boathouse one night,' Matthew said.

'See?' Susan exclaimed. '*Plus c'est la même chose.*'

Maggie twisted around in her seat to inspect her children. It always disoriented her to see them after a long absence. They had such fresh attractive faces, the kind she enjoyed looking at in airports and restaurants. By the time Maggie had reached Fred's age, she had already begun to withdraw. In every class photograph from the sixth grade onwards, Maggie wore the same solemn expression. Fred and Susan had open, confident faces. They were brown from four weeks of outdoor activities, except for the mosquito bites that dotted their arms and legs. Maggie smiled.

'Remember when you both had chicken pox for Christmas?'

Susan laughed. 'Yeah, and you gave us paint brushes with calamine lotion in our stockings and had us paint each other's spots.'

'Well, it worked. I just couldn't do you both every day. Together you must have had five hundred poxes. Anyhow, it kept you occupied.'

Maggie noticed that Susan had pulled her hair back into a

pony tail. It was streaked with gold. The soft hairs around her face were bleached white-blonde. 'You look very pretty, honey,' Maggie said. 'Being a counsellor must agree with you.'

'She was a pain at first,' Fred declared. 'Ordering everybody around, especially me so she wouldn't get accused of nepotism. But once she got over being drunk with power, she turned out to be a pretty excellent counsellor.'

'Gee, thanks,' Susan said wryly. 'He's always trying to worm privileges out of me, like not having to set tables.'

'I need all the support I can get,' Fred explained. 'I'm entering puberty.'

Matthew laughed. 'God knows it's rough to set tables with puberty lurking around the corner.'

They pulled onto the steep road that led up to the hotel.

'Who's the richest black man in the world, Dad?' Fred asked.

'I haven't the vaguest idea. Probably some king in Africa. Why?'

'What about the richest black *woman*?'

'Oh, Fred,' Maggie said. They turned into the parking lot and the children scrambled out of the back seat and raced for the hotel entrance.

'What do you suppose that was all about?' Matthew asked as they trailed along behind.

'God knows,' Maggie said. 'It never changes with him. Remember "If you dropped a penny off the World Trade Centre, would it make a hole in the sidewalk?"'

'I got "If you dropped *water* off the World Trade Centre, at which floor would it evaporate?"' He swung his arm around Maggie's shoulder. 'I wish we could take them home with us tomorrow.'

'Yes,' Maggie said. As she and Matthew stood adoring their children, she struggled to think about David and what he might be doing at this particular moment. But his image flickered evasively in the powerful light of the sunny Vermont morning.

After lunch, Hilary, Phyllis and Matthew made off for the health club. Maggie watched the children swim for a while,

167

but she soon tired of the shouting and splashing. Then she remembered hearing Stephen and Zachary making plans to ice skate, and thought the indoor rink might be a pleasant distraction. The rink was in a small log cabin up a wooded rise behind the main lodge. It was very cold inside. A bored adolescent attendant played video games while chewing an immense wad of gum.

'Help?' he asked Maggie without enthusiasm. The sound emerged from his mouth in a mist of condensation that smelled of Juicy Fruit.

'Just watching.' Maggie sat down on the rough pine bench and watched Stephen and Zachary through the plate-glass window. Since she could barely hear the music from inside their slippery cage, it was rather like watching a silent movie. Stephen executed a jump. He was confident and proficient on the ice. Zachary watched his father carefully and tried to imitate him, but his ankles kept collapsing inward. He could barely stand, let alone attempt the tricks Stephen was urging on him. As the cold began to penetrate Maggie's light summer dress, she realized that Zachary was wearing only shorts and a cotton shirt. Suddenly the boy fell. His ludicrous version of Stephen's leap had caused him to catch a pick in the slushy surface, and he went down with a thud. He grasped his knee and tried to bite back the tears. Stephen stood above him, talking and gesticulating while Zachary huddled in his wet shorts, one hand on his bloody knee and one hand extended to his father. Help him up, Maggie thought, but Stephen ignored the hand. Maggie could see tears forming raw streaks on the boy's face. He tried to struggle onto his feet, but the weakened knee would not support him and he went down again. Maggie could hear him cry out through the glass. *Help him!* Maggie thought. There was a ferocious pounding beginning behind her eyes. Zachary was sobbing now, and this time Stephen angrily thrust the child's hand away. At this, Maggie leapt to the window. She forced a smile and rapped hard on the glass. Stephen turned to her in annoyance, but Maggie just waved gaily. While Zachary began a painful crawl to the side of the ice, Stephen came to the door and poked his head out.

'Hi. We're learning the first rule of skating. How to get up after you fall on your ass.'

'I see,' Maggie said. 'I came to tell Zach that . . . that there's going to be swimming tonight until eleven. They've decided to keep the pool open later after all, in honour of the kids.'

Stephen gave her a strange look. By this time, Zachary had made his way to the door.

'Zachary Wheeler, you'll catch your death in that outfit!' Maggie exclaimed. 'You're soaking wet. How'd you talk your father into letting you skate like that?' Maggie rolled her eyes at Stephen. 'Teenagers. Come on and get warmed up before your mother skins you alive. You're probably the only person in Vermont to ever get frost bite at the end of July.'

Zachary thumped over to the bench and sank onto it gratefully. Stephen's face was menacing behind a polite smile. 'Next time we'll remember to bring long pants and a sweater. Zach, you just run along with Mrs Hollander. Go jump in the pool or something. I'll stick around here for a while.'

'All right,' Zachary replied. 'Sorry I'm such a clutz.'

'All it takes is confidence and tenacity,' Stephen said, then gave them a salute and closed the door behind him.

'Your dad's a good skater,' Maggie said on their way back to the pool.

'Yeah, he can never figure out how I could be so bad when he's so good. He can't accept the fact that it's hopeless.'

'I'm sure you're good at other things.'

'That's true. I have my strengths.'

Maggie looked down at the face half hidden with a summer's growth of shaggy black bangs. The thick eyelashes glistened in the sunshine from their film of recent tears. She thought about Zachary's reputed flirtation with drugs and laid her cheek against the top of his head for a moment. 'We haven't seen anywhere near enough of you, Zach,' she said.

When they reached the pool, the boy peeled off his shirt and dived into the water with his shorts. They were soaked anyway. Hilary and Phyllis were sitting nearby beside a pitcher of sangria. Phyllis waved at Maggie to join them.

'How was the skating lesson?' Phyllis asked.

'Stephen stood up and Zach sat down,' Maggie answered.

'I suppose my husband was his usual tolerant self.'

'I had no idea he was such an accomplished skater,' Maggie said. She poured herself a glass of the fruity wine.

'Oh, he has all kinds of secret talents,' Phyllis said. She glanced at Hilary, but Hilary looked away. Phyllis drained her glass and stood up. 'Well, ladies, time for my aerobics. Anyone care to join me?'

'Not a chance. I'm just going to lie here and contemplate my cellulite,' Hilary said.

'You don't have any, darling,' Phyllis said. 'See you later.' She walked away in her sleek black tank suit.

'Damn Phyllis,' Maggie said. 'Her body's exactly the same as it was in her Freshman year.' She leaned back in the chaise and closed her eyes.

'Mm,' Hilary said.

'She seems positively cheerful these days. I know she was pleased with Robin, but I'll bet there's a new lover lurking somewhere.'

Hilary was silent.

'You still there?' Maggie asked, eyes tight shut against the bright sunshine.

'Yes.'

There was a strangled quality in Hilary's voice that made Maggie sit up and take a close look at her. 'What's the matter?'

'Nothing,' Hilary replied.

'*Something*'s going on with you,' Maggie said.

Suddenly it was as if Hilary had peeled away a mask. The face she showed Maggie was full of conflict: excitement, torment, love, apprehension, and more. She looked very beautiful.

'Oh, Hil . . .' Maggie said, reaching for her friend's hand. 'What is it?'

The ugly scrape on Stephen's face at dinner last night flickered in Maggie's mind, and the way Phyllis had touched Hilary's shoulder this morning. Even now, Phyllis's subtle proprietary attitude. It all came together at once. Maggie's eyes widened.

'Oh, my God,' she whispered. She sat staring into Hilary's face, speechless, compiling evidence from days past. 'How long?' she asked finally.

'Since the party.'

'I'm so incredibly dense.'

'No, far from it. But you don't seem shocked.'

'I'm not. Surprised, maybe. Come to think of it, I'm not even sure I'm surprised.'

Hilary poured them each another glass of sangria. 'So what about our little bridge group? Robin's pulled a revolution and Phyllis and I . . . It's not exactly what we expected of our lives, is it?'

'Hardly.'

'You're the only one. You and Matthew and the kids. Thank God there's one normal corner in the square.'

Maggie sipped at her drink. She was very close to telling Hilary everything. She felt as if David were sitting right there next to her on the chaise. He was so real, so blatant. The words were just behind her lips, pressing against them.

'The weird thing is,' Hilary said, 'I'm happy. Oh it's difficult and there's this sense of being . . . alien, I guess. But the geometry of it, you know, three of us, seems exactly right. All these years I've been trying to be half of a couple. I'm just an ordinary girl from Greenwich, and look what I've got myself into.'

The moment passed for Maggie. She sighed while Hilary rushed on in her relief to be talking openly at last. 'I've analysed and projected. Christ, who knows what's going to happen in the end. But we've decided to just go with it. I think maybe the best thing is the freedom. The fantasies, you have no idea . . .' She paused, remembering. 'Well, God knows what you and Matt get up to. For all I know, he puts on a dress and you whip him with the cord from the Cuisinart. It's just nice to let everything out of the cage.' She laughed softly. 'Though sometimes I wonder if we'll all emerge from this thing alive. It gets pretty wild.'

'I don't want you to get hurt.'

'No, well, I'll admit my concept of violence has changed. I don't mean I approve of really maltreating anybody. But the fact is, no matter how we may try to deny it, people are aggressive and a lot of that aggression is sexual, and what the hell, if you can make it fun instead of scary, why not?'

Maggie thought about the many times Phyllis had turned up with nasty bruises on her face and throat. It was inconceivable to Maggie that David would be capable of such brutality. Nor could she imagine harming him in any way. But the presence of David in her life had also taught her to resist making easy judgements.

'I admire you,' Maggie said.

Hilary was so startled that she stopped talking and gaped at her.

'You took a risk. It can't have been easy. I think most people would have turned their back on a relationship like yours without ever putting it to the test.'

'You are absolutely amazing,' Hilary said. 'Everything *is* all right, isn't it? I mean with you and Matthew.'

'Oh, sure.'

Hilary threw her head back and looked up at the sky. 'God, it's beautiful. What a day! I feel great.' She stood up. Against the sun, she was like a seething mass of colour. 'You have no idea what you just did. What a good friend you are.' She walked to the edge of the pool and dived in, leaving Maggie blinking and dazzled.

Zachary and Fred bobbed in their rented canoe and watched the sun go down. The sky was dotted with round cloud puffs that gradually deepened from pale pink to an intense fiery rose. Zachary sat idly dipping his paddle to make rippled patterns of silver and ruby. Otherwise, except for tiny insects that skimmed the surface, the lake was still.

Fred lay in the stern against the gunwale. 'Think we oughta get back? It's after seven.'

'Nah,' Zach answered. 'God, don't you wish we could just hang out here the rest of the summer and the hell with camp? I hate the sound of that miserable cowbell at 6.45 every morning.'

'Maybe our parents figure we'll never end up in the army so we ought to get the taste of what military life is all about.'

Zachary felt the familiar tug at the corner of his eye. It was a quick teasing pull as if someone had laid a finger there to show the world how his eye would look Oriental style. He had discovered that by closing both eyes and taking deep breaths, the annoying twitch disappeared faster than if he swiped at it. Smoking dope helped, too. It was just that it was so hard to relax sometimes. He dipped his hand in the water. It felt warm and soft, more like a strange elusive living creature than a reservoir of ordinary liquid. 'I remember when Mom used to go away with my father for a weekend or something, my aunt would tell me it was for my own good, to teach me how parents always come home again. I figured what it taught me was how parents always leave.'

'My grandmother says camp is character-building,' Fred remarked. 'Anyway, I don't mind. It's better than frying in New York all summer. Besides, my parents are crazy about me when I get home. For a while, at least.'

'You've got a real nice mother.'

'Yeah, she's all right. Yours has excellent legs.'

Zachary laughed. 'I never noticed.' He was quiet for a moment, watching the insect skaters trace their tiny iridescent tracks. 'Who's got the best tits?'

'Oh, Vonderhyde, no contest,' Fred replied.

'My father's hot for her.'

'How do you know?'

'He's always finding excuses to help her on and off with her jacket and then he stares at her boobs.'

'But he'd never really *do* anything.'

'Sure he would, if he got the chance.'

'Yeah?' Fred sat up too fast and the boat rocked precariously.

'He always fools around with women. I walked into his office once when he figured the door was locked and there he was on the couch getting a blow job from this punk secretary with purple streaks in her hair.'

'Jeez, what did you do?'

'They were really freaked out. My father sat up so fast she almost fell on the floor. I just said, "Okay, let me just try that one more time". I went out, knocked on the door and came back in again. This time she was sitting in the chair and he was behind his desk trying to zip his pants.'

'God.'

'Then he took me out to dinner to this fancy place and we

had this man-to-man bullshit talk about trust. He was bribing me not to tell Mom, of course, which I would never do in a million years. I can tell she knows, though.'

'You think they'll ever get divorced?'

Zachary shrugged.

'Which one would you live with if they did?'

'My mom,' Zachary answered. 'She screws around, too, but at least she's discreet about it.'

Fred laughed. 'Sorry. I shouldn't laugh, but you're blowing me away.'

'It's everywhere. Your parents probably do it, too.'

'Not them, no way.'

'Few more years you'll be doing it yourself,' Zachary said.

'Never,' Fred said staunchly. 'I may get divorced a couple of times. You know, marry one type of girl for a while, then when I get sick of her, get divorced and marry another one. Once I have kids, though, that's it for good.'

Zachary handed Fred the other paddle. 'It's almost dark. They'll be sending a search party out in a minute.'

They paddled in silence back to the dock, leaving a long silvery train in the clean water.


When Maggie mentioned the subject of Robin and Jackson, Matthew's hands turned white on the steering wheel.

'Christ,' he said, 'the man already has a kid of his own. She knew that when she married him.'

'Why shouldn't she have one of *her* own?'

'It wouldn't be her own. It would be adopted.'

Maggie stared out of the window at the blur of pine trees and telephone poles. It was like the film of a parade speeded up to an unbearable velocity. 'I'm not sure it's just the issue of having children,' she said. 'It's his whole attitude . . .'

'Fuck attitude,' Matthew interrupted. 'She's acting like a spoiled child. I don't know, you women amaze me sometimes.'

'Oh, we women?'

'Jackson works his balls off trying to give her a good life and look what he gets for his pains. I suppose he's going to be paying two rents now.'

Maggie was silent.

'I see it all the time in the legal profession. The poor suckers get dragged into court and never crawl out from under the alimony payments. Meanwhile, the ex-wives keep the car and the fancy co-op apartment and the clothes and the antiques . . .'

'You know damn well,' Maggie broke in, 'that most divorced women never collect their alimony payments *or* their child support. You're really worked up about this. I'm sorry I mentioned it.'

'Isn't it something to get worked up over?'

'Yes.'

'Well, there's nothing we can do about it.' He snapped on the radio. *WPIX*. Love songs, nothing but love songs. Roberta Flack was singing 'The First Time Ever'. The first time ever Maggie had seen David Golden's face, his eyes had held her like a pair of gentle arms. She looked at the angry man who was glaring out at the road with clenched jaw and thought about Robin all by herself in her very own apartment. What Maggie felt was profound envy.

# Nineteen

'We're too goddamn solemn,' David said to her over the telephone.

Maggie was startled enough to hear his voice at ten in the morning. His light-hearted tone baffled her further. 'Oh,' she said.

David laughed. 'It's a beautiful day and we're going to enjoy it. Bring a warm sweater, jeans, and rubber-soled shoes and don't ask me any questions.'

'Aye aye,' Maggie said. There was sudden silence at the other end. Maggie knew that she had reached into his brain yet again and guessed correctly that they were going on a boat.

David was already standing at Riverside Drive and Seventy-ninth Street when Maggie got off the bus.

'Where are we going?' She gave him a quick kiss and allowed him to take her arm. Lately, her fears of being seen with David had dissipated. She thought perhaps it was because her life on the West Side had become so vivid and essential it now seemed inviolable. Sometimes she did wonder if there was an unconscious wish to be caught and thereafter forced into a decision, but the reality of such an event seemed so horrific that she repressed such notions as soon as they surfaced.

David led her across the intersection and along a path that bisected the ribbon of Riverside Park. Suddenly they rounded a bend and blinked at the dazzling spectacle of the Seventy-ninth Street Boat Basin. Maggie had seen the marina from David's windows, but the aerial view left her unprepared for the sight that confronted her now. But for the muted roar of traffic and ambulance sirens shooting past on the West Side highway, she may have been in some quaint fishing village. Dozens of tidy sailboats and powerboats nestled against the docks and bobbed in the September sunshine. There were some square-shaped

176

vessels as well, like boxes on platforms, a small barge with an ancient beetle-shaped Volkswagen aboard, and a jaunty red tugboat.

David followed her line of vision and gestured towards the tug. 'Fellow picked that up on the Jersey shore after it spent a long career towing sand barges. It's quite a house. There's even a baby grand piano nailed down in there.'

'David, didn't you tell me Eliza Austin has a boat here?'

'Yes. She lives on it.'

'I don't think I want to do this.'

'Liza's a good friend, Maggie. I want you to know each other.' Reluctantly, Maggie let him urge her along.

They made their way along the pier and off onto a spur to the left. David halted beside a thirty-foot fibreglass boat and rapped on the hull. A muffled voice called 'Come!' David climbed aboard, gave Maggie a hand, then disappeared below while Maggie stood awkwardly on the teak deck wishing she could hop back on the cross-town bus. Her feet in their battered tennis shoes were pointed toes inward like a schoolgirl awaiting punishment.

After a moment, Eliza Austin's grey cropped head appeared, then shoulders, and finally the entire six feet of her, clad in overalls and navy-blue wool turtleneck. It was difficult to accept the fact that Eliza was approaching seventy. She was slim and straight, and had the same type of face as David's, clean and spare, with nothing hidden by excess pouches of flesh. There were wrinkles, of course, but they only served to soften the severity of her high forehead and cheekbones. She might have been David's mother.

Eliza watched, amused, while Maggie made her surreptitious inspection. Then the older woman held out her hand. 'Welcome aboard. The overalls are a necessity. Sometimes it gets pretty hectic alone at the helm, so I always keep a supply of emergency equipment in here.' She reached into a roomy pocket and drew out two cigar-shaped pretzels and a can of grapefruit juice. 'And here. And here.' Another pocket held a pair of sunglasses and some bandaids, a third a miniature tool kit. She turned. 'David, ready to cast off?'

David stood at the bow. 'Any time you say,' he called.

Maggie sat down and watched as the two expertly manoeuvred the boat away from the dock, David pushing off with his foot and Eliza reversing with one hand on the wheel. Soon they were free of the marina and heading north up the Hudson. Although it had been quite warm back at the dock, there was a stiff breeze on the water. Maggie turned her face into the wind and let it whip back her hair. A tanker, moving seaward, split the golden surface of the river, leaving a foamy wake. Far ahead, the George Washington Bridge stretched in a graceful span from New York to New Jersey. Along the shore on the Manhattan side, the trees had begun to turn, mostly yellow with an occasional burst of scarlet from a sugar maple.

Eliza slowed the engine so that it was possible to talk. 'Come and sit closer,' she said to Maggie. 'David, go and get my straw hat, will you? It's on my bed.'

He disappeared below deck while Maggie dutifully edged closer to Eliza. 'Do you actually live on this?' Maggie asked.

'Yes. A lot of us do at Seventy-ninth Street. There's a big mess about who's in charge of the place at the moment, but we'll hang on no matter what. We're a tenacious lot.'

'I guess it's hard for me to imagine. Can you cook, take a bath?'

'All the conveniences, more or less. Sometimes if there's an awful ice storm in February I'll go hole up in my studio until it blows over. These old bones are a bit intimidated by winter gales.'

David returned to plunk a ragged straw hat on Eliza's head. When he sat down beside Maggie and threw an arm around her shoulders, Maggie stiffened.

'So what do you think about this old tub?' David asked.

'It seems glamorous to me,' Maggie answered.

'She's not even ten years old,' Eliza protested. 'What do you know about old age anyway, child?' She reached out to ruffle David's hair and he ducked. Maggie had never seen David playful. Perhaps he had been right on the telephone this morning; their relationship was pretty serious-minded.

'The marina lifestyle attracts unusual people,' Eliza was saying. 'Each of my neighbours chose it for a different reason.'

'Why did you?' Maggie asked.

'I spent twenty years in a stifling marriage.'

'Eliza and her husband ran a very successful advertising business,' David said.

'Howard ran the business. I designed packaging for our clients. Oh my God, how I suffered, trying to convince myself it was gratifying to draw Jello boxes. One day my husband came home from a trip on a sunny Saturday afternoon. He walked into the studio, looked over my shoulder and said, "You were supposed to have that finished yesterday." I don't know what happened to me. I just got up, said something about how a person has to know when to walk out into the sun, and I left him. Never went back.'

Maggie wondered how the husband felt about losing Eliza. When the image of Matthew's face bobbed into view, she tried to imitate Eliza and brush the vision away.

'But you see, I never had children,' Eliza said. Maggie felt David squeeze her shoulder. Eliza squinted at a floating carton ahead and swerved to starboard. 'I don't understand the power of it myself, motherhood, especially once a child is old enough to comprehend a sentence. I can see sticking it out for little ones. They're quite helpless. But once they reach eight or ten, they should be able to manage. I know I did. I was ten when my parents separated.'

The George Washington Bridge loomed high above them now. The two huge towers rose out of the water dwarfing the boat passing far below. The structure's intricate design and immense arches seemed to echo the Gothic splendour of St John the Divine which dominated the riverbank just to the south. Sunlight through the cables cast mysterious shadows on the river. Maggie felt as if they were gliding across a strange floating web.

'Where are we going?' she asked.

'Depends on how much time we've got,' Eliza replied. 'When do you have to be home?'

Maggie detected a hint of pity, or perhaps it was contempt, in the question. 'About ten.'

'Good. Bear Mountain for sure, maybe further. How about a beer? Hold the wheel, Dee,' Eliza said, and slipped below.

David winked at Maggie, but kept his eyes on the river. 'There's garbage floating around. I'm always afraid I'll crack into something.'

'You seem to know what you're doing,' Maggie said. 'What did she call you?'

'Dee? Silly nickname.'

Eliza emerged with three Molson's. 'Hope you can make do without a glass,' she said to Maggie. 'I like to keep the dish-washing to a minimum since it's pretty cramped in the galley.'

Maggie took a swig, enjoying the shape of the smooth glass opening against her lips. It had been years since she had drunk anything straight out of the bottle. She took another long draw, stretched her feet out and sighed contentedly. To the west, the Palisades made their steep ascent four hundred feet straight up. They had a raw scraped appearance as if the geological phenomena that formed them had happened in one violent night. Manhattan, far downriver now, was merely a haphazard assortment of children's blocks, like the *Lego* Fred used to snap together. Fred. According to Eliza's philosophy, Fred was far past the age of comprehension and Maggie was free to leave. Children were resilient. In time, they would surely adjust to a new family structure. They loved their father, but how could they not learn to care for David? She watched him now, squinting up at the sky and absorbing the shapes of the fat fluffy clouds. Eliza, back at the helm, reached out for David's beer. He handed it to her, she took a sip and returned it. 'Did David tell you about the squall we got into off Montauk this spring?' Eliza asked. 'He saved this boat, not to mention our hides.'

'No, he didn't.' Maggie was beginning to feel a rising sense of discomfort regarding David's intimacy with Eliza. Here was a part of his life he had never shared with her. She wondered why not. She chided herself for the absurd fantasy that he existed only when she was present, and somehow remained suspended each time she left. Besides, was her jealousy a fraction of what David must feel about her life with Matthew and the children?

'What did you do with that bomb hoist Ben dug up for you?

Was it any use?' Eliza was asking David, the Montauk squall forgotten.

'Not much. It's okay for hauling raw stone, but even then, I'm afraid I'll wind up chipping it or fracturing something.'

Maggie was too proud to ask for an explanation. Anyway, Eliza had now switched her attention to Maggie.

'I understand you've begun working in collage,' Eliza said. 'I'd like to get a look at the Hudson River piece sometime.'

Maggie flashed a glance at David. He seemed free enough conversing with Eliza about her. 'You have a gift for dramatic utilization of space,' Eliza went on.

'Your class was good for me.'

'Come and take another, though I don't know how much I can teach you now.'

'A lot.' Maggie hesitated. 'Are you working?' she asked finally. She was careful about asking a fellow artist such a question. But all was well with Eliza.

'Oh yes,' she replied with gusto. 'David took me to see a film recently, what was it, the one about the runners?'

'*Chariots of Fire*,' David answered.

'Yes, that's it. I like athletics.'

'Eliza's an exercise fanatic,' David explained.

'I must say that movie was an inspiration. I came right home and jumped into my leotard. All those slim bodies.'

Maggie remembered now that on the night of her first class, she had felt curious about the nature of David's relationship with Eliza Austin. Maggie had wondered about the possibility of a sexual history between them, then dismissed the notion as foolish. But why reject such a possibility when the only obstacle to their being lovers was Eliza's age? Maggie was certain that neither David nor Eliza would find such a consideration the least bit relevant. Maggie looked from one to the other. David was staring out at a pair of gulls swooping into the wake of the *Dayline* excursion boat that had overtaken them on its way upriver. Eliza peered through binoculars at a swampy area on the New Jersey side. It seemed clear to Maggie that there had been something, and just as clear that it was over, leaving them both with deep affection for one another.

Eliza handed her the binoculars. 'Take a look at that egret. Damn thing's always standing in the same spot. At least I like to think it's the same fellow.'

'Liza used to sky-dive, Maggie, just like that bird,' David said drowsily. His eyes were half closed. The sun had already put a flush on his cheeks and the ridge of his nose.

'Is it wonderful?' Maggie asked.

'Yes. I've always liked floating.' Eliza laughed. 'Look at where I live. But I finally broke a bone in my foot and had to give it up.' She gazed into the sky. 'That's a fine place to get ideas.'

'I know some of the work that came out of those dives,' Maggie said excitedly. 'About ten years ago, the exhibit at Higgens Gallery. Kind of ethereal patchwork, disorientating, like looking through the wrong end of these.' She handed the binoculars back to Eliza.

'Yes,' the older woman nodded with a grin. 'How marvellous that you remember.'

The river which had gradually broadened into its widest point at Haverstraw Bay narrowed suddenly around a long bend to the left. Mountains over a thousand feet high rose up on either side of them. As they passed beneath Bear Mountain, they saw the huge bronze stag's head which projected from the bare rock.

'I wouldn't mind mounting my carvings on that chunk of boulder,' David muttered.

They passed Buttermilk Falls which cascaded down the mountainside into the river. To the north was West Point.

'We're in luck,' Eliza said. 'David, give me a hand. See that mooring over there? Next to the blue yawl.' As she steered the craft alongside the large ping-pong ball, she explained to Maggie, 'There're only a couple of guest moorings here. On a weekend, it's usually hopeless.'

While they tied up, Maggie stared up at the brooding monumental pile of granite that was West Point Military Academy. The buildings were austere but handsome. She could see a jeep slowly climbing a steep road on the edge of the cliff.

Eliza smiled at Maggie's expression. 'Intimidating, isn't it?

Actually, they're very friendly at the office over there on the pier. Come, you must be starving. Let's eat.'

Eliza had loaded up on provisions at a kosher delicatessen. Maggie was astonished at her appetite. She wolfed down an overstuffed corned beef sandwich. Eliza handed Maggie a second one, turkey this time, dripping with Russian dressing. Maggie made it half-way through, and then lay back against the seat groaning.

'It's the water that does it,' Eliza said. 'I have to watch myself or I'll turn into a tugboat.' She poured coffee into plastic mugs. 'Cream and sugar?' she asked, and seemed pleased when Maggie shook her head. 'David,' Eliza went on, 'would you be a dear and see if you can do something about that shower head? It worked fine for six months the last time you tinkered with it.'

'Sure,' David said. 'I'd just as soon get out of the sun for a while anyhow. My nose is frying.'

Maggie watched him disappear below, and when she looked up, saw that Eliza had been studying her quietly.

'Tell me,' Eliza said. 'Do you think it's possible to be a good mother and a great artist simultaneously?'

Maggie cupped her mug as she thought. 'I don't know,' she replied finally. 'A good mother and a good artist, maybe. I don't think a great one.'

She sighed and looked up into the deep blue autumn sky. 'Children are like leeches, beautiful, amazing, delicious leeches. I remember the first time I went out to dinner after Susan was born. She was three months old and I had been completely absorbed in her. I was worn out from lack of sleep and constant self-denial, and I guess I thought if I hired a baby-sitter and left the apartment, everything would be the same as before she was born. I would feel free again. It took ten minutes at a candlelit table for the truth to sink in. I wasn't free any more and never would be, even when Susan was grown up and gone. She had become a part of me in such a profound, mysterious way that I knew I would never be able to stop thinking about her on some level, worrying about her, wondering about her. And it's been the same with Fred, the second one. I can't ever be . . . single-minded again. They're always in my thoughts, and it takes very little for me to be distracted away from my work if they need me. But maybe it's not the same for other women.'

Four Canadian geese paddled over to the boat, one of them honking tentatively. Eliza tossed a crust overboard and it was gobbled up.

'No, I think you're probably right,' Eliza said. 'Look at the history of art in this country. How many women made a success of their creativity? A handful – O'Keeffe, Nevelson come to mind first since they're so well-known. O'Keeffe never had children and Nevelson went off to Europe and left her child behind.'

'O'Keeffe used to paint from first light until the sun went down,' Maggie said. 'I can't imagine ever having that kind of unstructured time. Every moment I'm at work, I'm aware that there's a limit. Somebody's waiting for me to do something for them outside that door. No matter if I'm on the edge of an important discovery or if the light is just right at that particular moment. The kids come home from school or I'm required at some function. I know it has a deleterious effect. But I do think about later on when they're off on their own. Maybe then . . .'

'Do you ever think about running away?'

'Yes,' Maggie admitted. Then she added, 'but I never imagine it as permanent, just a week, even a couple of months, some time to myself. They're so much a part of my life.'

'Perhaps for you it's worth the compromise,' Eliza said.

'It is.'

'I always thought I'd have made a dreadful mother,' Eliza said.

'Is that why you didn't have any children?'

'Yes, partly. Howard was bent on building up the business. He had no interest in babies. I saw my friends with their families, how consuming it all was. It was frightening. I believed I would have been submerged, drowned altogether if I'd added motherhood to the stew.'

Maggie glanced towards the galley. 'How did you meet David?'

'At Ben Ginsburg's. He runs an art supply store and gets

artists together to drink too much and sound off about art.' She poured Maggie a second cup of coffee from her thermos. 'Ah, David was such a sobersides. We disliked one another enormously. Pompous, self-righteous type, he was. And he thought I was naïve, and probably senile to boot.' She laughed. 'We had some real set-tos the first few weeks he joined the circle. I remember asking Ben what on earth he saw in this idiot, and Ben just said "Wait". Then one day David stopped in at an exhibition of mine on Fifty-seventh Street. It was the first I'd had after leaving my husband, and there was a work called "Flight". A very large canvas with open sky and wings. Well, I found him staring at it as pale as a ghost, and the next Saturday night, he brought along this carving to Ben's, and it was eerie how it mirrored my painting. Wings, it was, really soaring so you could practically hear the wind rush. It was soon after he'd left New Orleans and I suppose the feelings that went into both works were very similar. That was the beginning. Not that we don't have some knock-down-drag-outs even now. I think he's a dreadful teacher.'

'But why?'

'Well, I'm overstating it. He can't tolerate mediocrity of any kind, and is forever discouraging people. My feeling is that art is for everybody no matter how limited their ability. What's wrong with some fellow making mud pies to set on his mantel-piece month after month? He's had the joy of creating some-thing with his hands, and he'll have a better understanding of what the rest of us are trying to do.'

Maggie had sat forward. 'I watched him finish off the career of a little old lady just last week. It was heartbreaking.'

'What are you going to do, Maggie?' Eliza asked suddenly.

Maggie stared down into her mug. The kindness in the older woman's voice had brought her close to tears. 'I don't know,' she said. 'I just don't know.'

'You're a forever thing with David,' Eliza said.

'I know that.'

'And how about you?'

'He's a forever thing.'

'Can you go on this way indefinitely?'

'It's getting very hard. I'm not good at deception.' She gave

Eliza a bitter smile. 'Oh, I've become an expert at lying. It's living with it that's making me miserable.'

'He'd be a good father,' Eliza said. 'He's always wanted children.'

Maggie shook her head. 'It sounds so reasonable. But it's doing it that's difficult. I must be an awful coward. And there's Matthew.'

'What about him?'

'I don't know what I feel. Whenever I try to figure him out, I get this feeling as if my head has just turned to cement, just a solid block of it.' She looked up at Eliza. 'Pathetic, isn't it?'

'Can you imagine yourself living with David?'

'Yes. I do imagine it all the time. I have trouble with the children, though . . . they don't seem to belong in this part of my life. Oh Lord.' Maggie rubbed her head. 'Here comes the cement.'

'I'm very fond of Dee,' Eliza said. 'I would hate to see him hurt.'

'Somebody's going to be, and it'll be me who's doing the hurting. It's pretty ironic, after making a lifetime career out of being nice to everybody.'

David's head appeared in the galley entrance, but Eliza managed a final remark. 'Forget being nice. Be honest, and you'll do the right thing.' She waved at David. 'All fixed?'

'Yup.'

'Good,' Eliza said. 'You gave us a chance to pick your character apart.'

'Uh oh,' he said. His face was glowing with sunburn.

Maggie pulled him down beside her. 'But we decided that you have a few redeeming qualities.'

'Like what?'

'Tolerance,' Maggie grinned.

Eliza hooted. 'Come over here, Maggie. As soon as we get untied you can take over.'

A train whistle blew in the distance. Its hollow echo bounced back and forth between the mountainous banks. Eliza glanced at her watch. 'Amtrak, more or less on time. All right, David? We're clear?'

'All set!' he called.

Eliza started the engine and they moved away from the mooring. 'We'll wait until we get out into the bay, then you'll take the helm.'

The craft was very responsive. 'Can we go faster?' Maggie asked.

*I could be very happy here*, Maggie thought, and surrendered to the rocking motion of the boat and the drone of the engine.

When she awoke, the sky was black. There were jagged splits in the cloud cover that allowed glimpses of stars. Eliza, whose straw hat had disappeared, smiled at her.

'How long have I been asleep?' Maggie asked.

'An hour maybe,' David answered. 'Take a look.'

Maggie sat up stiffly. Behind them, shimmering lights blurred, then came into focus. The twin towers of the World Trade Centre rose like splendid glittering columns out of the water. She turned towards the bow and caught her breath. To starboard, the Statue of Liberty stood draped in scaffolding. The intricate webbing of cables had been lit so that each strand was like a fine golden chain. Barely visible beneath the luminous veil was the shadow of the lady herself, imposing, dark, secret.

'Oh, look at her,' Maggie whispered. They were all silent as Eliza moved closer, then made a long arc and headed up the East River.

Bulky shadows passed back and forth as they motored up past Governors Island where headlights could be seen blinking through the black silhouettes of trees.

'Extraordinary.' Maggie gazed at the Manhattan skyline. 'It looks so fragile, as if it's all afloat, and could sink into the water at any moment.'

'Liza,' David said. 'It's almost nine. Maggie has to be back at ten.'

Maggie looked at him, startled. Time had ceased to matter. It was impossible to imagine stepping back onto dry land and leaving this magic world of reflections and darkness. 'I didn't want to hear it from you,' David said softly, putting his face next to her cheek.

It took very little time, with the engine near full throttle, to deliver them back to Seventy-ninth Street. The marina glistened against west-side Manhattan like a handful of diamonds tossed carelessly against the shore. When Maggie stepped off the boat onto the dock, she felt her knees give way. The solid planks seemed cruelly unyielding beneath her feet after the gentle roll of the river. Maggie held her hand out to Eliza.

'I don't know how to thank you,' Maggie said.

'Come again and again. That's how,' Eliza answered. She waved and disappeared below. David walked Maggie to the bus stop. Neither of them spoke. He kissed her once, lightly, and she stepped up into the phosphorescent glare of the cross-town bus.

# Twenty

'Forget the cards,' Phyllis said. 'Put them away, Robin.'

Robin looked at the others. Maggie nodded. 'Phyl's right,' she said. 'Nobody can concentrate.'

'Something tells me our bridge days are numbered,' Hilary remarked.

'What's the rent in this place anyway?' Phyllis asked. Maggie noticed that she had refused a glass of wine and was drinking Perrier like Hilary.

'Four twenty-five.'

'You know you could always move in with us,' Phyllis said. 'We have the sofa bed in the living room.'

'Thanks, you're sweet, but I need a place of my own.'

The apartment was in a new high-rise that catered to young singles. Rock music pounded through the sheetrock wall, and from the floor above, someone seemed to be dropping paperclips in an endless relentless rhythm. The apartment itself was bare, almost ascetic compared with the friendly clutter of Robin's home with Jackson. There was the card table where they sat, which also served as a dining table and a desk. There was a couch which opened into a bed, a small portable television, and one jade plant. There was not a single hooked rug in evidence.

'I saw a bevy of stewardesses in the lobby,' Phyllis said. 'And somebody's having a Halloween party. The elevator had a belly dancer, a witch and a gorilla in it. God, they're all so young.'

Robin had lost weight and given up her contact lenses. The combination of visible cheekbones and large tortoise-shell glasses lent her a sober appearance that was in marked contrast to the former little-girl softness. Over the past three months, she had gradually removed most of her wardrobe from the old apartment and sold it to second-hand clothing stores. With the

189

profits, she bought herself several pairs of slacks and some tailored dresses. Tonight she wore plain black wool pants and a cowl-neck sweater. Phyllis nodded approvingly. 'You look fine,' she said. 'I've got to confess, you shocked the hell out of me.'

'Leaving my husband? People do it all the time.'

'Not you. Christ, I've been bitching and moaning about my marriage for fifteen years and I'd never have the guts to do what you did.'

'How's Jackson?' Maggie asked.

'He calls a lot. He wants to date.'

'Will you?' Hilary asked.

'I don't know,' Robin said. 'I miss him, but I'm not sure it's a good idea.'

'It must be so strange, living by yourself after all these years,' Maggie said.

'It's lonely and it's very nice. Well, Hil, you know.'

Hilary smiled. 'It's different if you've never been married.'

Hilary and Phyllis rarely looked at one another. They arrived together and left together, but there was little conversation between them. Maggie wondered what it would be like to be with David in a room full of old friends. Certainly eye contact could be dangerously eloquent.

'Do you know I tried practising my shorthand today and I couldn't remember any of it?' Robin said.

'You're going to get a *job*?' Phyllis sounded so appalled that they all laughed.

'Sure. How else am I going to pay for this place? I blew all my savings when I moved in.'

'I thought Jackson was paying the rent,' Hilary said.

'He wanted to, but I won't let him.'

'You've lost a few bolts there, dear,' Phyllis remarked.

Robin smoothed her hair but it popped right back into its springy curls. 'This is *my* place. It's the first time I've ever had anything of my own, and I don't want to owe anybody, especially not Jackson.'

'Let me see what I can scare up,' Hilary said. 'But you know, secretaries use computers now. Think you could handle that?'

'I'll learn.'

'Christ,' Phyllis said. Maggie saw her reach into her handbag for an unopened pack of cigarettes. Before she could undo the cellophane wrapper, Hilary silently placed her hand over Phyllis's. Phyllis immediately put the cigarettes away and kept right on talking. 'We used to wear white gloves to work every day. Imagine that,' she said.

'Yes, and getting a swat on the behind from the boss was a token of his appreciation,' Hilary added.

'I don't know if there's any way I could explain how it was to my liberated daughter,' Maggie said.

As others began to reminisce about *Woman's Companion*, Maggie's thoughts drifted to David. Tonight they would be together all night long. Matthew had left on a rare three-day trip out of town, and the children were on a school outing at Sturbridge Village in Massachusetts. It was wonderful to imagine lying in David's arms all night, to think of falling asleep and waking to find him beside her. She was almost sorry that it was nearly time to leave Robin's. Soon there would be no more minutes left for this delicious anticipation.

'Hil's coming home with me tonight,' Phyllis was saying. 'You want us to drop you?'

'No, I think I'll walk, thanks. Matt's out of town so there's no need to hurry home.'

Phyllis's eyes narrowed briefly. Downstairs when Hilary stepped into the street to hail a cab, Phyllis said, 'Did you put my number down as a backup for the Sturbridge trip?'

Maggie nodded.

'Good,' Phyllis said. 'Just in case there's an emergency, God forbid, and there's something wrong with your phone. You wouldn't have to worry. I'd cope.'

Maggie thought. Some day I'll tell you how much I love you. As soon as their cab was out of sight, she flagged another one and headed for the West Side.

David was standing in the doorway in a pair of jeans and a t-shirt as Maggie ran gasping up the last flight of stairs.

'You couldn't possibly have found an apartment on the first floor,' she laughed, falling into his arms.

'Just a little closer to heaven,' David said.

'I'll say. No, don't kiss me yet. I'm all sweaty.'

David ran his tongue lightly along her cheek. 'Mm, delicious. Like *sashimi*.'

'You don't really eat that stuff, do you? Isn't it raw fish?'

'Such a sheltered life you lead, my love.' He drew her to the round table, sat down and pulled her onto his lap.

'Not sheltered any more. David, we have all night together.'

'I know.'

She weaved his long dark hair through her fingers. 'It's nice to be home.'

'Yes.' He unbuttoned the bodice of her dress and made her naked to the waist. She could feel him growing hard under her thighs.

'Take off your clothes,' she said. 'I'm going to eat you up.'

He lifted her in his arms, carried her to the bed and set her down.

'How did you do that? I weigh almost as much as you do.'

'You're a whole lot lighter than a quarter of a ton of Belgian marble.'

'Look at you.' Maggie stared at his penis, erect and slightly curved. 'How did you ever get that way?'

'Practice.'

Maggie laughed.

'Care to straighten me out?'

Maggie leaned back against the pillows and held out her arms. 'If it takes me all night.'

As their love-making became more intense, the light-hearted mood shifted. Maggie watched David above her as their bodies clung together and did their slow dance. His face reflected the same mingled pain and joy that she felt, and as her eyes filled with tears, his did, too. Afterwards she cried against his shoulder while he stroked her hair.

'David, what are we going to do?'

He lifted himself away and lay down on his side so that he could look at her. 'Do you really want to talk about it?'

She shook her head and held his hand hard against her cheek. Then they slept. When David woke up, Maggie was dressed and standing over him. He sat up in a panic. 'What time is it?' he asked.

'It's all right. We only slept for a few minutes. Are you hungry?'

'I could eat.' He rubbed his eyes with the back of his fists like a child. His hair looked soft against the hard lean muscles of his shoulder. 'All right, I know what,' he said. 'I'm taking you out.'

'Out. We can't go out.'

'It'll be all right.'

Maggie considered. No one she knew could possibly be dining at 1 a.m. in this neighbourhood on a Tuesday night. And then, she could not deny an appealing element of danger, even of defiance.

Columbus Avenue was lively, but not with the trendy elegance of the Upper East Side. Here long-haired women in faded jeans and no make-up, walked arm-in-arm, and bearded men with wire-rimmed glasses talked earnestly over espresso in the windows of cafés.

'Doesn't anybody ever go to bed?' Maggie asked.

'Eventually.'

The October sky was a clean navy blue. Maggie held David's arm and was practically delirious with proprietary love. A black man passed in dancer's legwarmers. He let his eyes linger on Maggie and gave her a smile. She knew her body told the street that she loved this man, and that she had just made love to him.

David steered her into a tiny Japanese restaurant with half a dozen tables and a counter. The place was nearly full, but they found a table at the back.

'All right. It's time you discovered *sushi*.'

'Oh dear,' Maggie said nervously. 'I was kind of thinking about a cheeseburger.'

'Don't be crude. Trust me.'

'I do,' Maggie said. 'God, I'm so in love it's sickening.'

David ordered several unintelligible items and two Japanese beers.

'What are we getting?'

193

'Don't ask. Just eat.'

Soon a lacquered tray appeared with what looked like a garden laid out on it.

'We can't disturb this,' Maggie said, poking carefully at a shiny pink rectangle fastened to a ball of rice with a seaweed belt.

David lifted a piece of raw tuna in his fingers, dipped it in soy sauce and popped it into Maggie's mouth before she could protest. She chewed bravely. The pleasant texture surprised her, and also the delicacy of the flavour. She had expected a heavy fishy taste.

'So?' David asked.

'Good. What's that?' She picked up something white and slightly translucent.

'Giant clam. It takes perseverance to get your teeth through it, but it's worth the effort.'

'Life with you is an adventure,' Maggie said. She worked at the tough clam while David kept his eyes on her. 'Eat something,' she urged with her mouth full.

'I am, in my way . . .' His feet grasped her ankles under the table. 'Tell me about your work. Did you have time this week?'

She nodded. 'I couldn't fall asleep Sunday night. I guess I was all jagged up from . . .' She nearly mentioned yet another uncomfortable discussion with Matthew about Robin and Jackson, but she could not bear to bring Matthew into the restaurant with them. 'I was just lying there thinking about that damn black surface in the cityscape piece and how I couldn't make the shapes come alive. I wanted it thick, you know, and round in this spot, but not static. There just didn't seem to be a way, and then suddenly I remembered Fred's hole punch. Revelation. I bounded out of bed and sat punching holes like a madwoman until 6 a.m. It works, David. I pain each little circle, and pile them up one on top of the other, but not rigid. They bend and twist. It's quite wonderful.'

'I want to see it.'

'You will. Aren't you going to ask me why I paint all the pieces when it's only the one on top that's visible?'

'I know why.'

Maggie picked up his hand, kissed it, and returned to her

*sushi.* 'Matt thought I was crazy, sitting there at Fred's desk making little piles of circles.' She stopped suddenly. David's face had flinched at the mention of her husband's name.

'I'm sorry,' Maggie said. 'I forget sometimes . . .'

'You live with him. He's part of your life. But it's worse when you call him "Matt".' He smiled ruefully and shook his head. 'I'm a very possessive man.'

'I know that.'

'How do you know that?'

'Because you can't part with your carvings.'

'I'll tell you what frightens me,' David said, draining his beer. 'Your kids will be home on Friday.'

'Don't be jealous of them.'

'I'm not jealous. I want them in my life. They're part of you. They came from your body.'

'I wish they hated their father.'

David shook his head. 'No, you don't. You can't bear to think of depriving them of anything, much less that.'

'David, I want to be with you all the time, not just a few hours in the middle of the day. It shouldn't be a novelty waking up in the morning with you beside me.'

'Then . . .' he began, and hesitated. 'I'm afraid to pressure you. I'm afraid you'll bolt on me.'

'Other people find ways when these things happen. Why am I paralysed?'

'Because you don't want to hurt anybody.' He sighed. 'I've always considered myself a non-violent person, but there are times when I'd like to have your husband shot.'

'He's a decent man, David.'

'If you tell me that one more time, I'll have *you* shot.'

A young woman in an elaborate kimono stood quietly beside their table. 'Everything okay?' she asked.

'Everything is fine,' David said. She bowed and disappeared with sandals slapping against tiny feet.

'I wish we lived in Japan,' Maggie said. The ambience of the place, with its perfectly ordered decor, its carefully presented food, its beautiful polite waitress, seemed so controlled and passionless. Perhaps in Japan, love affairs were never chaotic.

David read her thoughts. 'Ever take a good hard look at Japanese art?' he asked.

Maggie smiled, remembering the blood and the lust. 'Yes. I guess there's no escape.' They were both silent for some minutes, lost in yearnings. 'You know what,' Maggie said finally. 'I want to do a whole wall. A huge white space about eighteen by ten.'

'With your hole punch?'

'Yes, and other things. It's been struggling in my head. I'm going to need too much space, though.'

'Put it on my wall.'

'Are you serious?' But she saw that he was. She contemplated the open white rectangle that was washed with intense river light. 'It's about perfect.'

'I figure it ought to take you at least thirty-five years.'

'God willing.' She got up. 'Let's get an ice-cream cone and walk back home.'


She told Matthew that she was working on a project requiring space and that a fellow student from class had offered his studio for a few hours a day. Matthew asked no questions. In fact, he appeared not to have heard her.

'Did you hear what I said?' Maggie asked. Listen to me when I'm lying to you, she thought.

Matthew looked up from the *Times*. 'You'll be working in someone's studio, person from class. I heard you.'

Anyway, it wasn't even a lie, Maggie told herself.


Before long, David began to see her every afternoon. At first, he would stay home and wait for her. She would smile at him, hold his hand, even make love to him, but he felt all the while how she was drawn to that great white wall on the other side of the room. Soon he gave her a key and began leaving the apartment before she was due. Then when he came back to her much later, he was always rewarded with her exhausted, grateful smile.

She began by transporting the accumulation of many years' work across the park in her black leather portfolio. She kept the papers in a pile on the floor beside the wall and each evening when she had gone, David examined page after page, reading her past as if he were poring over a photograph album. There were early experiments with fabric designs, undisciplined but fabulously coloured. There was a series in various colour washes that from a distance seemed merely attractive nubbly-surfaced abstractions. Close up, however, row upon row of tiny faces, each different, peered out. There was another group portraying the surfaces of tree bark: oak, birch, pine, maple. There were several renditions of a baby's hands and feet that David found particularly poignant.

Sometimes when David was sketching to prepare for a new carving, he stayed and sat at the round table, looking up every now and then to watch Maggie. At first, she did nothing but sit on the floor and cut up her work with a pair of scissors. She would select a page from the pile, then study it carefully for what seemed a long time. When she began cutting, she often worked against the flow of the design to create movement and tension. This process went on for many days. Then one afternoon she arrived at the apartment in a state of agitation.

'What's the matter?' he asked. 'Is it that I'm here? I was going to sketch today, but I can do it at the studio.'

'No. I'm ready to begin on the wall today. I'm terrified.'

Like the first strike into the stone, it was a commitment. Even if you changed your mind later, the initial impulse reverberated with a kind of tyranny.

'Do you want me to leave?'

'No.'

He saw that it did not matter. She smiled apologetically.

'I won't let myself be jealous of your work,' he said.

She kissed him, shrugged off her coat and spilled the wild array of shapes and colours out onto his floor. David fixed himself a cup of tea, and sat with the sketch pad untouched.

For nearly twenty minutes, Maggie stared at the wall, sighed, sat on the windowsill and stared some more, then went to ponder the cutouts. Finally, with the unhesitating acuity of an osprey after a fish, her hand dived into the multi-coloured patchwork and picked up a piece. It was crescent-shaped, fashioned from a fabric design of bold green and burgundy. She strode to the wall and taped the fragment to the upper-left area of the space. Then she returned to the centre of the room and stared some more.

Pretty soon she swooped after another piece, this time a square of intricately-woven strips from the tree series. She placed it to the lower right of the first, then retraced her steps to stare again. This process went on all afternoon. David barely sketched at all, so enthralled was he with watching her redesign the fragments of her history.

He found Maggie particularly compelling when she was at work. There was a kind of radiant intensity in her face that might have been frightening had he himself not experienced the emotions that produced it. As she paced back and forth, he felt his eyes sear through the layers of flesh to the skeletal structure underneath. He saw the long bones of her legs swing as she walked, the flat pelvis pivot with each turn, the neat rounded skull and smooth cheekbones. He saw them all and appreciated their dance as he supposed only a man who loved stone could. But Maggie was living stone, warm-blooded and graceful. It had never occurred to him that a woman's presence in his home could produce this peculiar convergence of excitement and peace. And yet it had happened. Being with Maggie stimulated him to such a point that he assumed his nerve endings had been hitherto anaesthetized. But his heightened receptivity was not at all agitating. On the contrary, everything in his life seemed suddenly to make sense. There was coherence where there had once been restless discontent. If only that wall were not filling up quite so quickly.

Maggie flung herself down at the table. 'Whoa, maybe I'm too old for this. Got some tea for me?'

He poured her a cup. It was lukewarm but she gulped it thankfully. Both of them gazed at the wall for a moment.

'Why that particular spot?' David asked. 'Where you began.'

'I don't know, really. I always seem to work out of the upper-left-hand corner. It's where my focus is.'

'Ever try starting somewhere else?'

'Oh, sure, but I always wind up feeling lost. There's never any balance.' She took his sketch pad and saw that he had made only a single preliminary drawing. 'Oh, David. I'm not good for you. This is a shame.'

'You are good for me. You're the best thing to fall into my life since my first hunk of alabaster. In fact, I think I could give up my work before I could live without you.'

'I don't want that kind of power.'

'I can't help you there.'

'Besides,' she continued. 'I don't think I believe it. As long as you're still breathing, you'll be carving stone.'

He considered this. 'Tell you what, let's not test it, okay?'

After she left, he turned on all the lights and scrutinized what she had done. The wild collection of colours and the juxtaposition of fantastic shapes seemed to leap off the wall and dance in the air. David's heart began to pound.

'I know I shouldn't call you,' he said, 'but I've been looking at your wall. It's thrilling, Maggie. You're doing something extraordinary here.'

'Thank you.' She sounded pleased, with none of the usual strangled remoteness of other phone calls.

'I'll see you tomorrow.'

'Yes. I love you.'

His eyes kept returning to the wall. It was as if she was living there with him at last, singing, crying, and speaking in many voices from the other side of the room.

# Twenty-One

Maggie's fingers trembled as she picked up the telephone to dial her doctor. With one hand she gripped the receiver. The other she held unconsciously to her right breast.

'This is Margaret Hollander. I'm calling for my autopsy report. I mean, oh, sorry, my *biopsy* report.'

'Just a moment, please.' The cool voice seemed not to notice the slip. Perhaps it was a common blunder. While she waited with the dead air against her ear, the knot in her throat threatened to gag her. It felt a bit like the forbidden lump of laughter that used to choke her as a child at sombre occasions like funerals.

'Mrs Hollander, this is Dr Berg. It was negative. You're fine. It was just a cyst.'

'Oh, God, thanks,' Maggie said. 'What do I do now?'

'Go on with your life. I'll see you in six months.'

Maggie sat on the edge of the bed and tried to analyse her reaction to the news. The fact was, she almost felt let down. *Go on with your life*, the man said, as if that was such a simple matter. Checking into a hospital seemed like a respite. Major surgery would have kept her isolated for a few weeks anyway, and after that, if it turned out that they had not managed to remove every malignant particle, perhaps soon she would achieve a permanent reprieve. No guilt. No decisions. Her heart began to thump. Death. The word flew about the room like a huge black bird, beating its wings against the walls, the windows, her face.

The phone jangled. 'Hello,' she said, certain it would be David.

'Hi, Mags. Did you get your results yet?' It was Matthew.

'Yes. I'm fine. It was okay.' She could not remember telling him she would find out this morning. There was silence on the other end.

'That's great,' he said finally. She heard the catch in his voice. 'In a meeting. See you at dinner.'

As soon as he hung up, Maggie began to cry. What was Matthew doing, showing concern for her health? And what was *she* doing, reacting with tears, as if she were moved by this shred of evidence that he cared about her? Last night over a late dinner without the children she had stared at him with such intensity that he had finally asked her if he needed a haircut. But she was trying to imagine herself telling him about David. What was the kindest way to say it? *Matt, I'm leaving you and taking the kids.* Does one do such things over coffee and dessert? Or first thing in the morning, perhaps, when one was presumably stronger.

This situation is giving me lumps in my breasts, Maggie thought. I'm giving myself cancer. She got off the bed, washed her face, threw on a heavy jacket and went out. She walked aimlessly along Seventy-ninth Street until she found herself in front of the Metropolitan Museum. It was cold and damp, but not raining yet, so she sat down on one of the benches. The leafless trees looked like claws reaching up out of the pavement. I will watch these other people, Maggie thought. I will observe and I will learn.

A large yellow school bus stopped at the curb. The doors opened and released a tumbling chattering collection of Oriental children dressed in black uniforms. They chased across the plaza, settling on the empty benches like a flock of starlings on a telephone wire. Soon they were herded together by their chaperons and swept up the vast stone stairs into the museum. Two young women with strollers passed, eyed Maggie, and then sat down on a bench nearby. Out came the Smurf and Strawberry Shortcake thermoses and the plastic baggies full of raisins and whole-wheat cookies. The toddlers, freed from their strollers, began to grab at one another's snacks.

'Jason! We have to share. Melanie always shares with you. Give her a cookie.'

'That's all right,' Melanie's mother responded.

As Jason continued to hoard his cookies, his mother's voice began to lose its guise of reasonableness. 'Aw, share your cookie, Jason,' she wheedled. 'I'll be your best *freh*-hend.' She

201

wrenched a cookie from Jason's tiny fingers and handed it to Melanie. Jason promptly flung himself to the ground and began to wail. His mother stood over him helplessly. 'Jason, this is not appropriate behaviour. You know I love you, darling, but I do not love your behaviour.' Jason began to kick and flail. His mother looked at her friend. 'He didn't have a nap yesterday. He's overtired.' She picked up the howling child, ducking the swinging feet. 'It's all right, Mommy loves you,' she crooned. 'Come, I'll take you to MacDonald's and buy you a nice burger and fries.'

Maggie glared at the woman and tried to transmit her thoughts through the air. I hate you, Maggie said in her head. You are so stupid, so terribly criminally stupid you should have been sterilized. Your child will grow up sick and twisted and destructive because you are such a fool. You'll probably have three more babies and turn them all into monsters and the world will have to cope with them. I hate you.

Jason's mother turned to intercept Maggie's furious gaze. The young woman's face was full of bewildered love.

When Maggie and Matthew had first moved uptown, they used to see a woman who haunted these benches and the street near the museum. She was tall, slim, wore her hair in a neat pile on her head. Her face was weathered, but attractive, though it was difficult to guess her age. She was always just barely smiling, either sitting with her hands crossed in her lap or striding up Madison Avenue – in the street, never on the sidewalk. People always looked at her. But it soon became apparent that there was something off kilter. Either her otherwise impeccable attire was marred by stockings that hung in sagging wrinkles around her legs or it was mid-July and she was wearing a heavy wool scarf twisted around her neck as if it were January. Maggie constructed endless romantic tragedies around her. She was an heiress driven to insanity by a lover who had betrayed her. She was a brilliant artist who had forsaken her children to paint, only to lose her great gift. Maggie searched the benches, but there was no sign of the strange elegant presence. She glanced down at her own ankles. Her stockings clung smoothly. Her jacket was buttoned tightly to her chin like everyone else's. I am an ordinary woman, Maggie told herself. Plain-faced Radcliffe graduates from Stafford, Connecticut, are not equipped to live the role of a Tennessee Williams heroine. 'What I have to do is go home and cook dinner,' Maggie said aloud. Peripherally, Maggie saw Jason's mother turn her face away, quickly, the way one does to avoid eye contact with a crazy person.

And when I cross the street, Maggie thought, careful now to keep the words unspoken within her head, perhaps I shall be run over by the Number Four bus and be crushed into oblivion.

Matthew was jaunty at the table but he did not mention Maggie's test. In fact, he barely looked at her as if the intensity of his telephone call needed to be diluted.

'So, Frederick, your sister says you have a girlfriend,' he remarked.

'She's full of it, too,' Fred answered. His voice had begun to crack since the summer so that the last few words emerged half an octave lower than the rest.

'I don't know why you're so defensive,' Susan complained. 'She's only the richest girl in school, even if she does have bow legs.'

'Listen,' Fred said menacingly, 'I don't go mouthing off about your precious David, do I?'

Maggie's heart shut down completely for several seconds.

'Jeez, you must really have it bad,' Susan said.

'The trick is to be cool,' Matthew advised Fred. 'You always rise to the bait, which is why your sister can't resist giving you the business.'

'Don't take away all my fun, Daddy,' Susan said. Her braces were removed in late October and she had developed a dazzling smile.

'Who's David?' Matthew asked.

'If you mean David Zimmerman,' Susan said to Fred, 'we are strictly platonic.'

'To your disgust,' Fred said.

'Mother, don't you think Fred got surly over the summer?'

Maggie smiled at her son. His complexion had developed red spots and fine dark hairs shadowed his upper lip. He was much thinner.

'It's just adolescence,' Maggie said. 'You ought to know all about it.'

'Yeah, it sucks,' Susan said.

'Watch it,' Matthew warned.

'Anyway, Mom's not so normal either,' Fred observed. 'She's been in never-never land since we got home. Right, Sue?'

Susan chewed her dinner roll and nodded. 'We decided it was early menopause. Have you been getting hot flushes, Mom?'

'What *are* you talking about?' Maggie asked.

'You've gotten much too skinny, and you don't hear people when they talk,' Sue said. 'I told you three times about my play try-outs and this morning you asked me when I was having my play try-outs. I mean, really.'

'Last week Sue got my laundry in her drawers and I got all her stuff. Even a bra,' Fred protested. 'Size twenty-eight triple A.'

'Shut up, Fred,' Susan said.

'I don't know what to say,' Maggie replied.

'It was probably the breast lump,' Matthew suggested. 'You were probably more worried than you thought.'

'What breast lump?' Susan asked.

'It's all right,' Maggie said. 'I got the biopsy report.' She had to concentrate not to say 'autopsy'. 'I'm fine. It was nothing.'

'It's all that coffee,' Susan said.

Maggie let her lecture, glad to be off the hook. At the first opportunity, she escaped into the kitchen to dole out ice cream. Five minutes later she was still standing with the scoop in her hand, staring at the three pint containers and the four empty bowls. Fred wanted chocolate chip and cherry vanilla. Susan was for pralines only. Or was it cherry? Matt liked all three kinds. No, that was wrong. The scoop fell out of her fingers and she began to cry. Suddenly Susan was beside her.

'What's wrong, Mom?' she asked.

'I can't keep it straight,' Maggie choked. 'I don't know, I'm so tired. I just can't keep it straight.'

'I'll do it,' Susan said, pretending not to see her mother's tears.

'Thanks, darling.' Maggie excused herself and left Susan to portion out dessert.

In the bedroom later, Matthew ruffled Maggie's hair and told her to use the bathroom first. 'I think I'm going to take a quick shower so you go ahead,' he said. Maggie went into the bathroom with her nightgown and robe over her arm. She was washing her face when she heard the bathroom door squeak. With rising panic, she realized that Matthew had come in, but she was helpless, bent over the sink with soap all over her face. She heard him chuckle as he gave her a quick pinch on the rear end. Instantly, she swung around and with all her weight behind her, drove her elbow into his midriff. She heard the sound of air exploding from his diaphragm with a cartoon 'Ooof!' Eyes smarting from soap and naked body vibrating with outrage, she said, 'Don't ever do that again. Now get out.'

Matthew backed out of the room holding his stomach. His face was full of surprise, pain, and something very close to laughter. Maggie looked at herself in the mirror. The soap had dried in white splotches on her cheeks and her eyes were bloodshot. She looked ludicrous and formidable all at once, but she was free, invincible, and it had been so easy. She wondered why on earth it had taken her eighteen years to do it.

She woke up about 4 a.m. as usual, with the dreaded sense of disorientation that had begun to plague her over the past few weeks. She would snap out of her sleep as if a gun had discharged beside her ear, and lie blinking in the dark with her heart pounding. Something was wrong, she knew. Someone had died, or there had been some other awful tragedy. Then she would remember that it was David. Not that he was dead, but that he was not beside her. What am I to do? she thought. And before long, she would slip out of bed and begin the prowl that had become a ritual. She checked and re-checked the children, listening to their night sounds and recalling the murmurs and sweet sighs of their babyhood. Sometimes she stared down at Matthew and tried to unlock the swollen cache of emotion she had buried so deep inside her that it was no longer within reach. She was existing in two separate dimensions of time and space. During the day, it almost seemed possible to preserve the tenuous balance. But night had become a menacing expanse of hostile territory that she had somehow to cross. She woke earlier and earlier, dazed and miserable, like a prisoner in a time machine, forever repeating a futile journey between two centuries.

She sat at the kitchen table with her head in her hands. Then she got up and searched the drawers for a pencil and some paper. She found a red marking pen, but no paper, so she ripped off a paper towel, sat down again, and began making her list. It always started out the same way, with two columns, one headed *D* and one *M*. Under *D* she wrote Love, Peace, Fulfilment, Sex, Art. Tonight she added Self and underlined the word. Under *M* she wrote Years, Shared Experience. Then she crossed out Shared Experience since it fell under the same category as Years. She went on with Stability, Familiarity, Comforts, then Children underlined. One night by way of experiment, she had tried to shift Children to the *D* column, but it hadn't worked. The letters seemed to march on their own back to *M*. With a groan, she wadded the paper into a ball, buried it in the garbage pail and went into the living room. She stared out at the building across the street. There were only three windows lit out of many dozens of empty black squares. People ill, perhaps, or restless. Ordinary members of ordinary families, just like Maggie's. She felt the anguish rise up into her mouth like vomit and flung herself to her knees against the couch. She buried her face in the cushions and cried out, What am I going to do? Oh, God, what am I going to do?

# Twenty-Two

For the sixth time, Matthew slammed the squash ball into the telltale for a foul, losing the point. 'God damn it,' he muttered, and swiped at his sweaty forehead with the back of his wrist. Jack Foreman gave him an odd look. In the ten years the two men had played together, Jack had never witnessed a display of temper from Matthew Hollander. Ordinarily, in fact, he rarely spoke on the court except to check the score or clarify a point.

Matthew towelled himself off by the water fountain and took a long drink. He had never enjoyed losing, but usually he could put defeat behind him with a shrug and look forward to beating the pants off Jack the next time. Tonight he felt like breaking his racquet in half or smashing it over Jack's head. Jack, perhaps sensing Matthew's hostility, had already set off for the locker room.

'God damn it,' Matthew said again.

He stood in the shower for a long time and let the hot water pelt down on his face and shoulders. Perhaps the driving water would wash away the constriction in his head. He wondered how long he had been carrying this around, this not-quite headache. Many weeks, certainly. He thought he could even recall feeling it when they went to visit the children at camp. He had taken a couple of aspirins after the drive home. They hadn't helped, so he had never bothered with pills again. It was not pain exactly. There was just this constant pressure as if his brains were expanding inside his skull. There was heat, too, which made him think of the textbook illustrations of volcanoes in his high-school geology course – seething magma trapped in an underground chamber preparing to blast through layers of rock, and up the volcanic shaft into the open sky.

Things had been out of whack in the office lately also. He had misplaced an important document. He kept calling his secretary 'Marian' which was the name of his previous secretary, gone a year ago to have her baby. He lost his temper with a junior associate over the use of the semi-colon and had barely restrained himself from hurling *The Elements of Style* at the poor kid as he fled the office. Matthew was not accustomed to ransacking his life in search of the discordant note. Either something was wrong or it wasn't, and there was not a single thing he could point his finger at and say *That's it*. The children's summer had been wonderful. Fred slimmed down and gained confidence. Susan lost the belligerent attitude that had grated on him all last year. And Maggie was flourishing. She had embarked on this new rather curious artistic adventure which he found difficult to understand but which engaged her to an extent he had not seen in years. He missed the paintings, those marvellous assemblages of colour and line that so impressed him back in college, but if she was content with her output, that was what counted. She was a little run down at the moment, but basically she was looking great – vibrant, healthy, sexy. Men had begun to notice her on the street. Maggie was totally unaware of it, of course, she was so damn oblivious of her own sensuality. But Matthew was amused by the surreptitious glances as he walked down Madison Avenue with Maggie on a Saturday afternoon. His head pounded mercilessly so he turned the dial to cold, hoping that would help. Still . . . still . . . perhaps something was maybe slightly amiss there, or if not quite amiss, then unfamiliar. She had slugged him not long ago. Even more shocking than the blow to the solar plexus had been the sight of her face, all twisted with what amounted to hatred. He turned off the water. They had never discussed it. Probably it was past time to let up on the pinching and poking and ass-slapping. She was a grown woman, after all, no college kid. Maybe she was already beginning to experience some hormonal changes. Not that she hadn't been perfectly pleasant and cordial since that night, only it seemed almost as if part of her had disappeared, gone on sabbatical. Christ, his head hurt. Maybe he ought to try the aspirin again.

'You okay, Hollander?' Jack asked him. He was blowing his hair dry at the mirror. Since his divorce a few years back, the hair-drying ritual consumed half an hour. He had explained to Matthew that erotic women relate to a well-groomed head of hair.

'Headache,' Matthew said. He never bothered with the dryer, just towelled his hair fiercely and then combed it with his fingers. Jack snapped off the machine and studied Matthew. 'I don't know why I still bother to ask, but why not join me for a drink tonight? It won't kill you, and you might even enjoy yourself.'

It had become a joke between them that Matthew always declined Jack's invitations. But for the first time, Matthew hesitated.

'Come on,' Jack urged. 'Let's cure that headache.'

The children were out late. Maggie had phoned about an art function she wanted to attend and gave him instructions about heating up his dinner. Matthew had half-planned on returning to the office to put in a few extra hours, but suddenly the idea of companionship appealed to him.

'Okay, what the hell.'

'Attaboy!' Jack exclaimed. 'We're gonna make it a veritable pub crawl straight up Columbus Ave.'

Jack's enthusiasm was daunting, but Matthew admitted to a twinge of excitement. It seemed pleasantly racy to be out on the town with this self-proclaimed womanizer.

'First rule,' Jack said in the cab. 'No shop talk. Anybody mentions the legal profession has to buy dinner.' When his marriage disintegrated, Jack had moved into a studio apartment on the West Side near Lincoln Centre. He had since become the type of zealot who considered everything east of Fifth Avenue to be hopelessly dreary. 'None of your tawdry Third Avenue bar scenes tonight, my friend,' he said, and began to chatter about his favourite obsession, next to women. 'Later you can come up to my place. I've just finished another model, Stutz Bearcat this time. Best one I've done. Real leather upholstery, brass fixtures, I'm nuts about it. I told you I finally bought my first antique car, didn't I, but it's out on the island. I can't insure it in the city.'

'Yes, you mentioned it.' Matthew was beginning to regret his impulsiveness. Maybe it had been a mistake to allow his circumscribed relationship with Jack to seep out beyond the thick walls of the racquet club. Where would it end, this invitation to intimacy? Matthew imagined himself being dragged to antique car conventions in Bridgehampton. His head began to pound again.

'I visit the damn thing almost every weekend,' Jack said. 'Good thing Virginia and I never had kids. They'd never compete in my affections with that beauty.'

Matthew regarded Jack with pity. Where was the humanity in this well-coiffed fellow's life, the warm rough-and-tumble of a complex lively family? Matthew was struck with his own good fortune. If not for Maggie, he could certainly have wound up just like Jack, devoting his days to wherefores and hereinafters and nights to jigsaw puzzles or computer games. Matthew had always understood that there was much in his own character that reached for objects and ideas rather than people.

'I'm buying tonight,' Matthew said.

'No way.' Jack took out his wallet to pay for the cab.

'How're things going on that co-op conversion on Eighty-fourth Street?' Matthew asked.

'Okay, I get the point,' Jack said. 'But I'm buying the drinks.'

'Deal.'

The cab let them off on Columbus Avenue in front of a place called *Thimbles*. It was dark inside, with a long oak bar and tables in the rear. Jack was right. The people here bore little resemblance to the natty Upper East Side crowd that gathered at *Uzie*'s or *McMullen*'s. In fact, Matthew and Jack were the only patrons wearing suits. A young woman with a clipboard appeared beside Matthew. 'Dinner?'

'Christ, look at this,' Jack complained. 'Rose, why is it I can never find you when I come in here alone and now I've got this guy with me you're on us like flies on a cowpat?'

'You're so poetic, Jack,' Rose observed.

'A drink first, then dinner,' Matthew said.

'I'll put you on the list.' She smiled up at Matthew. 'Name?'

'Foreman,' Jack answered.

'You make yourself at home and I'll slip you in whenever you're ready,' Rose said to Matthew.

As she squeezed through the crush towards the tables at the rear, Jack muttered, 'Bet she would, too. Hollander, you just may be a liability to a horny single man. I've been trying to score with that piece of ass for two years now.'

They made their way to the bar and ordered a couple of beers.

'She's a class act, that one, a violinist when she's not at this place. I keep telling her it's not just for a quick stab in the dark. She's marriage material.'

'You want to get married again?' Matthew asked.

'Sure I do. Who wants to be stuck in an empty apartment with a pile of plastic model pieces and a tube of airplane glue? I was the one who screwed up the first time. I drove Virginia crazy.'

Matthew lifted his glass in salute. 'This was a good idea. Thanks for pushing it.' It was agreeable standing here with Jack surrounded by lively intelligent-looking people. While Jack began a comical litany of his faults as a marriage partner, Matthew studied the mob. An earnest-looking group of middle-aged people in jeans moved off to be seated. It was then that Matthew got his first clear glimpse of the dining area. It used to be difficult to make out the faces through the haze in a place like this, Matthew thought. Maybe people were finally beginning to heed the voices of reason and cut down on cigarettes. Off in the far corner, his eye caught the outline of a familiar profile. There was the usual rather pleasant jolt to the consciousness that he often experienced on the street or in a crowded department store. The eyes, minding their own business, pass over the milling faces, come to a halt, retrack and hold on a particular arrangement of nose, mouth, line of jaw. *We know that person,* the eyes tell the brain, *just in case you're interested.* Sometimes he was, most often he was not, and would lose himself in the throng so as to escape a meaningless exchange with someone he cared nothing about. A moment too banal to qualify as even a minor event in a busy man's busy day.

So why in this darkened place with the warm air full of animated voices had this ordinary moment of split-second recognition suddenly sucked the breath from his lungs and set the wooden plank floor tilting and shifting under his feet? *If*

*I look away*, he thought, in words slow and deliberate inside his head, *the sideways movement of my face will obliterate the scene before me like an eraser swept across a chalkboard.* But he could not avert his eyes. He stood immobilized like a jammed, malfunctioning lighthouse that could focus on only one particular wedge of treacherous sea.

The woman was distressed, perhaps in tears. She talked, mouth twisted in anguish, then listened with eyes that fastened on her companion's face as if she were drowning and he possessed the world's sole life raft. The man's face was angled away, but Matthew could see the shoulder-length hair. No mistaking him for a woman, at least not for long. There was too much sinewy muscular power in his body. As he spoke, he gestured with his hands. Once he caught the woman's fingers between his own and held them to his mouth. Her face crumpled, she dropped her eyes, and hid them with her other hand.

Jack had stopped talking. His eyes followed Matthew's to the corner table. 'See someone you know?'

Matthew exerted enormous effort and forced his gaze to meet Jack's. 'I thought maybe, but I was mistaken.'

Breathing was Matthew's immediate problem. His chest was paralysed. So he ordered his brain to tell his lungs to expand. They did, and he gasped. But his upper body refused to take the next step without further instructions. Exhale, he told his brain to tell his lungs. They did, and his body relaxed with a sigh. He kept his eyes focused on Jack's face, but what he saw was the replay of an incident he had witnessed several years ago in the subway station. Matthew had stood in the rush-hour crowd waiting at Eighty-sixth Street for the downtown express. There was a distant rumble, and finally the appearance of a bright headlamp at the far end of the tunnel. Then a scream as a young man in a red windbreaker was shoved off the platform onto the tracks. Women's shrieks mingled with the sound of brakes, but before the train could stop, the man had lost his leg. The whole thing took five seconds, maybe less. What Matthew found so horrible was the guillotine speed of tragedy. There was no preparation. If the fellow had suffered frostbite, for instance, there would be the hospitalization, the medical consultations, with warnings that gangrene might ensue. Then if weeks later the leg were amputated, at least there had been some groundwork. Five seconds, and a life was altered forever. Everything would now be sorted into two categories: before and after. So while Jack Foreman related his exploits concerning an apartment full of 'stews', Matthew watched the news feature of the day unreel itself in the flat air an inch in front of Jack's face: *Intense Conversation in West Side Bar*, starring Margaret Hollander, long-time wife and best friend of attorney Matthew Hollander. Co-star unidentified.

He had to get out. Now.

'Go,' he interrupted Jack.

'What?' Jack said, getting to the best part.

'Gotta go. Don't feel so red hot. Here.' He handed Jack a twenty dollar bill. 'Do it again some time. Next week. Sorry.'

He fled. It had begun to sleet, but the ice felt good against his face. He tried not to think, just walk and taste the cold air and breathe until the process became automatic again. He walked south past the damp glitter of Lincoln Centre with its limousines and fountains, then across Central Park South, ignoring the sodden horses and their half-frozen buggy drivers still hawking for rides. Next he headed downtown on Fifth. The apartment waited for him like a beast huddled in the dark up on Seventy-ninth Street. He wanted to avoid it as long as possible. Perhaps he never had to go back there.

By the time he reached Fifty-first Street, he had begun to think that of course, Maggie was in love. What a fool he had been not to see it. Or perhaps he had merely chosen not to see it. A businessman with well-trimmed hair and sensible horn-rimmed glasses passed by. Why not him? Matthew thought. Betray me if you must, but let it be one of my own kind, not that Bohemian with the sensitive hands and the turtleneck sweater. He was probably an artist, no doubt the 'fellow student' who had loaned her his studio. So many lies there must have been. So much deception.

Matthew began to shiver. The shock and the cold had penetrated his topcoat. He ducked into a restaurant on a side street near Radio City Music Hall. It was a glossy place that catered to the theatre crowd. This late, only half a dozen people sat at the bar. The bartender poured goldfish crackers into wooden bowls in preparation for the mob that would arrive in an hour's time. Matthew ordered a double scotch, swallowed it in a hurry and ordered another.

'You okay?' the bartender asked before complying.

'I have hate in my heart,' Matthew said. 'Other than that, I'm fine.'

The bartender studied Matthew dubiously. The snow was melting off Matthew's hair and dripping onto the polished surface of the bar.

'Look, I forgot my hat. I'm an attorney. Lost a big case today due to deceit and corruption. I don't usually drink much so it won't be long before I'm totally blasted. I'm a very quiet drunk.'

'Got a car?'

'Nope. I'm on foot and I live right up the street.'

'Okay.'

He poured and Matthew drank. The liquor felt good going down, but seemed to have little effect on Matthew's thoughts. To no avail, he huddled over his glass as if the whisky's warm comfort could reach into his soul. After he had finished his second double, a young woman sat down next to him and shrugged out of her wet trenchcoat. She wore an expensive navy silk suit with a Liberty-print tie and a bow at her collar. She smiled at Matthew. He smiled back. Why not?

'Bad day?' she asked.

'Bad of prodigious proportions.'

'You're an attorney, right?'

'I'm dismayed that it shows,' Matthew answered.

'Can't help but recognize a fellow traveller.'

'Oh shit,' Matthew said.

'You don't like woman lawyers?'

'Don't like any lawyers. Minds like steel traps, hearts like basalt.'

'I play the harp in my spare time. Professionally.'

'That's different,' Matthew said. 'My wife's fucking around.'

The woman looked at him.

'You hardly know what to say.'

'That's right,' she said.

'Neither do I.' Matthew ordered another double and a refill for the woman. She was drinking straight vodka on ice. 'It's what's on my mind this evening. My wife's fucking.'

'There're a whole lot of questions I'd like to ask,' the woman said.

'You're an educated woman. Know how I can tell?'

'No.'

'Most people would say "*there's*" a whole lot of questions, not "*there're*".'

'Ah.' She waited. 'About those questions.'

'Fire away.'

'When did you find out?'

'Tonight. I saw them. He's a fucking hippy.'

'How long have you been married?'

'Eighteen years.'

'What are you going to do about it?'

'Drink.'

'You're extremely attractive. I suppose you know that.'

Matthew was silent.

'I mean, if you need bolstering in the confidence department, I'd be very happy to oblige. I've had a long day myself.'

Matthew took a closer look at her. She had a soft face, not bony like Maggie's. She was blue-eyed, rosy-skinned and rather fragile looking. Her mouth was pink and full. It had been a very long time since Matthew had kissed anyone other than Maggie. He could take her to bed, no doubt about it. A soft round body might be a welcome change from Maggie's angularities. A sweet form of vengeance. The woman moved her chair closer to his. His face was no more than six inches away.

'Try it,' she said.

'Okay.' Matthew leaned forward and kissed her gently. His lips were numb from the liquor. It felt as if someone else owned his mouth.

'Nothing, huh?' she asked.

'Sorry. Should have tried it before the last round.'

'I have a feeling it wouldn't have made a difference.'

'The trouble is . . .' he began.

'Go ahead,' the woman sighed.

'I keep wanting to tell Maggie about it.'

'Who's Maggie?'

'My wife.'

'I see your problem.'

Her face expressed patient sympathy, but practised, as if she had heard it all before.

'The humiliation of it. Everybody always thought we were the perfect couple. Well, almost everybody, as it turns out.'

'What went wrong?'

'Nothing.'

'There must have been some . . .'

'Why?' Matthew interrupted. 'Maybe she just has the hots for him. A temporary hormonal derailment.' He caught a glimpse of the coat rack by the door. There were only two coats hanging, a woman's fur, and over that, a man's Burberry trenchcoat, the arms of which draped the fur in a protective embrace. The tenderness of it was too much for Matthew to bear. Once again, he was overwhelmed with the urgent need for flight. Pain kept tracking him down. If he could only find some respite, however temporary. He paid the bill and stood up.

'Good luck,' the woman said.

'I hope some nice violinist sits down in a minute. Stay away from lawyers.' He leaned over and kissed her again. He let his mouth linger this time. Maybe at least she'd get some kind of charge out of it.

He stopped beside the railing at Rockefeller Centre and looked down at the skaters. They were teenagers mostly. They fell a lot, but seemed immune to pain. At the west end of the plaza, a team of men pounded at the scaffolding surrounding the giant bare Christmas tree. Matthew imagined Maggie and her lover crucified, hanging there from the wooden braces like macabre holiday decorations. Christ, how maudlin it all was. He wanted to kill Maggie, and yet all the time there was this need to go straight home and tell her all about the miserable night he was having.

She had always been the best listener. He could picture her at the kitchen table, leaning forward on her elbows. Her expressive eyes watched him carefully as he spoke so as not to miss a word. She was the perfect person to unload on because she never trivialized the complaint. If he was having a difficult time with a new secretary, Maggie never said, 'Oh, but it will soon get better, you'll see,' which of course, he knew. Instead the response would be something like 'It must be difficult adjusting to someone you're so dependent on.' If his shoulder stiffened so that he could not play squash, she never said 'Aren't you lucky it's not serious?' Instead it was 'You really count on that game. You'll miss it this week, won't you?' She had such a gift for making him feel understood. How he longed for her tonight.

He wondered suddenly about Maggie. Where did she go with her pain? The question struck him full force. He supposed she confided in her friends. He remembered her stunned silence when he called to check on her biopsy report the other day. Clearly, she had been shocked at his interest. The fact was, he only remembered because his secretary had used her lunch hour to have a mole removed and was terrified it was malignant. Matthew crossed Fifth Avenue and stood looking up at the spires of St Patrick's cathedral, resplendent with its façade recently cleaned. He had liked it better grimy and grey, but then perhaps he was just uncomfortable with change. Christ, how long since he had wondered how Maggie was doing, or looked at her with careful eyes? He thought of her companion in the bar tonight. He was watching her, listening to her. Along with the renaissance in Maggie's creativity had come a new womanliness and confidence. This man had given her something in a few short months that Matthew had failed to give her in all these many years. At this moment, it seemed inconceivable that such a love affair could have occurred without Matthew's knowledge, but then it was just more evidence that he was oblivious to Maggie in some essential way.

'Oh, God,' he heard himself moan, and a passer-by gave him a suspicious glance. He sat down on the stone steps in front of the cathedral, not far from a bag lady who picked idly through her tattered belongings and sorted them into piles beside her feet. But all Matthew could see was Maggie's tormented eyes as they clung to the face of her new lover.

'All right,' he said aloud, but the bag lady did not seem to hear. It was time to sort this thing out. He had a legal mind. Then be a lawyer now.

Maggie had met this man, been strongly attracted, resisted, but finally succumbed, with what terrible guilt he could only imagine, knowing her deep family commitment. It made Matthew's stomach turn to think that another man had discovered the joys of this woman's sensuality, this thing about Maggie that he had gloated over like secret treasure. But no, he would not think of that. He needed to understand, not torture himself. He stared down at his hands. They were capable, straight fingers, but not long and sensitive like that other man's. How casually Matthew had abused her body all these years, he thought, pinching, slapping, wrestling as if she were some kind of toy.

Logic told him that Maggie was attempting to give him up, this lover. There was conflict between them. Perhaps she was trying to remain in the marriage, even if only for the children's sake. Assuming this was so, did Matthew still want her?

He thought of her face, the way she looked at the children with a kind of shy adoration, her hands which were so often stained with glue and paint, the way she stood all rumpled and sleepy at the kitchen counter each morning, her gentle voice. Whatever beauty there was in his life, she brought it. She was good and loving, and yes, he wanted her. More than ever in his life, he wanted her, and Matthew put his head in his hands and cried on the steps of the cathedral.

It was 2 a.m. when Matthew was finally sober enough to leave the all-night coffee shop on Seventy-fifth Street. It had begun to snow again. At the corner news-stand, there were tubs of flowers now lightly sprinkled with white. Matthew stared at them for a moment, then swooped them up, daisies, carnations, irises, lilies. His arms were so full of dripping blossoms he could barely get his money out, but soon he started off up Lexington Avenue towards Seventy-ninth Street.

Matthew bid the doorman a pleasant good morning as the flowers created a puddle beside the elevator. He studied himself in the elevator mirror on the way upstairs. He barely looked drunk.

Maggie was waiting by the door. She was ashen, with dark circles under her eyes. 'Oh my God, Matthew, where have you been?' She did not notice the flowers. 'I've been calling the office and the squash court and Jack didn't answer his phone. Oh God, Matthew.' She began to cry, standing in her bathrobe with her arms stiff at her sides. Matthew handed her the flowers which she took, opening her hands blindly. Matthew held her face between his hands and kissed her carefully. She wept with the flowers crushed between them.

'I thought you were dead. Oh, Matt, don't ever do that to me again. I was so scared, so scared . . .'

'Shh, shh,' he soothed her, touching her hair. 'Here, let's put these in water.'

She saw the flowers for the first time, staring down at her arms and their contents as if she had no notion how they got there. 'What's this?'

'Flowers.'

'Flowers,' she echoed. 'What are they for?'

'For you.'

'Flowers for me,' Maggie repeated.

'Yes, at two-thirty in the morning, flowers for you.' He put his arm around her shoulder and led her to the kitchen. 'Come on, let's get us all a drink, water for them, whisky for us.'

They sat at the kitchen table while Matthew tried to tell her what happened without telling her what happened.

'I think I had a mid-life crisis or something tonight,' he began. 'Oh, it sounds ridiculous, like some born-again nut. I hardly know how to describe it.'

Her eyes were beginning to lose some of their terror. She held her tumbler of scotch with both hands. 'Where have you been all this time?'

'Walking mostly. I even sort of went to church.'

She waited.

'I don't know, Mag, I just suddenly realized that I've lost touch somewhere along the line. Or maybe I never was in touch.' He reached across the table and took her hand in his. She dropped her eyes as they both thought of the darkened table in the restaurant on Columbus Avenue. 'I don't want to go to my grave a successful lawyer and half a human being.'

'What happened tonight, Matthew?'

'Oh, Christ, I don't know. Some silly bastard of a client was in today. Lost his whole family in an ugly divorce and he's falling apart. It's his own damn fault. He's not what you would call a thoughtful human being. He's about as tractable as a totem pole. I looked across my desk at him and suddenly I saw myself . . .' Matthew took a long pull on his drink. He had made it through the worst part. The lie was behind him now, and he saw that Maggie was eager to believe him. 'I need you, Maggie. I want you to help me be more of a person. It's a heavy load, I know, and I've got some hell of a nerve. Can you help me?' He felt dangerously close to tears again.

'I don't know,' she answered softly.

'I can't lose you. You are so dear to me.'

'I'm glad you're safe, Matt.'

'We've been together a long time. That counts for something.'

Maggie drew her hand across her eyes. 'I'm so tired.'

'Come. Let me put you into bed.' He walked her down the hall, helped her into bed, and sat down on the edge beside her. He bent over to kiss her, then snapped off the light. Her eyes stared up at him in the darkness. 'Please, Maggie,' he whispered. 'Don't let it be too late.'

Then he got up and left her, closing the door softly behind him.

But Maggie did not go to sleep. She lay on the bed with her heart beating so hard that she could almost feel the tug of her nightgown with each pulse. The fear had left a taste in her mouth, acrid and bitter like the chalky film from aspirin that would not go down. For so long, she had been trying to resurrect her feelings for Matthew so that she could examine them, but when she tried to think back to what had drawn her to him in the first place, there was only a sense of constricted confusion. Had she truly spent eighteen years married to a man she merely respected? It seemed unlikely, and yet nothing surfaced to deny it. Until tonight, in the long hours when he did not turn his key in the lock and she became certain he was injured or killed. Oh God, that there might never be Matthew on this earth again. The thought – in fantasy the solution to her dilemma – was in fact unbearable. The implications of her terror were too complex for Maggie to deal with. I'll worry about all that later, she thought. Just please, please, let him come home.

With the growing conviction of tragedy came the flood of memories, long buried beneath the heavy cloak of anger. She remembered the first time she had found a lump, years ago, in the other breast then. Doctor Berg drained off some fluid and had it analysed. The first report was inconclusive, and they had had to wait two dreadful weeks for the verdict. Matthew was a man who could not bear sleeping with anyone touching him. Nevertheless, every morning for fourteen days, Maggie had awakened with his arms tight around her. He never spoke of it, and when the good news came, he reverted to bounding out of bed first thing.

She remembered a game he used to play with the children. He would place an object, a shoe, perhaps, on the cocktail table. The children, delighted, would pounce on it and take it back to his closet. There in the empty pouch of the shoe rack they would find something else, perhaps a jar of spaghetti sauce. Off they would go to the kitchen to discover a pair of Susan's socks where the spaghetti sauce belonged. The game continued until they reached the treasure – a box of chocolates or some silly wind-up toy. Maggie once asked Matthew where he had learned such a game. He shrugged and said he made it up.

'Don't ever tell me you have no imagination,' she had told him then.

She remembered when she was first pregnant with Susan, going to spend a week by herself with her parents. The second day she began to experience stomach cramps. The local doctor prescribed bed rest, assuring them there was no reason for alarm, yet when Maggie telephoned Matthew that evening, he rented a car and showed up in the driveway at 5 a.m.

Recollections kept appearing one after the other, like marching bands in a raucous Fifth Avenue parade. Still Matthew did not come to bed. It was nearly light outside before Maggie remembered that last night she had spent two hours in a bar with David trying to figure out how to tell Matthew she was leaving him.

# Twenty-Three

Matthew and Jackson Brody walked downtown on Fifth Avenue. It was hard going, what with the slush underfoot and the crowds of holiday shoppers.

'Sorry to just drop in on you,' Matthew said. 'Christ, is it always like this up here?' He was nearly shoved into the street by a bulging shopping bag.

'Always at Christmas,' Jackson said. 'We'll be out of it in a minute though.' He guided Matthew along Thirty-seventh Street and through the doors of a restaurant called *Mary Elizabeth*. 'Ah, we're early enough. Ten more minutes and we'd have been out of luck.'

While they stood in line to be seated, Matthew looked around. There were long rows of tables in a large wainscotted room. Most of the patrons appeared to be elderly ladies wearing hats. He spotted one man, but he was accompanied by a woman and a child who was asleep in its stroller. 'What is this place?' Matthew asked.

'A little off the beaten track, isn't it?' Jackson replied.

There were two large glass cabinets on the wall above their table. One displayed a pair of green porcelain chickens and the other faded paintings of houses over which a poem was superimposed. Matthew strained his eyes but could make out only the first line: *To think I once saw grocery shops with but a casual eye* . . . None of the waitresses was younger than forty-five. Theirs flew past in frilled white apron, dispensing menus in her wake. But she reappeared in seconds.

They ordered. After the waitress whisked away, there was a long silence. The men smiled at one another and then quickly averted their eyes. Matthew took a deep breath. The idea was to get one's feet wet.

'Silly to feel bashful after all these years,' he said.

'I guess we're used to having the girls with us,' Jackson said.

'Jesus, keep your voice down, man. Your taking your life in your hands, using that term in here.'

Jackson looked at the sea of bobbing felt hats and smiled.

'What are you doing for the holidays?' Matthew asked.

'Just hanging out,' Jackson answered. 'With Robin away . . .' He let the sentence go unfinished.

'Come and spend Christmas with us,' Matthew said.

'Oh, thanks, I appreciate it, but I think I'm better off just . . . hanging out.'

There was another silence. Matthew was finding this more difficult than he had expected. He had figured that once he finally picked up the telephone and asked Jackson if he was free, the rest would follow easily enough. Jackson's aristocratic good looks were intimidating. Still, he had seemed genuinely glad to hear from Matthew.

'I'm not accustomed to . . .' Matthew began. He hesitated, and tried again. 'I don't have friends. Men friends. I'm used to just Maggie. There's a lot I'd like to talk about, but God damned if I can get started.'

Two bowls of vegetable soup swooped under their chins and settled on the table. 'I know,' Jackson said. 'After this . . . thing . . . with Robin, I really got myself tied up in knots. The only person I could talk to about Robin was Robin.'

'Exactly!' Matthew exclaimed. 'So what did you do?'

'Spent a lot of money drinking so I could complain to the bartender.'

'Well, look, I'm sure it's cheaper than psychotherapy.'

'There's a guy in a place on Madison and Eightieth who's not half bad,' Jackson said.

Matthew surveyed the roomful of women chattering eagerly together. A lady at the next table kept dabbing at her eyes with a white lace handkerchief. 'They don't have any difficulty,' Matthew observed.

'They're analysing their real estate portfolios,' Jackson explained.

Matthew tried submerging himself by gradual steps. 'So what about you and Robin? Are you . . . is she . . . if you don't mind talking about it.'

On the contrary, Jackson seemed eager. His voice was deep and rich. Matthew liked listening to it.

'She's got this job, you know,' Jackson said. 'With a film company. She's wild about it. They do a lot of public service shorts for television, things on the environment, health care, that sort of thing.'

'Doesn't sound like Robin to me.'

'Have you seen her lately?' Jackson asked. 'She wears glasses and these god-awful turtleneck sweaters. Hadn't put on a dress in two months as far as I can tell. I figured if she wanted to work I'd set her up in a little business of her own, maybe with crafts. Needlepoint, macramé, knitting. Not a chance. She wanted to do it completely on her own.'

'But didn't Hilary Vonderhyde get her the job?'

Jackson shrugged and smiled.

'It sounds as if you're still in touch,' Matthew said.

'Oh yes. We date.' Jackson smiled again, but he was forcing it. He had ten years on Matthew, but sometimes he seemed even older. 'It's not wonderful.'

Matthew decided that by now he was in up to his ankles. Time to go for the knees. 'Aren't you pissed off?'

'Yes,' Jackson answered. 'But not as much as I was at first.'

'But you were always so good to her, gave her every damn thing she wanted. You always treated her like a princess, unless you beat her when nobody was looking.'

'She says I gave her what I wanted her to have, not what she wanted.'

'So what does she want then?' Matthew's voice had risen. In his agitation, he nearly knocked his water glass over.

'She doesn't know. She's working on it.'

'Oh my God.'

'I know,' Jackson said. 'I've gotten to the point where I read the *Hers* column in the *Times* every Thursday.'

Matthew laughed. 'Me, too. What the hell, I figure I may learn something.'

The empty soup bowls turned into plates of toast smothered in melted cheese. 'I keep telling myself it's not easy for her either,' Jackson said. 'Robin can't inflict pain without suffering herself. She's got plenty of things to sort out right now.' He reached into his pocket, took out a roll of *Tums* and popped two into his mouth.

'Maybe we should talk about the stock market,' Matthew said.

Jackson laughed. 'Maybe if we dedicated a few lunch hours to discussing our wives we might even figure them out some day.'

The melted cheese and toast points had transported Matthew back to the dining hall at Andover. Life had seemed manageable then. It was easy just making grades and shooting balls through hoops. 'Do you think . . . this is none of my business . . . did she, was there someone else?' Waist deep. Really getting there at last.

'I don't think so. I'd know if there was.'

'One would think.'

Jackson studied Matthew as the younger man tapped restlessly on the place mat with his spoon handle.

'Of course, you and Maggie are an institution,' Jackson said. 'It must be tough for you to understand what I'm talking about.'

'Every marriage has its rough spots, ours included.' Matthew set his fork down too hard and it fell to the floor with a clatter.

'How about a commune? Men only,' Jackson suggested.

'Sign me up,' Matthew said.

'One of those rough spots?'

'Nothing we can't handle, but it's a pain in the ass.' Matthew looked down at his hands. It should be so easy to let the words spill out of his mouth, but they would not come. Still, he was sitting across the table from Jackson, wasn't he, after all those years of promising? It was a start.

They finished off their Welsh rarebit without speaking, but it was a comfortable, thoughtful silence now. For the first time in days, Matthew thought he felt a stirring of hope. It was elusive, like the tiny shimmering reflection off his watch crystal that danced on the wall beside him, but it felt good nonetheless. He looked up from his plate to see Jackson staring at him intently.

'Since we're into it,' Jackson said slowly, 'Robin's pregnant.'

'Oh, for Christ's sake.'

Jackson smiled sadly. 'What a mess. She doesn't even know if she wants it.'

'You have most certainly been in touch.'

'Once. We got a little boozed and forgot we're not supposed to be lovers.'

'Do you want it?'

'I wouldn't mind having a baby around,' Jackson replied.

Their waitress dropped the bill on the table. Matthew grabbed it. 'Next time you'll come down my way,' he said. 'We could walk over to the South Street Seaport.'

'All right, fine.'

'Any projections about what'll happen over the next few months?'

'Damned if I know,' Jackson answered. 'I'm taking it a day at a time. The only thing I know for certain is that I'm going to have dessert. Try the gingerbread. It'll remind you of the days when Grandma spent her afternoons baking goodies in the kitchen instead of producing documentary films or running for congress.'

'With lemon sauce, no less,' Matthew read. 'My grandmother was a golf pro.'

'Mine drove a cab.'

Matthew laughed and raised his glass. 'Well, here's to grandmas anyway. The myth and the reality. May they rule the world someday and give us a break.'

Jackson touched his glass to Matthew's and drank. 'If they don't already.'


'You feeling okay, Mom?' Fred asked as they stepped out of the taxi in front of the Higgens Gallery.

'A little queasy,' Maggie said. 'Must have been the Christmas pudding I had for dessert.' She ushered Susan and Fred up the steps ahead of her and wondered if David was already there. Under his steady pressure, she had finally agreed to bring the children to Eliza's retrospective exhibition. He had convinced Maggie that the gallery was an ideal place for a preliminary meeting.

'It's friendly and public,' he had said. 'You can ignore me if you like, or introduce us if you think you can. Just relax, look at Eliza's pictures, and let me stare at the kids.'

All night, Maggie had been practising a possible introduction. 'Fred, Susan, this is a friend of mine from art class, David Golden.' It seemed so simple. She had tried it aloud in the bathroom this morning, but her voice trembled so violently that she never got past the word 'friend'.

'Hey, Mom,' Susan was saying. 'Your stuff is just as good as this. How come you don't get a show?'

'Patience, patience,' Maggie said. So far, no David. But there were two rooms. He could be lurking just around the corner.

Fred drew her over to an abstract of white-yellow colour slicing through a black background. 'Pretty excellent,' he commented.

Maggie thought of the Montauk lighthouse Eliza had spoken about on the boat. 'What do you suppose she was getting at?' she asked Fred.

'Does it always have to mean something? Maybe she was just having fun with the colours.'

'I bet it has something to do with inspiration,' Susan suggested. 'Kind of like the cartoon with a lightbulb going on over somebody's head.'

'Crude,' Fred said.

Then she saw him. He was leaning against the far wall. Maggie watched his eyes move from one child to the other. There was the merest flicker when his gaze intercepted hers. Maggie felt her face flush red-hot. She was certainly not ready for an introduction today, she decided. Let this be the first step. He can see them with her, and perhaps the next time it would be easier for Maggie to initiate an actual confrontation. She steered Fred and Susan in the opposite direction. The next time Maggie checked, David had disappeared.

'Maggie Hollander,' he said.

Maggie jumped. 'Oh,' she said. 'Uh.'

'I'm David Golden,' David said to the children. 'I know your mother from art class.'

'Yes,' Maggie said. 'Fred, Susan, this is David Golden.'

'He said,' Fred remarked, giving his mother a sideways glance.

Susan held out her hand and stared up into David's face. Maggie had begun to feel far removed, as if this event were taking place on some remote planet.

'What do you think of the exhibition?' David asked.

'Extremely excellent,' Fred said.

'She has a fine sense of colour, hasn't she?' Susan said.

David nodded seriously. 'It's one of her greatest assets.'

'If you know Mom from class, you must be an artist, too,' Fred said, as if he were not quite sure he was getting the full story.

'Sculpture,' David said.

'A sculptor! How exciting!' Susan exclaimed.

Maggie said in a strangled voice, 'It was nice running into you. We haven't seen the other room yet.'

David's expression closed up, he waved to the children and turned away.

'He's *cute*, Mom,' Susan whispered. 'He looks just like a sculptor's supposed to look.'

'And how's that?' Maggie asked.

'Incredibly romantic, with that long hair and those wild eyes.'

'Probably hasn't had a bath in weeks,' Fred commented.

At the dinner table, Fred passed the rolls to his father, glanced surreptitiously at Maggie, and said, 'We met a friend of Mom's at a gallery today.'

'Oh?' Matthew said. Something in Fred's tone made him look up from his dinner.

'Yeah, the neatest-looking sculptor,' Susan said.

'He was far from neat,' Fred muttered.

Matthew stopped buttering his roll. He stared at Maggie who was poking carefully at the mounds of food on her plate. She tried to swallow a mouthful of zucchini, but it stuck just above her Adam's apple.

'You should've seen the way he looked at Mom,' Fred began.

'Oh, Fred, don't be absurd,' Susan said. 'It was a terrific exhibition, didn't you think so, Mom?'

Fred excused himself before dessert. Maggie tried to keep her eyes off Matthew's face until she felt her expression return to normal.

Matthew caught Maggie's hand as she started for the bathroom with her nightgown draped over her arm.

'Why, Mag?'

She looked startled.

'This.' He touched the soft folds of her nightgown.

'I'm just going to change.'

'I know that. Why are you hiding in the bathroom?'

'It's more . . . I'm just in the habit, I guess.' She had flushed deep red.

He drew her over to the edge of the bed and sat down beside her. 'Are you afraid of me, Maggie?'

Her eyes filled with tears.

'We've known each other so long. Since we were kids, really. How could you be afraid of me?'

'I don't know.' She was looking down. Her hair curtained her face, but he could see a tear glistening on the tip of her nose.

'What can I do?' he asked.

She shook her head.

'Do you know how long it's been since we made love?'

'No,' she said in a choked voice.

'Almost three weeks. I have the feeling it could go on this way forever as far as you're concerned.'

'I'm sorry. I'm not . . . feeling so great lately.'

He hooked his finger under her chin to make her look at him. 'I swear to you, I will never touch you again if that's what you want.'

'Oh, Matthew,' she said miserably.

'Look, we may as well get our mid-life crises over with at the same time.'

'But are they ever going to be over?'

'Maybe we can prod them along a little. But I'm going to need your help with mine.'

'How can I?'

'Show me how to be the kind of man you want.'

Maggie began to cry in earnest. He reached for her and she went into his arms willingly. He rocked her on the edge of the bed and let his own tears fall into her hair.

Later as she was succumbing to exhaustion in the dark she heard Matthew say something. 'What?' she asked groggily.

'I had lunch with Jackson Brody today,' he said.

'You did?'

'Yeah.'

'Well,' Maggie said. 'Well.'

Christmas morning, Matthew handed Maggie a large envelope. Inside were two airline tickets and a brochure for the Spindrift Hotel on Key Biscayne. Maggie stared at the papers in her hand as if the writing was in a foreign language.

Fred and Susan laughed. 'You know what our present is?' Susan asked. 'We're not going with you.'

'But where will you stay?'

'Here. Grandma's coming.'

'Grandma,' Maggie repeated.

'Grandma Rhoda,' Fred said.

Maggie looked incredulous. 'Don't worry, Mom,' Fred said. 'We'll take good care of her.'

'I thought she was in Sante Fe.'

'She was,' Matthew said. 'I told her it was an emergency.'

'Well, when? Oh, I guess it's on the tickets. January third. My goodness, so soon.' Matthew was beginning to look disappointed. 'Thank you, Matt,' Maggie said hurriedly. 'It's a lovely present. I'm just stunned.' She was already wondering how she would break the news to David.

'He knows,' David said over the telephone.

'How could he?' Maggie asked.

'I can't imagine. Christ!' David's outburst sounded uncharacteristically violent. 'I wish I could throw down a gauntlet or something. I'd like to take him on face to face and get it over with.'

'I'm the one who has to sort it out, David.'

'The man's not used to losing.'

Maggie was silent.

'Don't let him . . . oh, damn it. I wish I'd stayed away from that gallery.'

'I wasn't ready,' Maggie said.

'You wouldn't ever be ready,' David said. 'It's not that, it's Fred. I'm sure he guessed there was something. Can I see you before you leave?'

'No. I've got Rhoda here. I'm supposed to show her the ropes. It's so silly, the children are far more mature than she is. David I don't want to go. It'll be ghastly.'

'I have to say I hope so.'

'I'll be back in a week. We've been apart longer than that.'

'That was before he knew.'

'Happy New Year, David, my darling.'

'Happy New Year,' he said gloomily.


On the plane to Miami, Matthew said, 'This week is for fun only. No decisions. Real life is hereby suspended. Okay?'

'Okay,' Maggie said.

Before dinner, they walked on the beach, picked up shells and talked.

'What do you think about psychotherapy?' Matthew asked. 'Think it could help ease the mid-life miseries?'

'I would think so,' Maggie answered. 'But does this topic fall under the category of fun?'

'We're just not allowed to get grim,' he said. 'God, that sand feels so good on my toes. Maybe this is better than going to a shrink.'

'I always thought you were pretty much set against it in principle,' Maggie said. She pulled her sweater more tightly around her. The sun was nearly down, sending red streaks blazing across the sky. The breeze was thick with the smell of the ocean.

'I was.' He flung a flat stone into the surf and watched it skip four times. 'Not bad for an old duffer. What if I quit law?'

'Quit law!'

He laughed.

'That's like telling me you'll quit eating, sleeping and breathing,' she said.

'I met a fellow the other day, used to be with a big uptown firm. He's chucked it all and started a maple syrup farm in Litchfield County.'

'Oh, Matt. I can't see you in maple syrup.'

'You know what, Maggie?' He was suddenly serious. 'I'm trying to climb out of a whole bunch of ruts. Don't keep stepping on my fingers when you see them coming over the edge.'

'I'm sorry,' she said.

Over dinner, he asked her if she thought there was hope for modern marriage. 'Theoretically,' he added.

'Some people seem to manage it,' she replied.

'Name three,' he said.

Maggie thought hard. She might once have counted the Brodys. 'How about Ethel and John Miller? And the Epsteins. The Wilkersons?' She paused a moment. 'Well, maybe not the Wilkersons.'

'You can only name them because you don't know them very well.' He ordered two espressos. 'Remember when we used to sit up half the night drinking wine and planning our lives? Back in that minuscule apartment when we first moved to New York?'

Maggie nodded. 'I was going to be a great artist and you a criminal court judge and we'd raise children together, taking turns walking them to school and waking up with them in the night.'

'Well, Christ, look what happened.' She was silent. 'What can a man do?' Matthew asked. 'What do you women really want from a marriage?'

'Theoretically?' she asked, with a touch of bitterness. The candle on the table hissed and flickered.

'I never manhandle you any more,' he said. 'Give me credit for that.'

'Am I supposed to be grateful?' Maggie asked. 'After pleading for seventeen years and being ignored? You only quit it because I slugged you as hard as I could. Is that what I have to do to get your attention?'

'Not any more. I'm asking you to talk to me and you won't.'

Maggie glared at him.

'Come on, talk,' he challenged her.

'What I have to say isn't fit for elegant surroundings like these.'

Matthew stood abruptly, dug in his wallet, slapped fifty dollars on the table and held out his hand. 'All right. Let's go someplace that is.'

Out on the beach, the wind had quickened. Waves at high

tide beat up against the sand with a roar and retreated. A full moon dodged the clouds to provoke weird shadows on the shore. Matthew spun Maggie around to face him. She could distinguish every whisker and every wrinkle on his face in the strange light.

'Let's have it!' he shouted over the wind. 'What do you say?'

'You're an insensitive, selfish bastard,' Maggie began. 'No, you're not a bastard, that's what makes it even more terrible. You're a nice guy, but you don't *see* people. We're all factors, items, that get arranged to suit your convenience. If somebody says something you don't like, you don't bother listening. Being married to you is like flailing at the wind. Jesus Christ, Matthew, how could you not remember that Susan got her goddamn period!' It was all exploding out of her. She felt her face contort with the screaming and knew that nothing could stop her. 'You don't know your own daughter, or Fred, or me, you don't even know yourself! Well, maybe you should see a psychiatrist! Maybe that'd be a start!' She began to run. She felt wild, exhilarated, but it was hard going with the sand sliding away beneath her feet. She could hear Matthew just behind her.

'You can't lay it all on me,' he was shouting. 'You're a silent brooder. It's deadly. It eats you up and destroys everything around you. Yes, I heard you when you jabbed me in the gut. You should have done it years ago.'

'People shouldn't have to scream to be heard,' Maggie yelled back.

'Sometimes they do.' He grabbed her arm and she struck out at him.

'I hate you!' Maggie howled. She pummelled his chest with her fists. He pinned her arms against him and they both fell to the sand. She struggled, but he held her fast against him.

'I hate you, I hate you,' she sobbed again and again until finally all the energy went out of her and she lay still.

'Anything else?' he asked her after a while.

'Yes,' she sniffed and sat up, brushing sand out of her hair. 'You were my friend and you let me down.'

Back in New York, Maggie realized that during the entire week, Matthew had not once tried to make love to her.

233

# Twenty-Four

The evening was unexpectedly mild for February. Maggie wore her down coat open while Matthew was content with a wool sports jacket over his sweater. They walked alongside the park, with Fred and Susan a few paces ahead chattering about the dance production they had just seen at school. Every now and then, the children would take turns flinging themselves into the air in a parody of the dancers. Maggie took a deep breath. She always drew hope from the false Spring contrived by a February thaw. It assured her that Winter would truly end one day.

Matthew took her hand. It was smooth compared to David's bony roughness. Guiltily, she glanced down on the sidewalk as if David might materialize to find her walking hand-in-hand with her husband.

'What are you thinking, Mags?' Matthew asked.

'Oh, I don't know. About springtime, I guess.'

'Pretty sober face for such a pleasant topic.'

'Do you know, Matt, I bet you've asked me half a dozen times this week what I'm thinking.'

'Have I? I'm curious, that's all. You get this Mona Lisa expression.'

'I'm not complaining. I'm just not used to it.'

Far across the park a siren wailed followed by a thin eerie echo of a dog's howl. Maggie shivered and belted her coat. The children had pranced far ahead now. She peered into the twilight and made out a cluster of moving shadows at the fringe of the park by the Eighty-fifth Street entrance.

'Matt . . .' she said, and tightened her grip on his hand.

As the shadows spilled out onto the sidewalk to surround Fred and Susan, Matthew pressed his hands hard on Maggie's shoulders as if planting her in the concrete, and took off.

Maggie's eyes caught the glint of something metallic in the

scuffling group. 'Mommy!' she heard Fred cry, and she began to run.

'Get out, you little bastards!' Matthew shouted, as if he were expelling intruders from his home. Seconds later, six youths scattered like ninepins struck by a hurtling ball. Susan and Fred clung together as Matthew chased two of the boys into the giant shadows cast by the construction site behind the museum.

Maggie put her arms around the children. 'Come and sit on the bench,' she said. 'Tell me what happened.'

Fred was crying. Susan's face was a circle of white paper with holes cut out where the eyes should have been.

'They had knives. They were going to hurt us,' Susan said. Matthew arrived panting, and she threw herself into his arms. 'Oh, Daddy!'

'I lost them, every last little creep,' Matthew gasped. 'They couldn't have been more than fourteen, fifteen years old. It's okay, honey. You're all right now.'

'They touched her,' Fred said in a low voice. He sat stiff and straight on the bench. 'One of them put his hand on her face.'

'Shouldn't we call the police?' Maggie asked.

'I want to go home,' Susan said. 'Can't we go home?'

They listened at the kitchen table while Matthew telephoned the local precinct. When he hung up and joined them, Maggie said, 'I gather nothing's going to happen.'

'These kids are hit-and-run packs,' Matthew reported. 'They use the park for cover and mug people on Fifth and the side streets further uptown.'

'So what are they gonna *do*?' Susan asked.

Matthew shook his head. 'There was no property loss, no injury, and we can't help them out with identifications.'

'How can they not even try to catch them. No injury!' Susan rubbed her cheek. 'That part of my face will probably grow some disgusting fungus on it.' Her eyes were very bright. Matthew smiled at Maggie. There was obviously a certain dramatic appeal in the evening's events. 'Tomorrow you wait, I'll wake up and there'll be things like mushrooms sprouting . . .'

'Fred?' Maggie interrupted. He was sitting very still with his eyes on the formica tabletop.

Susan stopped talking and stared at her brother. 'What's the matter with you?' she asked. 'They didn't lay a finger on you.'

'They touched her,' Fred said. 'They would have . . . hurt her. I just stood there.'

'I should hope so,' Matthew said.

'Oh, sure!' Fred accused. '*You* didn't just stand there like a wimp.'

'You did exactly as you should have. If it ever happens again, I want you to behave exactly as you did tonight.'

'Again! I'd never live through that again!' Susan howled. 'I was practically prostate with fear!'

'Prostrate,' Maggie corrected her.

'Well, anyway,' Susan continued, 'what makes him think he was supposed to save me? I'm the older one.'

'Yeah, but you're a girl,' Fred replied.

'Oh, Lord,' Maggie groaned.

'I may be a girl, Fred Hollander,' Susan said gently, 'but you're an asshole.' She got up, went around the table and kissed her brother on the cheek. 'Come on.' She dragged at his arm. 'Let's go and start making calls. We'll take turns. Ten minute limit, toss for first dibs. I can't *wait* to tell Roz. She got exposed to by some derelict and thinks she's this tragic heroine. Wait 'til she hears this!'

'I don't feel like telling anybody,' Fred said.

'You're a real New Yorker now,' Susan urged. 'Come *on*. Don't you even want to tell Zach?'

'Yeah,' Fred said, and got up.

Matthew watched them leave. 'Best thing to happen to her since she had her braces off,' he commented.

'Fred's pretty shook up.'

Matthew held his hands out over the table. His fingers were trembling. Maggie went to the refrigerator and took out a bottle of champagne. She handed it to Matthew. 'Here.'

'Where'd that come from?'

'Left over from New Year's. It's only going to spoil. Let's drink the whole damn thing.'

Matthew opened the top expertly. There was a tiny pop and

236

foam spilled out into their glasses. 'To survival in the urban jungle,' Matthew said, raising his glass.

They drained those and Maggie poured them each another one. 'I'm beginning to feel a little better. How about you?'

'I'm scared to death,' Matthew said. 'Delayed reaction, I suppose. And there's a funny kind of dirty feeling. As if *I* did something reprehensible, not those little Neanderthals.'

'Me, too. I feel guilty as hell. I think I'll drink this right down. Lord, I'll be very drunk in a minute.'

'Guilty, that's it. I feel guilty. Why do you suppose that is?'

'I know why *I* do but I'm too ashamed of myself to tell you,' Maggie said. She was feeling very light-headed. 'Guilty and giddy.'

'It's your duty to tell me.' Matthew poured himself glass number three. 'We got any more of this stuff?'

'Why's it my duty?'

'Because you're my wife and you have to obey me. It's in the vows.'

'Fuck the vows.'

Matthew hooted.

'I'll tell you because you're my friend,' Maggie said, 'but don't get mad at me and don't tell anybody. All right?' Matthew nodded solemnly. Maggie leaned across the table and whispered. 'I feel guilty because I was so scared for Fred I hardly thought about Susan. I knew if I had to save one of them, it would have been Fred.' She stopped and waited for the pronouncement to sink in. 'Isn't it disgusting?' But Matthew was looking at her with interest rather than horror. 'You don't look disgusted.'

He shook his head. 'Isn't that something? Know what spurred me on, running like hell after those kids? They were going to hurt my little girl. It was this real primitive thing. She was a fragile flower and I had to protect her. Poor old Frederick.'

'At least they've each got a champion. How dreadful if we both favoured the same one.'

'I didn't know I had a favourite until tonight.'

'Do you suppose it's Oedipal? Me and Fred, you and Sue?' Maggie held out her empty glass.

'Or maybe we're just disgusting after all.' He filled it for her.

'So we should drink to forget.'

They were quiet for a moment. Then Matthew put his hand over hers. 'Remember how we used to do this when we first got married? At that tiny table with a cheap bottle of wine?'

'We had it all figured out,' Maggie said.

'The arrogance of youth. Why didn't it end up the way we planned it, Mag? With you filling the galleries with your paintings and me sharing the domestic load?'

'Forces of history. Realities. Not wanting it enough.'

'You know what I turned out to be? One of those bugs that skates on the water, we used to call them skimmers. I've never really gotten wet, just zip along the surface. You think it's too late for me to submerge?'

'I don't think I could know that.'

'But you're an expert.'

'I don't understand. Maybe I'm too drunk.'

'You're in it up to your neck, aren't you, Mag? You've had babies. I mean felt the pain and bled. You've mopped up their vomit and worried all night over them.'

'You have, too.'

'I worry until I get out of the door in the morning, and then I leave it all to you.'

'But you care about your clients.'

'My clients. That's not family, that's pieces of paper. They come and go. There's no impact on my life. Just ripples on the surface. You make things, beautiful permanent things, with your hands. You're involved with . . . your friends. Get all messed up in their lives. You're not afraid of that, of the mess. You feel things, I know, so deeply, and you suffer . . .'

Maggie dropped her eyes. Matthew's grip on her hand became tighter. 'Do you think it's too late, Mag? Once a skimmer, always a skimmer?'

She looked up at him. 'No. I don't think it's too late.'

'I don't ever want to lose you.'

'I know that,' she said.

'Do you think children tend to bind parents together?' Matthew asked.

'Sometimes. I think our children do.'

'Should we go and see how they're doing?'

'Yes.' She rose, tottered, and clutched at the back of her chair. Matthew, none too steady himself, put his arm around her waist and together they made their way down the hall.

She woke herself up screaming. Matthew snapped on the light.

'What is it?' he asked.

'Nightmare.' Maggie's face was soaked in sweat. Damp tendrils of hair clung to her cheeks like claws. 'It must have been the champagne.'

'Or the business in the park. Can you remember the dream?'

Maggie sat up and tried to unpeel the nightgown from her back. 'It was only a few seconds. I was me, now, but sort of a child, too. I was in this kind of tent, I think at my parents, and I was all alone. This person came and he . . . no, it was a woman . . . she had a long knife, and she cut a circle in my stomach and pulled out my insides. I was eviscerated. Emptied out. There was just this dark hole left. I looked down into it. The odd thing was, I didn't fight her at all. I was completely passive. There was this sense of inevitability. It just had to be, that's all.'

Matthew put his arm around her. 'It was the mugging.'

'Yes, I'm sure,' Maggie said. But when Matthew turned out the light again, she lay next to him and thought about David and how he had made her feel rich and full, as if she were pregnant with marvellous secrets. She pressed her hands flat against her stomach and hoped that he was lost in the sweet oblivion of sleep on the other side of the park.

'I have to see you,' Maggie said into the telephone.

'What's wrong?' David asked.

'I can't talk. Matthew's still here.'

'I was just about to leave for the studio. Meet me there.'

'All right.' She hung up and moments later Matthew came into the kitchen to pour himself a cup of coffee.

'Who was that on the phone?'

Maggie buried her face in the newspaper. 'Phyllis.'

'A bit early in the day for Phyllis. I didn't think she ever crawled out until noon.'

'She wants me to meet her for lunch.' Maggie's cheeks were flaming. It had been so easy when Matthew was indifferent.

She knew that if his eyes could penetrate the page, he would surely guess the truth. But Matthew did not press her. Maggie noticed that whenever he came close to the truth, he backed off or circled around it. Sometimes she wondered exactly how much he suspected.

'How about dinner tonight?' Matthew asked. He glanced at his watch and bolted the last of his coffee.

'With the kids?'

'No. Just us.'

'Where?'

'I'll surprise you. Call at six and I'll tell you where to meet me.' He bent to give her the usual brief morning kiss, then lingered to kiss her again, slowly and thoroughly. 'Wish I could stay home today.'

'I get that impression.' She eyed the wall clock. 'You've never left this late in your life.'

'One of these days I'm going to knock your socks off and stay home altogether. We'll make love and go to the movies in the middle of the afternoon.'

'I think I would faint dead away.'

'Don't believe me?' He had made his way to the kitchen doorway but could not seem to step across the threshold.

'Nope,' Maggie answered.

'I could never bear a smug woman. You wait.'

'Matt, it's nine-thirty.'

'All right.' He saluted her and went off down the hall bellowing *Will you still need me, will you still feed me, when I'm sixty-four?* A minute later she heard the front door slam.

Maggie's body felt like stone, but leaden, not full of movement and grace like David's carvings. She dragged herself to the bedroom, pulled on a pair of slacks and a sweater that did not really match, slung her bag over her shoulder and left. She was deaf to the doorman's good morning, and his bewildered concern went unnoticed.

As soon as she stepped out of the freight elevator, Maggie heard David's air hammer pounding. It was a comforting sound. The only thing she ever truly dreaded for David was that he could not work. Creative silence was the great unendurable

240

terror, and she believed that he would prefer annihilation to the death of his art.

She had to beat on the door to be heard over the din. David was covered with marble dust. It clung to his hair in streaks and frosted his eyelashes and eyebrows.

'Where's your mask?' Maggie asked.

'I forgot,' he said. When he closed the door, a choking cloud swirled around them. Maggie began to cough. 'I'm sorry,' he said. 'Let me get you some water.' She sat on the folding chair and drank. It was painful to look at David's face. Sweat and dirt traced deep lines beside his mouth. His eyes seemed to have sunk into dark caves beneath his forehead. Maggie tried to calm the sick trembling of her stomach by concentrating on the uncut stones that lay in jagged heaps on the floor. She knew that if David were to rinse away the thick film of dust, their rough beauty would be revealed. The texture and translucency would emerge, veined in lovely patterns of blue, rust, grey, white. David had performed that magic trick with her, too, Maggie thought, when she had been as drab and inert as that raw marble.

'Do you want to see what I've been doing?' David asked.

'Of course.'

On the long shelf lay ten new pieces protected by canvas drapes. One by one, David removed the covers and wet the sculptures with a spray bottle. Each was carved from dense black marble. Some were sharp spears, like shards split by lightning. The others were perfectly round highly-polished masses whose interiors had been roughly gouged out. The gaping holes were all the more disfiguring in contrast to their serene surfaces. Maggie took David's arm and buried her face against the chalky denim of his work shirt. 'I'm so sorry,' she murmured. 'How long have you been . . . ?' She gestured at the dark shapes.

'Since we met in the bar. I've had bad feelings about what's coming.' He touched one of his carvings. 'I call these pieces "Omens". They are omens, aren't they?'

Maggie took his hand in both of hers and held it to her breast.

'Do you love me, Maggie?'

'Yes.'

'Why can't you leave him?'

'Because he's trying so hard. Because he's the father of my children. Because I can't imagine my life without him.'

'He's a habit, not a lover. Not even a friend. It's because of the children.'

He extracted his hand and it hung like a dead thing against his side. Maggie felt the strain of sharing the same space without being physically connected.

'It's not just the children,' she said. 'It's Matthew, too. He's so much what I am.' She saw David flinch. 'Oh, God, I have to tell you, don't I?' He nodded, and she went on. 'If I had met you years ago – David, don't you know it would have all been different? But we didn't meet, and I married Matt and had a family, and they're as much of what I am as my hands and eyes and bones. I can't start all over again, pulling all the pieces apart and redefining myself.'

He took a step backward as if seeking shelter from the black stones.

'There's another one I haven't shown you,' David said. He lifted the drape that covered a medium-sized carving in a corner by the window.

Maggie gasped. It was a bust of two young faces, one elevated slightly above the other. The top of the boy's head was level with the girl's temple, and each pair of eyes gazed out at Maggie with the penetrating confidence of youth. David had even captured the asymmetrical shape of Fred's eyebrows.

'Oh my God,' Maggie said, and began to cry.

David reached for a manila folder and handed it to her. Her fingers trembled, and the folder slipped to the floor. The preliminary sketches of Susan and Fred lay at Maggie's feet.

'You can keep those,' David said, kneeling to gather them together. 'But not the carving.' He stood and put his hand on the statue, his fingers gently cupping Fred's chin. 'It's all I'll ever have of them.'

'What you don't really believe,' Maggie said through her tears, 'is how much I love you and how much I wish there was a way. My heart is breaking . . . it sounds so pitiful and lame, but it's true. I wasn't even half a person when I met you. David, are you going to be all right?'

'No,' he said. One of the hooks on his overalls had come undone. She longed to fix it for him. She would never touch him again, never see him grow older.

'I'll never see you get old,' he said.

'Oh, David.' The cry was wrenched from some primitive place inside her in a voice she did not recognize. She took one last look at him, and fled.


Maggie dutifully called Matthew at six o'clock. She was to meet him in the bar at *Windows on the World* at the top of the World Trade Centre. She went through the motions, bathing, dressing, checking the pantihose for runs. Her cabby was friendly. When he asked how she was this fine evening, she wanted to reply, 'In mourning.' Instead, she answered, 'I'm well. And you?' As she had hoped, the question set off a monologue that lasted the entire trip downtown.

The cavernous elevator at the base of the World Trade Centre catapulted her up a quarter mile of concrete and steel. Matthew was waiting at a table in the bar. He rose to kiss her.

'I wanted to see what kind of a night it was going to be before I decided on this place. Spectacular?'

Maggie gazed out over the pinpoint lights of the harbour. There was still enough twilight left to reflect off the water, turning it into a shiny slate-grey mirror. Helicopters winked far below them like fireflies kneehigh on the immense Goliath pillars of the twin towers. Maggie felt the comfort of being suspended far above the earth. She closed her eyes and listened to the music from the three-piece jazz band – *Fly Me to the Moon*. They seemed half-way there already.

'Come on,' Matthew said. He stood up and held out his arms.

'We haven't danced in a hundred years,' Maggie protested.

'Time we got back into shape.'

They had enjoyed dancing in the early days in New York, but once the children arrived, they got out of the habit. Maggie was usually so exhausted from sleepless nights that an evening out seemed most appealing if it required nothing more than sitting down for two hours and being served something edible on dishes she did not have to wash herself. After so many years, she was surprised at how easy it was to let Matthew guide her around the tiny dance floor, expertly, graceful as he always was. They had once choreographed a dance of their own, an elegant lindy-like combination of steps. When the music swung into a Cole Porter medley, Matthew began the first moves and she found herself remembering, gliding along with him. It was gratifying, this effortless collaboration of movement. Maggie remembered David's accusation, that Matthew was really no more than a habit.

'Can we sit down now?' she asked Matthew. 'I could use a drink.'

She sipped her wine and looked out of the window. Jewels scattered on black velvet as far as the eye could see. So many lights, so many people, so many tragedies. She was tinier than that speck landing way off at LaGuardia Airport. What did her pitiful love affair signify in the face of all that vast glittering display? But she felt herself slipping down, down, as if she were back in the draughty elevator, plunging down the shaft, through the bottom of the building and down, down into the black dense suffocating swamp of lower Manhattan. She glanced up suddenly, feeling Matthew's eyes on her. She smiled at him feebly.

'You okay?' he asked.

'Yes,' she answered.

'Nope,' Matthew declared. 'Want to talk about it?'

'Must be hormonal,' she said.

'You're too young for menopause.'

'I'm not. But it's all right. I'll adjust.'

He took her hand, laid it flat open on the table and traced the lines. 'About that phone call this morning,' he began slowly. Maggie's heart started to thump. 'Did you manage to set up a bridge game finally?'

'No.'

His voice was casual, but he still did not look into her face. 'Do you think there'll be any more?'

Maggie could feel the thundering reach her temples now. 'They're over,' she said.

'That's said.' Matthew picked up her hand and kissed it.

'Yes, but life changes. Things happen to people. They grow and change.'

'If I can help, Maggie, if you get lonely. Those times you would have been . . . at the bridge table. Will you call me? I promise I won't put you on hold.'

'You are a dear man.'

'I love you, and that's a fact.'

'I know.'

'Do you really know?'

'Yes. Now tell me about your day.'

'What do you want to know?'

'What you did, who you talked to, which clients.'

He leaned back in his chair. 'Well, let's see, first I worked on a merger agreement between two little film companies. Do you really want to hear this?'

'Yes,' Maggie said, 'but I have a confession. At least half the things you tell me about your work go right over my head. I may look as if I know what you're talking about, but I don't.' It was true. Over the years, Maggie had learned little catch phrases to give the impression that she understood him. She was like her deaf grandmother, nodding brightly as if she had heard every syllable when in fact there was merely a bewildering hum. 'You'll think I'm incredibly stupid when you see how much I don't know, but I'd like you to explain it all to me as you go along. If you've got the patience.'

'Why?'

'I want to understand what it is you do for that huge chunk of time I'm not with you every day.'

Matthew smiled at her but did not talk.

'Well?' Maggie said.

'In a minute,' he replied, and kept on smiling.

That night in bed, he held her without making love to her, just allowing her to snuggle against him for comfort like a child with a nightmare. She could not help but think about David and wonder where he was now, with no warm reassuring body to curl up to. She imagined him standing alone among the cold stones in his darkened apartment, looking out over the icy water of the Hudson. She shivered, and felt Matthew's arms tighten around her in his sleep.

# Twenty-Five

The telephone call came just after midnight. Groggily, Maggie reached for the receiver and said hello.

'It's me. We've got big trouble, Maggie.'

'Hilary?' Maggie barely recognized the voice. It sounded flat, remote, colourless.

'Yes. I'm with Phyl at my apartment. There's been an accident.'

Maggie felt the soft hairs on the back of her neck stand on end.

'Stephen's dead,' Hilary said.

'Oh, God.'

'Phyllis is terribly shaken. I don't know what to do. Should I call the police?'

Maggie snapped on the light and rechecked Matthew's side of the bed. He was not yet home. 'He's . . . Stephen's . . . there with you?'

'Yes,' Hilary said.

'You're . . . sure he's . . . ?'

'He's very dead, Maggie. I've got to do something. She's hanging on by a thread.'

'Call the police. No, don't. Wait a minute.' She sat up on the edge of the bed. 'Let me get Matt. He's still at work. Will you be all right if I hang up for a minute?'

'Yes, but don't make it too long.'

'I'll get right back to you.' Maggie's fingers were shaking so badly she could barely dial Matthew's private line. 'Thank God,' she breathed when she heard his voice.

'What's wrong?' Matthew asked.

'Hilary just called. Something awful's happened. She seems to be in shock or drugged. She says Stephen's dead. There at her apartment.'

Matthew was silent for a long moment. 'Is she alone?' he asked finally.

'No. Phyllis, too.'

More silence. Then he said, 'I'm going over there. You call and tell Hilary not to see anybody or talk to anybody. No police, no ambulance. Just wait for me.'

'I'll meet you there,' Maggie said.

'No. I don't want you involved.'

'I am involved. Matt, wait, what should I do about Zach? He's asleep on Fred's floor in the sleeping bag. Stephen just told me the other day how he's so grateful to us for Fred, that Fred's such a good influence on Zach . . .'

'Let him sleep,' Matthew interrupted briskly.

'Sorry,' Maggie said. 'I guess I'm pretty shaky. I'll see you in a few minutes.'

She dressed quietly, pinned a note to the bedroom door (GONE TO MEET DAD FOR A LATE DRINK), and slipped out. On the way down to Soho, Maggie imagined the terrible scene awaiting her. She had never seen a dead person, not even in a funeral parlour. How could she prepare herself for the visual shock, Stephen whom she had known for years, whose rough cheek she had kissed hundreds of times? There was very little traffic. In fifteen minutes, she was in the elevator to Hilary's apartment. Hilary greeted her at the door with a face like a mask, white and cold. Her eyes had no light in them, and when she moved her mouth, words came out like a collection of syllables from a robot.

'Thanks for coming,' Hilary said. She drew Maggie inside. Phyllis was huddled in one corner of the couch with her arms hugging her chest, rocking back and forth. Her mouth was drawn into a wild expression of sorrow. There was a slice under her left eye. Tears had washed the blood down onto her collar and stained it with pink blotches.

'Oh, my poor friend,' Maggie whispered. She knelt on the floor and put her hands on Phyllis's elbows. Phyllis looked at Maggie through the unceasing deluge of tears and cried, 'No, no, no, no, no!' Maggie put her arms around her and rocked her. The doorbell rang. Maggie heard Matthew's low voice. In a moment he was standing by the couch looking down at

Phyllis in Maggie's arms. Then he glanced at Hilary.

'How sensible do you feel?' he asked Hilary.

'I'm all right,' she replied.

'He's in there?' Matthew asked, indicating the sleeping alcove.

Hilary nodded.

'Come in here with me. I don't want you to say one word, not one. Understand?'

'Yes.'

He took her arm and they disappeared for what seemed a long time. Maggie succeeded in calming Phyllis to the point of low rhythmic moans. Finally, Matthew and Hilary emerged.

'What's she got in her?' he asked Hilary.

'Nothing. Two swallows of wine.'

'Got any tranquillizers?'

Hilary nodded.

'Give her one and take one yourself. Let me think a minute.'

'I'd better do something about this cut,' Maggie said. Phyllis's wound had begun to swell and darken.

'Leave it alone,' Matthew said. Then he perched on one arm of the couch with his trench-coat hanging open. Maggie remembered that when his law firm first contemplated purchasing an expensive computer, one of the senior partners had questioned the need, 'since they already had Matthew Hollander'. She watched him now, with the rather vague expression on his face as if he were day-dreaming, and knew that his brain was operating at full throttle.

Hilary returned with a capsule and a glass of water.

'I'm afraid to let go of her,' Maggie said.

'Stay with me,' Phyllis whispered.

'All right, honey,' Maggie said. 'Now take this.' Phyllis looked up at Hilary as if seeking approval. Hilary nodded and Phyllis swallowed the pill.

'Now you,' Maggie told Hilary.

'I already took two.' Hilary sat cross-legged on the floor. 'Is she going to be all right?' she asked Maggie.

'Yes.' Maggie tried to sound convincing. She kept feeling her eyes drawn to the sleeping alcove. What used to be Stephen was in there, dead. For reassurance, she glanced at Matthew.

His jaw muscles were working, which meant that he was about finished thinking things through. In a moment, he looked up.

'How do you think she is now?' Matthew asked.

'I'm all right,' Phyllis said. And indeed, her voice sounded nearly normal. 'It's just that I keep thinking of Zach.' At this, her mouth trembled and she began to cry again, but softly now.

Matthew came to sit beside Maggie on the couch. Everyone waited for him to speak.

'I'm going to ask you what happened, Hilary,' he began, 'and I want you to answer very carefully. Then we're going to call the police and you're going to tell them. Think you can manage that?'

Hilary nodded.

'You said he had a lot to drink, isn't that right?'

'Yes, he was very drunk.'

'You're positive,' Matthew pressed.

'Yes,' Hilary said.

'But the two of you were sober.'

'Yes.'

'There will be blood tests.'

'They'll bear me out.'

'Stephen gets belligerent when he drinks, isn't that so?'

Phyllis answered this time in a hoarse voice. 'Yes.'

'He's struck you before?'

'Yes.'

'He became very abusive tonight. You argued and he hit you.'

'He hit Hilary, too,' Phyllis said. 'She was trying to get him off me and his ring sliced her back . . .'

'Never mind that,' Matthew interrupted. 'He became increasingly violent and you were terrified, certain he was going to kill you. Hilary reached for the telephone to call the police, and when he lunged for her, you picked up that heavy marble clock and hit him on the back of the head. You only wanted to stun him, but he went down hard. You tried to revive him with artificial respiration, which is why there are lipstick traces around his mouth. But it was too late. By now, both of you were very frightened and in shock, which is why you telephoned your friends instead of the police.' He paused. The

249

three women were transfixed. They stared at him, waiting. 'Isn't that about it, Phyllis?' Matthew asked. Phyllis nodded slowly. 'Hilary, you have anything to add?'

'No,' she said.

'Good. It's not complicated. Very simple and very tragic.'

'It was strange that he was in the bedroom, wasn't it?' Hilary said.

'I'm sure Phyllis and Stephen wanted privacy to keep the argument from you,' Matthew said.

'But I became alarmed when I heard Phyllis cry out.' Hilary's face had lost its numb look. In fact, Maggie observed, the golden eyes were glittering now. Maggie had seen that expression once before, when Hilary described the attempt of a fellow vice president at CinemInc to boost himself up the executive ladder into Hilary's job. She liked challenge.

'Are you ready for me to call the police?' Matthew asked.

'Go ahead,' Hilary said.

'Phyllis?'

Phyllis nodded.

The police arrived in ten minutes. Maggie watched the proceedings with bleak fascination. The men were clearly sympathetic. Hilary's flushed face and tousled hair, and the lines of her body under the jeans and sweater, received many covert glances. When she told their story, Phyllis began to cry silently. It was clear that she was deeply affected, and by now her wound was impressively ugly. After an hour, Matthew and Maggie were permitted to leave.

'Phyl,' Maggie said at the door. 'What shall I say to Zach? Shall I let him sleep?'

'Yes. I'll come to you as soon as I can. When he wakes up. I'll tell him.'

'Are you going to be all right?'

'When they get him out of here, I'll feel a lot better. I can't stand him being in there like that. He should be . . . resting.'

Maggie held her tightly for a moment. Then Phyllis freed herself to embrace Matthew. 'I don't know what to say, Matt,' Phyllis said. 'We would have been lost without you.'

'It's going to be tough,' he said. 'But you'll get through it. Just keep thinking of Zach.'

In the taxi, Maggie began, 'Matt, what do you think . . .'

'Later,' Matthew interrupted, indicating the back of the driver's head. He took her hand, and they rode uptown in silence. By the time they got to Seventy-ninth Street, their fingers were welded together like cold white fragments of steel.

They shut the kitchen door and sat huddled over cups of coffee. 'Jesus Christ, Mags,' Matthew said. 'I've never been through anything that gruelling in my life.'

'You seemed composed at the time.'

'My knees are still shaking. In fact, I'll skip the coffee and have a double shot of scotch.'

Maggie got up to pour him a drink. He downed half of it in one gulp and sighed, with eyes watering.

'What do you think really happened there?' Maggie asked.

He shook his head.

'Why did you do it? You can't bear Phyllis, and you hardly know Hilary. My God, Matt, if it ever came out. You've always played it so straight. I don't want them to go to jail, and he was an awful man, but . . .'

'Awful enough to be killed?'

Maggie was silent. Matthew swallowed the rest of his scotch. 'It's Zach,' he said. 'I saw those ruined lives. One man dead, those two living through who knows what kind of torment, but the worst is that kid. He's a good little guy. I guess I figured screw the scruples and try to salvage something for him.' He put his head in his hands. 'Christ, what a night.'

Maggie pulled him to his feet and led him down the hall to the bedroom. She helped him off with his clothes, gave him a gentle push and he tumbled onto the bed.

'What was it you said a while ago about my not minding the mess?' she asked. 'Matt, when you decide to submerge, you sure do it in a very big way.'

But he was already asleep. She turned out the light and went to check the children. Zachary lay cocooned on the floor in Fred's sleeping bag. With one hand curled under his chin and the thick dark hair shadowing his forehead, he seemed like a small child. She touched him lightly, acknowledging the fugitive wish that Phyllis be locked away, leaving Zachary here with them forever.

# Twenty-Six

❦

Maggie walked north on Fifth Avenue past the wrought-iron gates of the Frick Museum with its soft green lawns and flowers blooming thick along the verges of the formal gardens. There was still a bite in the air, but the exercise of walking from the Fifty-seventh Street galleries had warmed her. She switched her heavy portfolio to the other hand and drank in a deep breath of May that was only slightly polluted by traffic. Surely Robin would be outside on such an afternoon. Maggie turned into the park at Seventy-sixth Street and strolled down towards the boat pond. A painter had set up his easel halfway down the hill. Maggie glanced curiously at the pleasant if unoriginal oil rendering of the silvery water. Though she had been required to work in public several times, she had never enjoyed painting under the eyes of inquisitive onlookers and sidewalk critics. Still, there was no point in attaching herself to a gallery if the idea of public display intimidated her. She smiled at the artist and moved on.

There was no Robin on the benches circling the pond, only nannies and here and there a drunk stretched out to bask in the sun. Maggie turned right and was nearly knocked over by a roller skater with a bare chest and earphones. But the *Alice in Wonderland* statue reposed unperturbed in bronze splendour on its vast platform. As always, children clambered up Alice's slippery surface, clinging to sides worn shiny by the many wriggling bodies that preceded them. Maggie had always wondered at the choice of bronze as a medium for Alice. Surely some type of stone was more whimsical than this heavy sombre metal.

Maggie climbed the steps, and there beside the statue sat Robin. Maggie watched her for a moment, smiling at the scene. With one hand, Robin held a copy of *People* magazine unopened in her lap. With the other she rocked the baby carriage. Her face had the vacant, exhausted look typical of new mothers. She seemed stunned, as if she had been confronted with some monumental fact that she could not absorb.

Maggie sat down on the bench. 'Hi,' she said.

Robin blinked. 'Hi. Well, hi!'

'I figured I'd find you at your usual spot on such a pretty day.'

Robin squinted up into the sky. 'Yes, it is nice, isn't it?'

Maggie laughed. 'Did you sleep last night?'

'Oh, we're doing much better. She made it from eleven until three, her first four-hour stretch.'

'You've been up since three?'

Robin nodded. 'Mostly, and look at her now, the little beast, peaceful as can be.'

The minute figure in the carriage was barely visible under her quilt. Tiny spiky eyelashes lay against a pink cheek.

'I wish she'd get up so I could hold her,' Maggie said.

'Drop over any time between 3 and 6 a.m.'

'When are you going to get some help, Robin? You'll wear yourself out.'

'Soon.'

'God, I don't remember Susan's ever being that small.'

'She probably wasn't. Phoebe's still underweight.' Robin adjusted the quilt. 'Jackson's so glad she was a girl.'

'That's because he lost the one he had, the one you were.'

Robin nodded. 'It's awfully easy to slip back into that. I was in too much of a hurry moving back in.'

'But with the baby?'

'I know,' Robin said. 'Still, I think we could have managed all right, Phoebe and I.' She smiled at Maggie's troubled face. 'Oh, we're fine, really. It's not Jackson, it's me. I have a long way to go.'

'You sound as if you've got regrets.'

'I regret the timing of things more than the way they turned out. I love Jackson. I love having his baby. I just wish I'd been on my own more. Before, years before, when I first came to New York. I wish I hadn't found him so fast. I sound like a nut, don't I? An ungrateful nut, with all these poor women out there who can't find a decent man.'

'You're not a nut. Timing's . . . well, crucial.'

'I feel as though I never got a chance to grow up.'

'I wonder if we ever do.'

'Oh, Maggie, you were always a grown-up.'

'Maybe that's my trouble. I wasn't ever a child.'

'Is there something wrong?' Robin asked. 'I hate to think of you having a problem.'

Maggie sighed. 'I'm not supposed to, I'm so strong and sensible.'

'No Mag, that's not what I meant. I hate to think of you hurting, because I love you.'

Maggie took Robin's hand and squeezed it. 'I'm sorry.'

'Are you going to tell me?'

'Yes, but not today.'

'Just tell me if you're all right.'

'I am. Please don't worry about me.'

Robin glanced at the carriage. 'It's that I've been so preoccupied.'

Maggie smiled. 'Don't you dare feel guilty. We'll have a long talk in a few weeks. Look what I'm hauling around with me today.'

'You've got your portfolio,' Robin said.

'I've been hounding the galleries trying to get somebody interested in my stuff.'

'But you can't show your wall, that big wall.'

'I have photographs of it. There's been some interest, but nobody can figure out how to mount it for a show. The damn thing's twenty-two feet long. I've got an appointment with somebody down in Soho tomorrow who thinks he might like to put it in his loft gallery. Not much exposure, but it's a beginning.'

'Is it that friend of Hilary's?'

Maggie nodded. 'She and Phyl showed him a polaroid without telling me.'

'They sent Phoebe a beautiful sterling silver baby cup from Tiffany's. But they haven't been to see us since the hospital.'

'They're pretty busy with the move.'

'How does Zach feel about being uprooted?'

'He told Fred it gave him the creeps living up here with his father's ghost. He'd much rather live in Soho.'

Robin sat in thoughtful silence for a moment. 'They're much better off down there anyway. People won't give them a hard time.'

'Do you really think anybody would figure it out?' Maggie asked. 'I mean, two friends, one widowed, living with a child?'

Robin gave her a wry look. 'Come on, Mag. You can't be around them for two minutes without getting the picture. I never saw either of them so happy.'

Maggie laughed. 'I don't know how I can laugh. Stephen dead, poor Zach, and those two nuts together.'

'Zach is much better off than he was with that creep always on his case. So what if his parents are both the same sex these days?'

'Robin, you astonish me.'

The baby had begun to whimper. Robin picked her up and rocked her, resting her cheek against the soft fuzz of her head. 'Don't cry, don't cry, Mommy loves you . . .'

'Rob,' Maggie said, 'what do you suppose will become of them?'

'Oh, they'll be all right. Hilary will be president of CinemInc and Phyl will get eccentric . . .'

'Actually,' Maggie said, 'I didn't mean them. I was thinking of Susan and Phoebe. I was wondering what it'll be like. It's all been such a mess for us.' She touched Phoebe's hand and smiled as the tiny fingers curled around hers. 'Poor Susan's got this boyfriend now. They both entered a writing contest and she's afraid she might beat him. You can be sure he doesn't feel that way. He just wants to win.'

'You know something? It's just as rough for the guys,' Robin said.

'Yes, I guess it was just fine when all they did was tromp out into the forest and bring home dead animals for dinner. What's a pioneer supposed to do when his wife looks at him with a jaundiced eye and says "you don't give me enough space, honey"?'

'They'll get there, too.'

'How?' Maggie asked.

'We'll teach 'em.'

Maggie laughed.

'Come on,' Robin said, 'We'll walk you home.' Phoebe began to cry the moment Robin laid her in the carriage, but the rocking motion soon quieted her. 'I'm so happy,' Robin said. 'I always knew a baby would make me happy and she has.' They walked up the path away from the boat pond. 'I wish you would be happy, too, Maggie.'

'I'm not unhappy.' It was true. The searing pain of those first months without David had eased. When she felt too miserable, she turned to Matthew and he was always there to comfort her, requiring no explanation other than her feeling low. And she found relief, and sometimes even joy, in her work. She felt like an amphibian who was slowly, inexorably, evolving into a land animal. She would drag herself out of the surf only to flounder as the heavy spray broke over her head. She splashed about for a while, then touched the sand beneath her feet and began the struggle all over again. It was sad, abandoning that watery world, and sometimes she longed to flip back into the waves and let them wash her down, down. But dry land rose ahead, and she liked the firm feel of it, liked directing her own steps rather than drifting with the current.

She and Robin strolled slowly north along the plaza in front of the Metropolitan Museum. Sunshine glistened on the fountains when Maggie's heart suddenly caught in her chest. It happened often, and each time the jolt left her shaken and tearful. There was always some familiar feature, a lanky walk, an angular face, a gesture from long fingers. She strained to track him as up ahead he weaved through the throng like some slim and elegant sea creature swimming among the reeds and tall grass only to disappear forever in the shimmering light of the water. As always, she lost him, but there was a rainbow dancing in the spray from the fountain as they passed.